CHRISTMAS IN WINTER VALLEY

JODI THOMAS

CHRISTMAS IN WINTER VALLEY

HQN™

ISBN-13: 978-1-335-14636-6

Christmas in Winter Valley

www.HQNBooks.com

Printed in U.S.A.

CHRISTMAS
IN WINTER VALLEY

CHRISTMAS IN WINTER VALLEY

CHAPTER ONE

December 10

Cooper Holloway barely noticed the beauty of his ranch from his huge east-facing windows. The grass had already turned brown and tumbleweeds spotted the prairie like ghostly Christmas bulbs scattered across the ground. His favorite time of year, he thought, but today was turning out to be a nightmare and it wasn't even noon. He glanced at the hills, far in the distance. Winter Valley was hidden there, along with his vital work. He had to make it to the hills by dark.

He tossed two worn pairs of boots, along with half a dozen shirts and jeans, into a duffel bag as he mumbled every swear word he'd ever heard. He stuffed in a handful of mismatched socks and yanked the bag's drawstring. Forget underwear or a shaving kit. He had to get out of the old ranch shack as fast as possible.

The cousins were coming and if they saw him, he'd be delayed for hours.

"You ready, Coop?" his brother Elliot yelled from the ground-floor foyer. "I see the dust cloud. The vans have turned off the county road." Elliot's words echoed through the spacious rooms and up the wide oak stairs.

Cooper's duffel bag hit the saltillo tiles at the bottom of the stairs and echoed off the entryway walls. "You got Hector saddled?" Cooper shouted as he looked around for his hat.

"Yeah, he's out back, ready to run. Creed and a few boys have already left in the truck loaded down with supplies and medicine. They're hauling an extra mount just in case you need one. Hopefully they'll be waiting for you at the entrance to the pass, but the road will take them longer than you crossing open country on horseback."

Cooper came down the stairs so fast Elliot had to jump back to keep from being run over. "Coop!" Elliot yelled. "You don't have a posse gunning for you. It's Sunlan's cousins just getting together before they head home for Christmas. How bad could three women in their early twenties be? At least one is still in college, so she'll probably be studying for finals. It's not like they're kids we have to babysit. When they planned the visit they picked the ranch so they could see Sunlan, not us. Now, with Sunlan's father ill, who knows if she'll even make it in before the cousins have to leave.

"Griffin said they are all drop-dead gorgeous and can't wait to see you again."

"College! The redhead is taking her senior year for the third or fourth time, which leaves me to believe she's probably not into studying." Cooper picked up his bag. "They think I'm the ranch pet. Last time I saw them, one of them actually scratched my ear. I took Sunlan into the family when Griffin married her, but I refuse to accept the rest of her kin."

"They can't be that bad." Elliot's attempt to look on the bright side wasn't even working on Elliot himself. He looked as miserable as Cooper felt.

"If you ever left the ranch, big brother, you'd learn what women are like these days."

Elliot shook his head. "I've got too much work to do to travel around talking to women I have nothing in common with."

"Good—now you can entertain them right here. I took my turn at the stock show last summer. I'm not doing it again. Just because they're closer to my age doesn't mean I'm the one who has to be sacrificed to my sister-in-law's crazy relatives."

He stormed toward the back door. "I met them in Fort Worth, having no idea what I was in for. At first I thought I was there just to haul luggage and drive them around, but as we headed up to their rooms, two of them started trying to take off my clothes. One claimed she'd never seen a real cowboy up close." Cooper shook his head. "I got to tell you, brother, it wasn't easy holding on to my dignity and the luggage at the same time."

They hit the back door and the youngest Holloway broke into a run. "Working with the wild mustangs up in the hills will be far more fun."

Elliot followed. "But you'll be out there alone, Coop. No one within miles. No cell service. If you run into trouble, there'll be no one to help."

"Great. Sunlan can't call me and talk me into anything. Why'd Griffin have to marry someone so smart? None of us can say no to her." Cooper stopped suddenly. "Promise me, Elliot, that you will never, ever get married. I don't think I could take another sister-in-law. Especially not one with cousins."

"No problem. I haven't had time for a date in two years. Sunlan's cousins are too young for me. I have a feeling I'll grow into the old uncle who takes the odd place at the holiday table every year."

Both men slowed as they neared a wooded area where their great-grandfather had planted a forest a hundred yards behind the ranch house. Apple trees on the left of the path. Peach trees on the right. He'd told each respective wife when he'd married her that he wanted either a peach or an apple pie served at every meal. The first three ladies must have objected and divorced him, but number four had been a cook.

A ranch hand passed Cooper the reins to his mount. "Good luck, Coop," he whispered, as if this might be the last time he would see his boss.

"Thanks." Cooper nodded once. "Look in on the mares in the barn at least twice a day. That one who got cut up by barbed wire needs to be watched, and that new mare looks like she'll be dropping a foal any day."

The man nodded.

"Good luck," Elliot echoed. "How long before I send old Doc Westland up to check on your progress with the mustangs?"

"Give me a few days to round up the herd. Then, when the doc arrives, we'll tag what I've corralled. Who knows how far back in the canyon they'll be."

"I could ride up with the doc." Elliot sounded like a big brother. "Creed said he'd go help guide the old guy in if it snows. He's the only one besides Griffin who can find the place. I'm not sure I could, even with a map."

"No need. The doc will find me. I left him with detailed instructions after last year. Besides, I'll be looking for him. Too much activity would scare the mustangs off. This is a job for one rider, two at the most. That herd is wild, but they still need care to stay healthy through winter. I'll be lucky if they accept me. Last year I couldn't get close to a dozen of them."

Elliot slapped his brother's horse, starting him along. "You'll smell like them when you get back, and be lucky if we let you enter the house. Make sure you're back for Christmas."

Cooper gave Hector his head and they were off and running full-out toward the hills, toward Winter Valley. He wanted isolation. He always saw this one job as a challenge, a quest. One man against the wilderness. One cowboy riding among a herd of wild horses, some that had never seen a human. The timing had to be just right—late fall, when pastures had turned brown, but the snows hadn't started. Like the wild mustangs, Cooper knew it was time. He felt it in the air. Sunlan's cousins coming in just started him along a few days earlier on an adventure he loved.

"See you when the job's done." He laughed, knowing he was already too far away for anyone to hear.

Griffin and Elliot could run the ranch for a while. All Cooper wanted was solitude.

Before dark he'd be so far back into the canyons that Coop could almost believe he was traveling back in time. His great-grandfather had built a cabin miles away from any road almost a century ago. He'd found the mustangs the winter after he'd homesteaded. Legend was he'd loved watching the wild horses that lived so far back in the rough canyons more than he'd loved any of his four wives. He'd made a promise to keep the herd strong and protected from diseases and rustlers. Every generation of Holloways had kept that promise.

A few weeks alone was exactly what Cooper needed. Peace, nature and no women. He swore that December was the opening of husband-hunting season in Crossroads, the nearest town. Parties, dinners, fund-raisers, church festivals. All the local single women needed a date and he seemed to be the first unattached man they thought to ask.

December was the perfect time to disappear.

He wouldn't worry about the ranch house. How much damage could three young women do with manicured hands? Besides, Sunlan promised she'd be there to help. As soon as her father recovered she'd fly down and join the girls. Maybe she'd take them shopping or something. From the looks of the boxes that had rained down on them yesterday, the girls had already started shopping online.

Cooper glanced back at the headquarters and saw dark clouds moving across the northern sky. For a moment he thought it might be the cousins, then he realized winter's first storm was thundering in.

He didn't care. He'd spend his solitary days in mud. He wasn't going back.

Freedom pounded in his veins to the beat of Hector's hooves.

Elliot Holloway watched his brother disappear. Cooper was a man born out of his time—he was tall, lean and wild as the wind. He should have been a Texas Ranger, or an outlaw back when Texas was untamed. The modern world hemmed him in.

Part of Elliot longed to run away with Coop, but Elliot had always been the logical one. He'd do what was right, what was needed. Griffin, eight years older, had taken the reins of the ranch when their parents died, but Elliot had come home from college and taken responsibility for the books. While his brothers became working ranchers, he'd taken classes in programming, the stock market, bookkeeping, taxes. Elliot might dress in boots and jeans, but he rarely climbed on a horse.

He walked back toward the huge three-story house that they called simply "the headquarters." With both his brothers gone, Elliot felt alone. Surely, Griffin and Sunlan would be back in time to decorate. Cooper might make a show of wanting to be alone up at Winter Valley, but he loved the holidays, too. He'd come riding in time to celebrate, cousins or no cousins. Until then, Elliot would take over.

He'd loved growing up on the ranch, but he'd always thought that once he left for college he'd never return, except to visit. His dreams were in the big city. Wall Street, maybe. For him, numbers, patterns, programs were far more interesting than horses or moving cattle from one pasture to another.

But those dreams of walking the canyons built by skyscrapers in New York hadn't come true. He'd been pulled back before he'd finished college. His dad had died, and his brothers needed him. He'd thought he would only be gone a semester, a year at the most, but the finances back home were in terrible shape. The Maverick Ranch wasn't just land and cattle. His father had investments in dozens of other ventures. Some were paying out, but most were dripping blood. The first few years he and Griffin worked hard just to hold on to what three generations of Holloways had built. When drought hit one year and fire two years later, they were barely surviving by the time Cooper was old enough to pull his share.

Then Griffin had married Sunlan, and she'd poured money into the Maverick. She'd also added property in Colorado she wanted kept separate, but she swore no one could manage the books but Elliot. When Grif and Sunlan's girl was born, all three men had spent time helping out on the Colorado ranch, knowing it would someday go to the newest Holloway.

Or Holloways. Sunlan would spend time with her father, make sure he was recovering from his respiratory infection, then come home to the ranch. Her parents might travel from their ranch to Washington, DC, but the Maverick Ranch was her home now.

She'd be popping out another Holloway by spring.

Elliot swore. Sunlan would let him have a piece of her mind if he talked like that. She'd spent the past two years loving Griffin and picking on Elliot and Cooper like the clay wasn't dry in their molding. Griffin once told both brothers that they were masochists because they seemed to love listening to her lectures.

Elliot told himself he didn't mind taking on both ranches' books. It was all in the family.

He stretched, barely noticing the cold wind blowing in from the north as Cooper disappeared from sight. His little brother would have his free days, and Elliot would try to play host to the three cousins while he spent midnight hours with year-end details.

Maybe he'd take them into the café in town tomorrow. Maybe he'd get out the Monopoly game, or, if that was too juvenile for them, they'd play poker.

Walking back into the house, he noticed the stack of boxes piled in the foyer had grown. Elliot smiled. Sunlan had said the cousins had ordered a few things for the days they were staying. Maybe they'd brought their own games. Or books. That would be quieter.

He'd ask Creed to take them out for a ride. The young foreman was close to their age. That'd kill an afternoon. Creed would hate the chore, but he'd be too quiet to complain, and Elliot wouldn't trust anyone else to watch over city girls.

"I can handle this and still get my work done. No sweat," Elliot lied to himself as his words echoed through the hallway.

After all, it was only for a short visit. Sunlan had even commented on the phone that her father was getting better every day. When Elliot had talked to her a few nights ago, he could tell she was longing for home, and home was here.

CHAPTER TWO

December 10
Wyoming

Tye Franklin walked the rainy-day shadows of the rodeo grounds. He was into his forties and hard as leather, and most agreed that he was usually one drink past being drunk.

He never bothered to argue. In truth, he rarely talked to anyone. His job was to haul in rough stock for small rodeos across the West. He'd made sure the pens were loaded with hard-to-ride broncs and bulls flashing Satan's fire in their eyes.

He'd lived so long around the mud and blood of the rodeo that it was more home than anywhere he'd ever been.

As he passed from one floodlight to another in the silence of a cloudy arena, he watched his shadow beside him. Long and lean. He wore his Stetson low, even after sundown. His back was bowed just a bit from fatigue, and he had a limp he carried like a badge of failure.

Tye smiled at his shadow. Sometimes he wondered if he was the echo and the dark carbon copy that paced him was real.

They weren't that different. Both almost invisible. Both silent. Both broken.

"Franklin," someone yelled from the row of empty stands. "You still out here?"

Tye recognized Harden's voice. "I am, Trooper, but you can't arrest me for being a walking drunk."

The lawman didn't bother to laugh. "Damn it, Tye, you're the hardest man in this state to find. If I hadn't seen that tin can of a truck of yours, I never would have found you. A Texas Ranger down in Austin I know has got me looking for you." His words came as fast and sharp as his steps on the metal bleachers.

Tye didn't move. He'd figured trouble would find him soon enough without him running toward it.

Harden was out of breath when he reached the mud of the arena. "Double damn. If it rains again tonight, we won't be able to have the rodeo tomorrow. Folks around here look forward to it all year long."

"You just come out to give me the weather forecast, Officer?" Tye pushed back his hat so he could meet the trooper's eyes. In an odd way, they were friends. Tye had done what he could to keep the lawmen in this area in business. Running stoplights. Being drunk and disorderly. Occasionally picking a fight in a bar just so he could feel the pain.

Harden glared at him. "I came to deliver this to you. It's traveled across several states to find you." He slapped a brown envelope against Tye's chest. "Tonight it appears I'm just a mailman, nothing more."

Tye grinned. "The Texas Rangers after me again?"

"No, it's from a lawyer. I think the Rangers were just helping find you."

Tye rolled up the envelope and put it in his coat pocket. He cared less about what was in it than the trooper did.

Harden spit in the dirt. "Hell. I came all the way out here and you're not going to tell me what's in it?"

"Nope."

Turning, he walked away with Harden describing, in detail, what he planned to do the next time he arrested the cowboy.

Tye didn't care about the letter or the threats or much of anything.

His body was strong. Hard work kept him fit, but Tye knew deep down inside he was dying. A man without a heart could only pretend he's alive for so long.

Not one person would mourn him when he died. Tye had no one who'd care, and he planned to keep it that way.

CHAPTER THREE

December 10
Late afternoon
Maverick Ranch

Cooper used the extra mount to haul medical supplies and extra provisions up to the line shack. Creed's pickup could have made it within a mile of the little house, but Cooper had met the foreman at the opening to the pass and loaded up. He was in a hurry to be alone.

The air was crisp where canyon walls widened and rose to Heaven. It was so quiet he swore he could hear the clouds floating by. In the warmth of the late-fall day, everything around him seemed still, as if nature rested in the warmth before sundown.

A hawk floated above him without a sound, and the tall grass waved in the wind. Cooper could feel this country calling to him. Reminding him that he was from this land, as much a part of it as the soil and rocks. Here, out in the open, he didn't need to-do lists or deadlines or even conversations. He was a man who needed solitude, and this land welcomed him to that paradise.

This part of the ranch wasn't good for grazing—too rocky, too uneven to drive cattle and impossible to truck them in or out. Maybe that was why he loved it so much. It had no purpose but to be.

He rode toward the base of Winter Valley, hidden away among the hills blanketed with cottonwood and juniper. Shrubby mesquite was peppered between them, a bothersome squatter. Once at the base, he climbed through trees to the highest hill. The wide basin was covered in fall colors on the bottom. Splashes of golden leaves and rich browns and oranges were spread over patches of still-green grass. Near the north wall, a stream moved as silently as a huge snake between the cottonwoods and sage.

Cooper saw tracks and knew the wild horses had already arrived. They'd winter here, where the canyons would shelter them. And, if he was lucky, they'd let him take care of them.

There were rumors of bears up here and maybe a mountain lion or two, but a healthy horse wasn't likely to become prey. Snakes would be belowground by now. The horses would need shots, maybe doctoring from old wounds to weather the winter. They'd need him, even though they wouldn't welcome him.

He rode toward the shack his great-grandfather had built. The original log wall still blocked the north wind, but the other three sides of the line shack had had layers added, more than being rebuilt. Log walls covered with wide planks of oak boards.

The first Holloway on this land had hauled the wood for the line shack by mule, then cut enough logs so winter wind wouldn't freeze him out. Legend claimed he'd started it the summer his first wife had left him. By the time the third one left, he'd disappeared from the headquarters so often, he'd had time to build the shack solidly. Cooper's dad had told him once that he remembered the old cowhands called it Holloway's Hideout.

Cooper had no idea if wife number four had driven him here, or if the old man had just grown used to the silence by the time she came along. Coop was just considering that he'd inherited that trait as his home for the next few weeks came into view.

The place had never been painted. There was no real porch, just a low roof that shaded the front door but left the rough board steps open to the weather. If a Realtor ever saw it, she'd probably describe it as worthless and rustic. One room with no bath, but with a nice view.

Grinning, he thought he'd made it to Heaven.

Before dark, he'd unloaded the medical supplies, mended the corral for his horses and stacked all the staples he'd need inside—a case of soups and chili, a box of spices and basics, a tin of crackers, coffee and a cooler packed full of peanut-butter cookies and sealed with duct tape.

More food than he'd need, but Dani Garrett, the new cook, insisted on making sure he had enough. "You might get snowed in," she'd said, "or have company come to dinner, and I want you prepared."

Cooper liked the way she took care of everyone. He and his brothers had called her Momma Dani from the day she'd moved in. She could cook pretty much anything, even those funny foods that Sunlan liked. Beans made into hummus and little noodle bags packed with a teaspoonful of meat.

When Sunlan was home, Dani would make funny little appetizers with raw meat or seafood, but on nights it was just the men, she cooked chicken-fried steak or slabs of ribs that hung over the edges of their plates.

Cooper decided he'd rather haul in more than he needed than hurt her feelings. Who knew—by Christmas, he might be as fat as a bear. If he timed it right, he could miss all the pre-Christmas mess and just make it home for the gift opening.

The brooding sky was almost dark when he climbed up the bluff behind the shack and looked over the valley. Every year since his dad had first brought him here when he was five, the first view from the cliff always took his breath away. Cooper sat down and watched evening spread across the land so slowly it was fully dark by the time he realized he should be off the cliff.

As he stumbled down, he cussed himself for not even bothering to bring a flashlight. He'd probably step on the last snake heading into hibernation.

Thank goodness he'd hung the solar light on a nail at the sunny side of the roof. It hadn't had the seven hours of sunshine to fully charge, but maybe it would shine enough to show him the way to the shack.

He was almost down from the cliff when he noticed a low light. Though it was putting off the glow of a dying firefly, it was enough for him to get his bearings.

Cooper made it to the shack's overhang and reached for his flashlight, which was tucked away in his saddlebags, along with a Colt. He always hung necessities, like matches and firearms, on a peg shadowed under the overhang. That way, day or night, inside or out, he knew where they were when needed.

He looped the bags over his shoulder, turned on the flashlight and stepped into the cabin, where he'd unloaded the supplies.

One sweep of the beam told him someone, or some*thing*, had been there. The bags were tossed around, spilling medical supplies and canned goods all over the place.

Cooper backed slowly outside and reached for his Colt. If the intruder hadn't found what he was looking for, there was a good chance he was still in the cabin. Maybe the door had swung closed and whatever had entered was trapped inside.

A man might hide, but a cornered animal would fight when threatened.

With the door wide-open and his gun at the ready, Cooper tried to tell himself he was prepared. He'd threaten any stranger who'd invaded his place, or hopefully frighten away a curious animal.

The whole world was silent. Dried leaves rushed along in the wind, seeming to whisper of danger in the darkness outside. A dove cooed, and its partner echoed the call.

Cooper didn't move. He barely breathed as sweat dripped from his forehead. He hated waiting. But something had invaded, and right now they seemed to be playing a game of chicken to see who would make the next move.

Then he heard a crunching sound. Maybe the animal inside had found food, or maybe he was gnawing his way out between loose boards at the back of the shack.

The sound came again. One of the floorboards creaked.

"You'd better come out," Cooper said, feeling foolish—he was probably talking to a raccoon. "If I have to come in after you, I'll come in firing."

Silence.

"I'll count to ten." Cooper almost hit himself in the forehead with the Colt. Raccoons couldn't count. "One...two."

Nothing.

"Three...four...five." Cooper leaned in, trying to see something moving in the shadows, but the flashlight's beam only passed over dust. The stranger could be behind the old potbellied stove or under one of the two small beds.

"Six...seven...eight." Hell, he *was* going to have to go in shooting.

"Nine." Cooper took a step, the barrel of the Colt pointed ahead of him.

"Don't shoot me, mister," a squeaky voice said.

Cooper lowered the Colt, swung his flashlight back and forth and watched as a kid crawled from beneath one of the bunks. He held a box of crackers in one hand and an old, beat-up hat in the other.

Cooper stared at the intruder. Eight, maybe nine years old. Filthy. Body so thin his clothes hung on him as if he was no more than a coat hanger. Brown hair and light blue eyes shining up at Cooper as if he thought he was meeting Satan himself.

"What's your name? What are you doing here?"

"Tatum, sir. I ain't a thief, mister, I promise. I was just so hungry, and I couldn't wait around to see if you were coming back." He held out the almost-empty box of crackers. "I didn't eat them all. You can have the rest back."

Cooper walked to the lantern and flipped it on. He was thankful the batteries were fresh.

The kid watched his every move as though he'd already figured the cowboy would turn around and strike at any moment.

Cooper had a dozen questions, but he guessed he'd frightened the kid enough. "You want some soup or chili with those crackers?"

Tatum looked like he feared a trap, but hunger must have made him brave. "You got a can opener? I looked for one. I'll be happy with anything. You don't even need to heat it up."

Smiling, Coop relaxed. "Sit down, kid. I'll warm you a can of soup. This place gets cold once the sun goes down, so I was planning to start a fire, anyway."

He tossed a few logs into a potbellied stove three times older than him, then pulled a starter stick from his saddlebag. While the wood caught, Cooper moved around the small space, putting up supplies. Food on the top two shelves, too high for the kid, or any wild thing, to reach. The duffel bag of clothes hung on a peg in case it rained and the place flooded. He'd shoved his old rifle back above the cabinet. The rest of the supplies went on a shelf inside a cupboard he'd made when he'd started coming out to work with the horses. It didn't have a lock, but the latch would keep out varmints.

Ten minutes later, Cooper handed the little boy a mug of soup. "Eat slow, kid."

As he ate, Tatum never took his eyes off the pot. That told Coop all he needed to know about how hungry the boy was.

As the boy finished, Cooper made coffee and dug out the first bag of cookies. Dani had told him she'd packed one bag for each day he'd be out here, so when the cookies were gone, he'd better be heading home.

Cooper would have laughed, but with no cell phone and no electricity, there was a good chance he'd lose track of time.

He pulled out three of the cookies and handed them to the kid, then ate his three for supper.

Tatum handed back the empty mug, his big blue eyes never turning away from Cooper.

"I wash dishes in the stream." Cooper kept his voice low, friendly. "If you stay for breakfast, you'll have to do the dishes tomorrow morning."

"You going to let me stay, mister? I'm not trouble. You'll barely know I'm here."

The doubt in the boy's tone broke Cooper's heart, as did the fact that this shack was his best option. What kind of people had this kid been around to have him skeptical of simple kindness? "Yeah, you're welcome to stay. I got two bunks. From the looks of it, a northerner is coming in. Won't get much below freezing tonight. Probably won't see but a dusting of snow, but the place will be warmer than outside."

"Thanks." Relief shook the boy's thin frame.

A hundred questions still stood between them, but Cooper thought the kid looked like he might fall over any minute. He tossed the boy a blanket and his only pillow. "Better settle in before I turn off the lamp. The fire will offer enough light." He sat the flashlight on the room's tiny table and flipped the latch on the door. "I'll leave the flashlight here in case you have to go to the outhouse in the night, but you be sure and turn it off when you get back."

"Which bunk do I take?"

Cooper finished off his coffee. "The one closest to the door. That way if a bear breaks in, he'll eat you first."

Tatum crawled onto the smooth, cowhide-covered slats. "I wouldn't be more than a few bites, mister. If a bear does break in, he'll just step over me and go straight for you."

Cooper laughed. "Way my luck's been going, you're probably right, kid."

He studied the child. His clothes hadn't been washed in at least a week, and they probably had been little more than rags to start with. As soon as his head rested on the pillow, the boy was asleep. Cooper wondered how many days he'd been out here, probably rarely sleeping and never eating. He was miles from a road or any farm. Maybe he'd been riding a horse and gotten lost, but if that had been true, someone would be out searching, and this was Holloway land. If men were on his ranch hunting for the kid, they'd probably never find the cabin. Cooper's ranch hands would spot them long before they reached Winter Valley.

Tomorrow, after breakfast, maybe the boy would explain the mystery. Then Cooper would have to find a way to get him back to civilization quickly, before Cooper lost too many days of peace.

He stretched out and tried to solve the puzzle.

There was nothing worth stealing for miles around, so the kid wouldn't have traveled in with smugglers or thieves. Farther south, an intruder might find Holloway equipment and cattle, but no one could get there without being noticed. No campers would venture onto the ranch by accident.

"Nothing of value anywhere worth taking," Cooper whispered. But then a thought sent a chill up his spine.

Nothing but wild horses.

His muscles tightened. If someone was after the herd, they'd have to get past him first, and he didn't plan to make that easy.

CHAPTER FOUR

December 13

Tye Franklin sat on the bed in his thirty-dollar-a-night hotel room and stared at the envelope the trooper had said was from the Texas Rangers. He never got mail. As far as he knew, he had no living relatives except a pair of old aunts, and he hadn't checked on them in years. Every time he passed through Amarillo, he stopped by his post-office box to collect all the junk mail. He'd drop off a dozen postcards, too—all addressed to his first boss. At ninety, the old guy had lost his memory. He couldn't remember who Tye was, but the nurses at the VA said he liked getting the cards.

In Tye's grand days, when he was riding high over the rodeo circuit, he'd be asked to endorse a product or make an appearance at some store opening for extra money. But those days were long gone. He hadn't even had to show up drunk that many times before the word got out. The offers had stopped about the time his luck at the rodeo played its last hand.

No one ever asked why he drank, but if they had, Tye would

have lied. It was no one's business. Hell, most days he didn't have enough sense to figure it out himself.

He set the newly delivered mail beside him and pulled off his boots, but for once, he didn't reach for a beer.

The envelope drew him. It had several addresses crossed out and rewritten. What could be so important that a lawman had tracked him down to deliver it?

Slowly, he opened the big battered envelope and pulled out a thick file folder.

Moving to a wobbly, scratched table by a dirty window, he turned on the best light he had in the dingy room and shoved aside a half-dozen empty beer bottles. Slowly, as if something might pop out, he opened the folder.

One piece of notepaper sat atop what looked like a yellowed journal.

To Tyson Jefferson Franklin, only child of Jefferson Allen Franklin, only grandson of Adam Tyson Franklin.

Tye smiled. He'd already learned something. He'd been named after his grandfather. His father had told him once that *his* old man had been an outlaw as well as a certified drunk. Tye's dad would have known how to recognize a drunk—after all, Tye never remembered his dad sober. Legend was Adam Franklin ran drugs up from the border in the sixties and had killed more than one friend who'd turned on him.

Some folks said he'd died in jail; others claimed he'd just disappeared somewhere south, near Big Bend.

Tye didn't care. Adam hadn't been any more of a grandfather than Jefferson had been a father. Tye had been raised by his single mom, and he used to think of his old man as a horror vacation dad: once in a while he'd drop by and take Tye for a week, and while the planned trips always sounded grand, they never panned out. He'd forget to make a reservation, and they'd end up sleeping in the car, or whatever they'd traveled hours to see was closed. Once his grandfather had come along for the vacation, and it'd been a double disaster. The two had stopped in for a drink and ended up leaving Tye in the car all night and most of the next morning. Tye's dad made no apology, but his grandfather brought him a pocketful of peanuts from the bar.

Picking up the journal, Tye tried to figure out what would be so special that it had to be hand delivered. The notebook was just one of those cheap ones sold in school-supply aisles in discount stores. The pages had yellowed and the corners had worn away. The circle of wire that held it together was bent so badly it was hard to lay the book flat on the table.

Still fighting the urge to reach for a beer, he flipped through the pages. He needed to be stone-cold sober to figure this out.

He opened the first page and read.

This is my last will and testament. I want my grandson to be the only person who goes beyond this page. I curse any other man who does.
Adam Franklin
June 1989

Tye didn't believe in curses. He didn't even believe in luck, unless it was bad luck.

Slowly, he turned the page and saw a pencil drawing. Open prairie with cattle grazing. The next picture was almost the same. Barbed-wire fence in the foreground, rolling hills in the background.

He kept turning. The sketches began to look familiar. Small-town streets. A tiny post office. A big old two-story house. A town square built in a triangle. A café front with windows showing booths pushed up against them.

Tye closed the book and went to bed. If this was his inheritance from his grandfather, it was worthless. From the looks of it, his grandfather had little talent.

As he dozed, the black-and-white world in the notebook began to whirl in his head. Somewhere in his dreams the drawings became a town. A real place, not just sketches. It was like he knew his way well enough to walk the streets, even though there were no streetlights.

Tye woke at dawn, his head hurting as usual. For once, he didn't reach for a drink to self-medicate. He simply pulled on his boots and stepped out into the fall air. His hotel was across from the rodeo grounds, so his commute was easy. The last thing he needed to do for the job was check on the stock, then he'd make sure the rodeo was a go and his job was done. Another guy was due to take over when the rodeo moved on this time.

An hour later he was finished and heading back to pack. Tye had drunk two cups of coffee and made sure the arena was dry enough for the rodeo to open. Usually he stayed around until it was over. Sometimes he even helped with loading the stock for their ride back to Colorado Springs.

But this time, he had something else to think about. Somewhere else to be. He went back to his room and, with clearer eyes, looked through the pages one more time. Drawings of old houses. Ranch land bordered by a gate branded with a huge *M*. Horses running the fence line next to a dirt road. The sketches were primitive. Worthless. The setting could be anywhere on the plains. They could have existed a year ago or a century ago and they'd look the same.

One comment was written in the middle fold along the edges.

Follow the lone star. Find Dusty Roads. My gift to you waits.

Tye thought of adding one more label to his grandfather: crazy. He'd only seen the old man a few times, and that had been when he was barely in grade school.

Tye had been in his early teens when his mother told him the old man went to jail. A year later she mentioned that Tye's dad had died. She'd never added details. When he'd asked, she'd simply said, "What does it matter?" His grandfather was in jail and his dad was dead.

Why would a grandfather who'd never remembered a birthday or Christmas leave him a gift now?

As he studied each drawing, he swore he'd seen a few of the scenes before. Maybe in Western magazines or posters on a wall. Or maybe he'd seen the real places the artist had depicted. But only one drawing gave a location, and even that just showed a Texas county-road sign with bullet holes shot through the metal.

Lone star. The site of the drawings had to be in Texas.

Another ranch gate was in the corner of a drawing. This one looked old, broken-down. But Tye could clearly see, outlined on the crossbar, what looked like a wild horse rising to fight.

Maybe it'd be worth looking for, Tye thought. After all, he had nothing to do until spring, when the rodeos started up again.

After an hour spent memorizing the drawings, he packed his gear into the bed of his pickup and made a sandwich with the two heels of bread and the last of the bologna. Time to drive south toward Texas. The notebook mystery was probably nothing, but Tye had time off and nowhere else to go. He'd start with ranch land where he'd been before. If the drawings looked familiar, maybe he'd get lucky. The brand on a gate might appear next to a dusty road and there, sitting in the middle of it all, would be a huge box. His gift. *Fat chance.*

He didn't bother with a map. He'd just drive until he got tired. Then, anywhere there was land and stock, he'd find work.

It dawned on him that the artist was traveling through a place as he drew. Sometimes the corner ending one picture would appear in the next frame.

A wide ranch gate framed one page. Tye had seen a dozen

gates that could match the drawing. Maybe he'd drive until he found one.

There were maps wiggling across a few pages of the book, but there was no starting point, no ending and no scale: markers like a stand of trees or a windmill could have been twenty feet apart or twenty miles.

Tye finally closed the book, frustrated with himself for allowing a dream to form. You'd think after over twenty years on his own, he'd give up on dreams. There was no happily-ever-after.

On the back cover of the notebook, scratched in the cardboard, words were written… *Never stop looking.*

In a slit in the cover was a small yellowed newspaper clipping announcing one of Tye's first wins at a little rodeo in West Texas. The second clue, maybe?

If this had been written by his grandfather, who'd disappeared thirty years ago, and he was trying to tell Tye something, the memories had to be in Texas. Tye decided he'd head south toward Ransom Canyon. His grandfather had never lived there, but his two great-aunts, his grandfather's younger sisters, had settled near there. It seemed as good as anywhere to start. Tye had cowboyed a few off-seasons on some of the ranches nearby. He figured he could find work there.

It was the end of the season this far north, so he was heading that way, anyway. He had enough money to hole up for a while if he was careful.

But being careful had never been in his vocabulary.

The last time he'd seen his grandfather was in a little town somewhere in the Panhandle. His father had been working the oil fields, and Grandpa had taken Tye to eat at a fancy two-story house, then shopping for everything he thought a six-year-old needed.

Tye flipped to the middle of the book. The two-story house. He'd start there. Find a ranch gate with an *M*. A two-story house that looked familiar. Maybe even find the rodeo ground where he'd won and made it into the paper.

All he had to do then was find a dusty road and the gift his grandfather had left him.

As he drove, Tye remembered a ranch owned by a family called Holloway. The Maverick Ranch. An *M* over the gate maybe. Too many drunk nights had washed away facts, but he'd start there.

CHAPTER FIVE

December 14
Just after midnight
Maverick Ranch

Elliot Holloway stepped away from his U-shaped desk and stretched. Even with company for a couple of days, he'd managed to get in three hours of work every night. They'd slept off their flights the first night and shopped online until they were exhausted the second night. Tonight, boredom was setting in.

He left his office and headed to check on his guests. Grinning, he decided he'd been the perfect host to his three, slightly tipsy, almost cousins. He'd settled their luggage in their rooms upstairs and shown them the kitchen, which was stocked with snacks. Then he'd pointed toward a supper of sandwiches and little cakes the cook had set out in front of the huge fireplace in the great room every night. What else could he do?

As he'd walked away the first night, he'd said, "I'll give you three time to relax. Have fun."

They hadn't seemed that interested in much until he'd mentioned this morning that their UPS boxes were stacked in the foyer. From the squeals, you'd think it was Christmas morning, not two weeks away from the holiday.

He'd left them to talk and open packages from stores he'd never heard of. According to his sister-in-law, the three went to schools in different states and always got together for a few days to catch up before they went home to their folks. This year, the Maverick Ranch seemed to be their private bed-and-breakfast of choice.

Why they picked the Maverick Ranch was anyone's guess. The short one with blond hair claimed she hated the outdoors.

When he'd heard them laughing, he'd closed the big oak door to his office, not wanting them to think he was eavesdropping.

Three hours later, without warning, he opened the doors to the great room and stepped into chaos. The main room, big enough to hold a dance, looked more like a lingerie boutique. If Cooper had still been around, he'd be having a fit. It appeared the three young ladies had turned the long coffee table into a runway. Bras were hanging from the antlers of the deer Cooper had shot one winter. Nightgowns were draped all over the two long leather couches, and tiny house shoes that weren't designed for comfort or warmth were scattered everywhere.

So much for his belief that they'd mailed books and games.

The wide end tables had perfumes and all kinds of beauty products. One bottle had tipped over, and was dripping a green liquid onto the tile.

None of this bothered Elliot. He was the sensible brother, he told himself. The old house had survived many parties. These ladies were his brother's wife's cousins. Griffin was crazy about Sunlan. If she said she wanted to go to Mars, he'd start packing, and if she wanted her cousins here, Elliot wouldn't argue.

Cooper would be yelling about now, but he'd vanished, the coward.

That left him, the middle brother, the brains of the whole Maverick operation from ranching to oil to farming. Elliot knew what he had to do. He had to take charge. He locked his fists behind him and walked toward his guests as he kicked empty UPS boxes out of the way.

The mess could be cleaned up, but what was he going to do with the three drunk cousins who'd invaded? They hurried to the kitchen to get more food and champagne. "We'll be right back," one said, while another announced that Elliot would have to join them in the fun.

Elliot picked up the phone and dialed the bunkhouse as he walked toward the front door.

Creed, the ranch foreman, answered. "Yeah, boss." Creed never wasted words or time.

"You got a few men mature enough over there to help me get three drunk cousins up the stairs?"

"Can't Dani help?" Creed's answer was low and polite, but Elliot swore he could hear the cowboy groaning. "That sounds more like a housekeeper's job than mine."

"She's out with her two sons tonight celebrating."

"Celebrating what?" Creed asked.

"Dani's boys finally got jobs. At twenty, it's about time." Elliot glanced back at the three drunk fairies in satin and lace dancing into the great room. Their nightgowns, which didn't even fully cover their bottoms, flowed around them like cotton candy.

The pretty little blonde, who looked like the youngest of the three, was hiccuping in rhythm to the music. The tall redhead, obviously the leader of the pack, was singing off-key, and the third cousin, who had black-and-white-striped hair, had started doing yoga. At least, he thought it was yoga.

He thought she'd said her name was Apple.

They were in their twenties, but their brains must have stopped growing at sixteen. A triple dose of trouble.

Creed's next questions came through loud and clear in Elliot's ear. "What idiot would give those two nitwits Dani gave birth to jobs? Together they're about four hundred pounds of bumbling."

Now it was Elliot's time to groan. "Me. I offered them both jobs. It's better to have them working here than driving over every day to check on their mother. We'll let them eat breakfast here in the headquarters' kitchen, so they can see her, then I want them on the east pasture rounding up strays. I figure they'll make it two or three days before giving up the hard work and going back home."

"All right, boss. The only thing those two boys can do is cowboy and they don't even do that well. I swear I caught a couple of heifers giggling at them."

Elliot fought down a laugh. Creed's sense of humor always got him. "Forget the brothers for now. I need a few good men to be perfect gentlemen to three drunk ladies."

Creed let out a huff, sounding like a deer blowing out the smell of humans. "On my way, boss. Oh, and a man showed up at sunset today, looking for work—I'll bring him, too. Rodeo guy by the name of Franklin. He's old enough to be their father. Maybe they won't give him much trouble. He said he worked for us once before, years ago. He claims he's good with horses. Don't know about women. I told him he could join us for supper at the bunkhouse and sleep over tonight before talking to you about a job tomorrow morning. I figured you had your hands full tonight."

"You're right." Elliot glanced over his shoulder. The girls had started dancing in a circle as they passed around a bottle. "Grab the stranger and get here fast."

By the time he opened the door, he could hear help riding in.

Elliot nodded at his foreman and the cowboy at his side as they swung from their horses. The newcomer named Franklin was thin, but solidly built, as only a man who'd lived in the saddle could be. When the tall cowboy nodded once, Elliot saw steel in the stranger's eyes and guessed he could handle any job—even this one.

"I'm Franklin, Mr. Holloway. Folks call me Tye." The man's hat looked expensive but well-worn.

"Call me Elliot. There are enough Holloways around to use the *mister*. This chore isn't going to be an easy one and it's above and beyond normal around here, but I'd appreciate your help. Consider it a job interview. Or maybe just a favor you don't owe me, but if you help, I'll owe you one."

The new hand followed Creed inside, his wolf-gray eyes missing little, Elliot guessed.

"Ladies!" Elliot moved to the double doors of the great room and yelled over the country music. "If you don't mind, we'd like to escort you all upstairs to your rooms. It's getting late and your music is keeping the cows awake."

All three women turned on him, looking like Victoria's Secret models, pouting and preparing to rebel.

Elliot glanced at Creed, but the foreman just stared. He was shy around women—even the middle-aged housekeeper, Dani. Creed, at twenty-six, was not much older than the cousins. These three ladies were way out of his league.

Turning to the new man, Elliot raised an eyebrow, silently asking for suggestions, any suggestions. Sunlan would never forgive him if he was rude to her kin, and he wasn't sure the room would survive an all-night party.

The cowboy nodded slightly and stepped forward. "Evening, ladies. I'm Tye Franklin and I swear I've never seen such beauties. Royalty must run in your family, because three princesses are standing before me."

They giggled at his obvious line of crap, so he continued,

"Would you do us the honor of allowing us to two-step you up to your rooms?"

The redhead moved so that she was nose to nose with Tye. "All the way up, cowboy?"

"All the way." He smiled, and Elliot had no doubt this new man had charmed many a dance-hall beauty in his day. A slow grin crossed his sun-worn face.

She laughed, a bit nervously.

Without another word the stranger put his arm around the redhead's waist and danced her around the room.

She giggled. "A cowboy who can dance. A rare sight indeed."

Elliot offered his hand to the blonde with hair falling down her back to the hem of her nightgown. "You're Bethany, right?"

"I am," she said and bowed slightly. "Elliot, right?"

He tried to dance like the stranger, but his skill was poor at best. Bethany didn't seem to notice. Her skill barely matched his, but damn if she didn't feel good in his arms.

It had been so long since he'd held a woman, he'd forgotten how good they could feel.

They were halfway up to the landing when Elliot looked back and noticed Creed was just standing there. His feet seemed to be stuck to the floor. The tall, thin foreman still had his hat on, reminding Elliot of a Western floor lamp.

The third cousin, Apple, swayed as she headed toward the foreman. Her dark red pajama top, made to look like a man's shirt, fit her just right, even if it did clash with her black-and-white-striped hair.

Her eyes were the color of a winter sunset. Or at least he thought they both were. He'd only seen one. The other eye was covered by the strands of skunk-colored hair.

She twirled to the music, caught the corner of the coffee table and stumbled into Creed's arms.

To Creed's obvious shock, she passed right out. For a moment he just stood there, as if someone had tossed him a newborn and he had no idea how to handle it.

Finally, he slid his arm beneath her legs and picked her up. Slowly, he carried her toward the stairs. When he reached the steps, he glanced at Elliot, silently asking for help, but Elliot had his hands full, and all he could do was motion for Creed to follow.

Since the three were already wearing their pj's, the men put them in the three guest bedrooms, covered them up and rushed back out into the hallway. Then, like frightened boys, not gentlemen, they ran down the stairs.

"You think we got them in the right rooms?" Creed whispered as if he might wake them.

"Who cares? I'm just hoping they stay there. Come morning, they can straighten it out." Elliot glanced over at the desserts stacked on the breakfast table. "I say we don't let their snacks go to waste. Dancing cousins up the stairs burns a great many calories."

Ten minutes later they were drinking the last of the coffee and laughing when Dani walked through the side door that opened to her kitchen.

She took one look at them and froze. "What are you men up to?" As the mother of sons, she recognized mischief, even in grown men.

Elliot told the housekeeper what they'd done, then introduced her to the new man. "Tye used to rodeo, Dani. He's used to handling wild stock and wild women, I'd guess."

"I'm sure he is." She offered her hand, and Tye smiled without saying a word.

Elliot thought the ex-rodeo man held her hand a bit longer than necessary, but they were both old enough to gauge time.

As everyone parted in different directions, Elliot couldn't help but think that Tye and Dani might become friends. Maybe this cook would stay around a little longer if she had someone her age to talk to now and then.

When Creed hesitated at the door, Elliot whispered, "Bring Tye over here for breakfast tomorrow. He's hired. Maybe he should sit between Dani's sons. The last time I invited them to the table, they got in a fight and broke half a dozen plates. If that cowboy can handle cousins, he can be the referee between the Garrett twins."

"I could leave them in the bunkhouse. The men take turns frying up eggs and bacon. Dani always sends over enough biscuits or cinnamon rolls to go around."

"No, I promised them they'd get to see their mother every morning. I'm not sure if they need to know she's all right since she moved out, or if they just miss her cooking. She told me she tried everything to get them to grow up last year when they both finished high school. When they didn't, she decided it wasn't worth the arguing, so she just moved off the farm and left them with the chores."

Creed nodded. "Pete claimed he wouldn't leave home until Patrick did. After all, Patrick's the oldest by five minutes. He should go first. Short of starving them, she had no option."

Elliot agreed. "She loves them."

"Yeah, boss, the way a mother possum loves her babies no matter how ugly they are."

"Thanks for your help tonight."

"Anytime, boss. I got the easy one tonight. If she remembers me carrying her to bed, she'll probably cuss me out in the morning. I might ride out to the far pasture with the Garrett boys."

Elliot didn't argue. He just closed the door and smiled. If Sunlan didn't show up soon, he might have to bring in reinforcements. A visit he'd thought might be just a weekend was stretching longer, with no mention of when they'd be leaving.

CHAPTER SIX

December 14

Long, thin beams of light flickered into the cabin through cracks in the boards around the front door. Cooper rolled over, realizing the fire had gone out sometime during the night. He remembered tossing the extra blanket over the kid before the air chilled.

He opened one eye and groaned.

The blankets were there, but the boy was missing.

Before all his brain cells were awake, Cooper considered the possibility that he'd dreamed of having a kid as a cabin guest. Only he never dreamed about anything except wild horses and naked women.

No, the boy was real. He didn't have that much imagination to fill in all the details. Light blue eyes set in a thin little face. Hair the color of sand. Clothes worn and dirty. He'd said his name was Tatum.

"Tatum?" Cooper said aloud.

No answer.

Cooper sat up and pulled on his boots as his eyes adjusted to the shadowy light between the sunbeams. The blanket he'd layered over the kid was folded. The coffee cup and Tatum's bowl were gone, along with the spoons they'd used last night.

Footsteps stomped outside on the porch. Cooper leaned back and pretended to be asleep.

The boy, wrapped in a blanket tied around his neck like a cape, slipped through the door. He carried the tin dishes in one hand and a few logs tucked under his arm.

Cooper watched as he set down the bowl, both spoons and the cup, then—with no skill—tried to start the fire in the old iron stove.

"You need some help?" Cooper asked, his voice low and calm.

To his credit, the boy didn't spook easy. In fact, he didn't even look up from his task.

"If you show me, mister, I'll learn." The boy finally turned to face him. "I got to figure things out by myself most of the time, but you could help."

Cooper sat up. "Lighting a fire in a hundred-year-old stove isn't something I'd think you need to know. Shouldn't we be talking about how to get you home? I've already let you stay too long. You looked so hungry a few days ago I wasn't sure you'd have the energy to hike down."

Tears filled the boy's eyes, but he blinked them away. "I ain't got no home."

"Parents?"

The boy shook his head. "My dad died before I was born. He was in the army. That's all I know. My mom was killed in a car wreck when I was in the first grade. No one ever told me much about it. A woman just came and got me in a big blue car and took me to my grandma's house. She packed my clothes in a trash bag and said my grandma said not to bring any junk like toys."

"What about other relatives?"

"Only had one grandma. She said she had a daughter, but she never came around. I don't think they got along. My grandma didn't wake up a few weeks ago. Her hand was cold when I touched her, so I got dressed and went to school. When I told my teacher, she took me to the office and made me wait there for a policeman. He took me back home to talk to my grandma, but she was still cold. The policeman told me not to touch her."

"What happened then?"

"A nosy neighbor saw the police car and came over. Grandma and her weren't friends. They just yelled at each other now and then about the trash spilling over or the lady parking in Grandma's spot." He looked like he might cry, then he shrugged and continued, "The neighbor said I carry death wherever I go, so I been thinking I got to live on my own."

"How old are you, Tatum?"

"Nine. I'm small for my age, but my grandma said I'll grow. I can read and write. I read all the mail to her."

"You remember what her address was?" Cooper asked.

Every time the boy said something, a dozen more questions popped up. Suddenly, Cooper saw panic in his shy blue eyes and fear so deep it seemed a permanent part of him. He held one of the logs in a warrior's grip and twice he'd taken a step backward toward the door as if it might be time to run.

Cooper could smell the desperation.

The questions faded from Cooper's mind. They'd wait. He had to gain this kid's trust first. Cooper looked over at the stove. "I'll show you how to light a fire since you washed the dishes. Seems like a fair trade. Then, after breakfast, we'll talk."

Slowly, as if moving toward a wild colt, Cooper showed him how to build a fire. While the kid poked at the blaze, Coop grabbed the nearest can on the shelf.

"Chili sound good for breakfast?"

"Sure, mister."

"You drink coffee?"

"Sure."

Cooper grinned. "Nothing better than chili and coffee at dawn." He pulled down the camp coffeepot, washed out the cobwebs and filled it with water from the two-gallon jug he'd brought. "My dad told me once that my grandfather put the grounds in a sock to boil, but I use a filter."

The kid watched each step.

As the chili and water boiled, Cooper poured Tatum's cup half-full of milk. Soon after, breakfast was ready.

They ate in silence for a while, then Cooper leaned back in his chair. "Nothing better than hot coffee on a cold morning."

Tatum had to push with his toes to lean even an inch back. "Nothing better," he added.

Cooper reminded himself to latch the small cooler holding milk and cookies and set it aside. The luxuries would be gone soon. One by one, along with the candy bars, they'd disappear and he'd be down to trail mix and canned goods. Now, with the boy here, his supplies would be eaten fast. When he took the boy home, he'd be wise to pick up extra. If they started soon, they could be home before dark and call the sheriff to come pick up the kid. He'd have to wait until tomorrow to come back. The cousins might not even know he was near if he slept in the bunkhouse.

The kid ate the rest of the crackers with his chili.

"You want more?"

Tatum eyed the cooler with the cookies.

"How about we have cookies for dessert?"

"Dessert comes with breakfast?"

"Out in the wild you eat what you have, and we got cookies." Cooper pitched him two small bags. "Take your time. We'll need to feed the horses, then head down when breakfast is over.

Like it or not, even folks who live wild need supplies, and they need to check in now and then."

The boy gobbled up the dessert, too busy eating to ask questions. Cooper leaned back, drinking his coffee slowly. "You don't carry death, Tatum. That's not what people do. You had nothing to do with the people around you dying."

"I do." Innocent eyes stared up at Cooper, and the boy added, "The neighbor wasn't the first to tell me I was nothing but trouble. My mom used to say my dad wouldn't have re-upped for three more years if I hadn't been born. I figured if I walked far enough away from town, I could live like a wolf off the land, but it wasn't as easy as I thought. I was about ready to give up, but I knew I could never find the way back. Then I saw you sitting up on that ledge. I thought maybe you were someone like me—one of the wolf people. I headed toward you to ask directions, but I found this cabin first. I swear I wasn't going to steal more than I could eat."

"Where you from?" Cooper kept his voice low, casual, as if they were simply passing time. "We got to be honest with each other, Tatum. That's how it works out here in the wild."

Tatum looked up as if suspecting a trap. "Oklahoma. The morning Grandma died, I heard the neighbor say I didn't have any kin to go to. She said I was half-wild and they should take me to the pound. The policeman said he'd call someone to come pick me up. He looked around and noticed I'd vanished."

He looked at Cooper. "I knew what that meant. The lady in the blue car was coming and the next place would be worse than where I was. I didn't want to go with her.

"I was hiding inside the back of Grandma's old couch. The back was ripped just enough for me to slip in. The cop searched the whole house but couldn't find me. When he and the neighbor went outside to look for me in the sheds, I stuffed my backpack with anything I thought I might need and slipped away. I caught the school bus a block over. Darted in the back and hid in the last seat when everyone else got off."

Cooper was impressed. "None of that means you carry death with you."

"Yeah, it does. I got to keep moving. I got to learn to live off the land. If rabbits and squirrels do it, I should be able to. Grandma said I was smart."

"How'd you get to Texas?"

"At the bus barn I heard the men talking. One said he was taking a load of football players to watch a game at Texas Tech. While they were gassing up I hid behind the last seat. It wasn't comfortable, but I was warm. When the driver stopped outside Lubbock for a potty stop, I climbed out. I just started walking."

Cooper leaned closer. "Lubbock is almost thirty miles from here. The rest stop is maybe another twenty or more."

"I don't know how to figure miles. I just walked all day and slept in the bar ditches so no one would see me. A few times folks stopped to offer me a ride, but I told them I was close to home. I picked smaller roads whenever I could. They finally ran out so I followed trails. From then on I just slept in tall grass and headed toward the sunrise every morning so I wouldn't go in circles.

"Once I found the stream, I followed it. At least I had water. My food ran out the third day. About the time I thought I might starve, I found a grove of pecan trees. It took me a while to figure out how to crack them."

"Where were you heading?"

"I don't know. Just away from people. My grandma told me if she hadn't taken me in I'd have to go to a bad place where no one would ever care about me." A fat tear drifted down Tatum's dirty face. "I'd rather stay out here and eat nuts. I got water. Until it got so cold yesterday, I was doing fine. If I can just figure out how to stay warm, I can survive."

Cooper studied him, almost believing the nine-year-old

might just be able to do it. "I have to take you back, Tatum. It's not safe out here alone."

"You're out here alone."

"I'm here to doctor a herd of wild horses. It's my job. I won't be out here all alone long—a doc will drop by in a day or two to help with the horses. I try to get any horses he needs to check rounded up before he gets here."

"I can help with that. I learn fast."

"No. You can't. A wild horse will run right over you to get free."

Tatum set his jaw and looked up at Cooper. "If you take me back, I'll just run away again. I don't want someone I love to die. I carry death with me, the neighbor said so."

"I'm not dead. That alone should prove the neighbor's wrong."

The kid glared at him. "I'm not sure I even like you, mister. You're probably safe."

Cooper stared back, feeling like he'd been outdebated by a nine-year-old. "All right. We stay here today. One more day, that's all. I need to check up on things. If I have to ride all the way back to headquarters, I don't want to have to make another trip for supplies I could have picked up when I drop you off."

Cooper grabbed his leather vest. "Take off your coat and put this underneath it. It'll be warmer than that blanket. Stop calling me mister. Name's Cooper, but to you it's Coop. That's what my brothers call me."

The kid followed orders, then tied the blanket back around his neck. When Cooper raised an eyebrow, he said simply, "It's not a blanket. It is a cape."

"All right. Can you ride a horse?"

"No."

"Then we ride double 'til you get the hang of it. When we get close to the herd, if we get close, I don't want you saying a word, understand?"

"Understand."

Cooper walked out into the cold, cloudy day with the kid two steps behind him. Tatum didn't talk except to answer a question, but he watched everything. They walked the fifty feet to the small corral where Hector and one of Creed's cutting horses were kept. Hector snorted at the newcomer, but the mare let the child pat her nose.

When Cooper finally swung into the saddle, he looked down at his unplanned guest. Tatum looked so small and frightened, but he took Cooper's hand and climbed up behind him.

"Hold on, kid," Cooper ordered as he began the short trek down to the water. He'd be lucky to see one horse today, but the best place to start the search would be near the stream. He'd pick up tracks there.

By noon, snow had started with flurries but quickly changed to lazy flakes drifting in the wind. Most of the tracks they'd found were from small animals. Coop taught him to recognize each. Tatum seemed to love the game. He had a hunger to learn.

As Cooper talked about reading the weather, he gave the kid a health bar and they ate as they sat on a rock and watched the river. "We're turning back. Eat up and make sure you don't drop the wrapper."

The boy asked a few questions about fishing, then folded his arms exactly as Cooper did and studied the stream.

"You ready to ride?"

"Yes, Coop, I'm ready."

Cooper lifted up the boy and decided to walk beside Hector. The kid needed to feel like he was really riding.

When they were in sight of the line shack, Cooper turned the reins loose. He walked near and let the boy ride alone. Tatum held the reins easy in his hands, like he'd seen Coop do.

To his surprise, Cooper found himself explaining things to Tatum that the kid would probably never need to know.

By the time they'd fed Hector and put him in a stall built into an overhang that blocked the wind, Cooper noticed the boy was almost sleepwalking.

"You go on in and start the fire, I'll heat up some stew after I work on the corral awhile." When the boy hesitated, Cooper added, "Make a pot of coffee. I'll be needing a cup when I get in. Snow's falling faster."

Tatum headed into the shack, and by the time Coop finished working on the corral and had come inside, he found the boy curled up on his bed, already asleep.

He poured himself a cup of coffee and listened to the wind howling outside as light from the lantern flickered across the walls. If he hadn't found the boy, or more accurately, if Tatum hadn't found him, the kid wouldn't have survived this night. The sun wasn't all the way down, and he could already feel the temperature dropping below freezing.

The knowledge that Tatum might have frozen up here tore at his heart. He would have died alone, without one person who cared about him. He'd die thinking that he was the cause of everyone he loved dying.

Cooper liked women, but he'd never met one he wanted to live with. And he liked kids from a distance. So the chances of him ever having children were slim, but if he ever did, Cooper wouldn't mind having one as tough as this one. Tatum hadn't complained once, but he'd be sore in the morning from holding on when Hector crossed uneven terrain.

An hour after dark, he woke Tatum and the kid asked questions while he ate supper.

Then, with nothing else to do, they turned in for the night.

It was silent for a while, except for the wind rattling the walls and the fire popping. On nights like this, it seemed that the animals were talking to each other. The cry of an owl, the rush of feet, the howl of a coyote. This was usually Cooper's favorite time. He was alone, away from everyone. He could almost believe he was living a hundred years in the past.

"Mister," Tatum said in the darkness. "I mean, Coop. You awake?"

"Yes." So much for being alone.

"You hearing all that racket outside?" His voice shook slightly.

"It's just nature saying good-night. You want to howl back?"

Tatum sat up and howled. Cooper did the same. Then they both plopped back on their bunks and laughed.

The cabin grew quiet and Cooper relaxed, thinking he might start howling good-night every night.

"Mister? You asleep?"

"No."

"I just wanted you to know that this was the best day of my life."

"Go to sleep. We've got a long ride tomorrow." Cooper stared into the darkness and realized he felt the same way.

CHAPTER SEVEN

December 15
Maverick Ranch

Danielle Garrett had never been called by her proper name. She'd always been Dani. Just plain Dani, as if her full title was simply too much for such an ordinary woman. Forty and plump. A good cook. An overprotective mother. A failure at pretty much everything else in her life.

While it was still dark outside her kitchen window, she cracked two dozen eggs, added milk, salt and pepper, then set them aside. There was no telling what time the three ladies upstairs would come down for breakfast, but the men would have boots under the table by dawn. The round kitchen table on the Maverick Ranch was command central every morning. The Holloway boys, the foreman and sometimes others would eat breakfast and plan the work that needed to be done that day.

Dani figured that after three months as cook, she knew all that was happening on the ranch, but she never said a word. Never offered advice. That wasn't her place. She cooked.

But she loved the excitement, the unpredictable happenings, the heartbeat that pounded through the place as if the headquarters was a living, breathing being of its own.

Dani had settled into the routine nicely. She'd grown up down the road on a farm, even babysat the Holloway boys when she was a teenager. Coming to work here was like coming home. Griffin's wife had repainted the huge old place when they'd married two years ago. She'd added all kinds of art and rugs and plants, but the bones of the hundred-year-old ranch house were still there.

Dani's favorite part of the house was her quarters behind the kitchen. No one but her was allowed there, so for once she had her very own space. A big bedroom with windows facing south and a bathroom all to herself. Between meals she could watch whatever she wanted on TV or read in silence or even nap. Before she'd arrived at her first hired job, Dani hadn't had a nap in twenty years. On her farm, there were always ten chores waiting.

She even had a side garden here, where she might grow herbs next spring. Then, on warm nights, she'd sit out in a swing and just watch the night.

As the cinnamon rolls baked, she dusted the bacon with brown sugar before sliding it onto the bottom rack of the oven. She fried up two pounds of sausage while she reviewed her life as if rereading a novel she'd read a thousand times.

She'd married six months out of high school. A year later, she was pregnant with twins. Her husband had been a long-haul trucker whose runs seemed to last longer and longer. When she'd told him she wanted to go back to her parents' little place in Texas, he'd said simply that if she left, not to bother coming back.

Apparently, marriage wasn't what he'd thought it would be, and he took his frustration out on her with words first, then with blows. He'd declared that the last thing he needed was kids. He blamed her for the pregnancy and said the babies would be her problem because she'd known how he felt from the first.

At twenty, she'd moved back to her parents' little farm with a son in each arm.

Life was hard at first. She'd stayed up most nights with the babies. Every morning her mother would watch the boys and she'd be her dad's unpaid ranch hand. Dani could cowboy as good as most men, and she'd never backed down from hard work.

About then she began to think in "someday" terms. Someday she'd have time. Someday she'd find another man who'd love her. Someday life would be easy.

Only someday never came. Life just kept moving on as her dreams slowly died. No man was interested in a woman with two sons. She took on more and more of the ranch load as her dad grew older. There was never any time for the things other girls her age did. No parties or dates or even time to paint her nails.

Once the boys started school, she'd thought it might slow, but then when her mom had gotten sick, she took on the housework and cooking, as well. The years were now counted in seasons. The boys grew up. She'd taught them to work the land. But life never got easier. She felt like she'd skipped the fun part and now was too far into middle age to even hope for anything new.

Dani flipped the sausage and set her mind back on track. She had a dozen things to do this morning, but still life did seem calmer here. She had a pretty room with sky blue curtains on the windows and a sunshine-yellow bedspread and fancy pillows on her bed. It had made her smile when she'd found out that Sunlan, the only lady of the house, had ordered all new things for Dani's quarters. Dani kept the bedspread folded over a cedar chest most days.

Elliot walked into the kitchen, reading a paper as he went. His glasses were atop his head in hair that hadn't been combed and his clothes looked like the ones he'd had on last night. "Morning," he said without looking up.

"Morning," she answered as she poured his coffee.

He nodded his thanks, picked up his cup and turned. "Ah…" He looked at the round kitchen table set for six and the dining table set for four.

Dani smiled. She swore Elliot sometimes looked like a young version of an absentminded professor. They said Elliot was the smartest of the Holloway men, but this morning he couldn't seem to find his chair in two tables of empty places.

"I thought your houseguests would probably want to eat in the dining room. I set four places in case you wanted to join them. Then I set you a place at the kitchen table in case you needed to talk to Creed or Cooper or even my boys over breakfast."

Elliot downed half his cup of coffee, then handed it back to her for a refill. "Cooper went up to Winter Valley about the time the guests arrived. Not sure when he'll be back but leave the extra plate. A new ranch hand will be joining us along with your boys."

She grinned, wanting to thank him again for hiring her sons. Once they rode for the Maverick brand, they'd be able to get jobs on any ranch around. With luck, they'd find jobs far enough away that they wouldn't be able to bring their laundry home.

They were good boys, really, in a gnawing-puppy kind of way.

Before she could say a word, the back door opened with a bang. Her sons marched right toward her. Both gave her a kiss on the cheek and she handed them coffee cups. Pete took his black. Patrick preferred a few splashes of cream.

Without a word she turned back to her cooking. She didn't need to talk to her boys. Seeing them was enough. They must have felt the same way.

Pouring the eggs into an already-warm cast-iron skillet, she sprinkled cheese on top. From the sound of the wind shaking the window over her sink, she guessed everything from coffee to food needed to be hot this morning.

When she noticed her boys were still standing in front of the bar, she shooed them on with a wave. "Take your seats here at the kitchen table. I'll have breakfast ready shortly."

Both Pete and Patrick nodded politely at Elliot and took their places as far away from the boss as possible.

Creed and the man who'd introduced himself as Tye Franklin last night stepped inside next. Both thanked her for the coffee and took their places at the table.

Dani set hot apple-cinnamon rolls on the table, and the men treated them like appetizers while she put out the rest of the meal. All talking stopped as the eating began. All five men had been up working for at least two hours and were hungry.

When she passed behind Tye Franklin, Dani asked, "You don't like plum jelly on them hot biscuits? It's made from the plums that grow on the ranch, but I could set out strawberry jam if you like."

The cowboy slowly raised his eyes as if noticing everything about her. "I like honey on my biscuits, ma'am, but I don't want to be any trouble."

"No trouble." She had a feeling they were communicating on another level for a moment, like they were almost flirting. Then the absurdity of such a thing happening made her feel like a fool. "I'll make sure it's on the table from now on."

She moved away, listening to the men talking. Elliot and Tye discussed repairs that needed to be done to the horse barn before the snow hit. Dani noted that big ranch or small farm, there was always a to-do list waiting.

It was obvious Elliot must have hired Tye this morning and had already showed him the fancy horse barn, which everyone called Sunny Barn after Sunlan.

Creed, as always, didn't say much. If Cooper had been present, they would have talked about what had to be done on the ranch, but Elliot seemed happy to let Creed set the schedule for the men while Cooper was at Winter Valley. Cooper and Creed were the same age. They'd been friends through school, even rodeoed together for a few seasons. But Dani had never seen them just talking or heard Cooper call Creed by his first name. She thought it might be John, but she wasn't sure.

Her sons were quiet for a change. When Elliot told them to follow Creed's orders until they learned the way the ranch ran, both boys seemed happy with that. She loved her sons, but she'd failed them. Somehow, she'd forgotten to tell them to grow up, stand on their own, live their own lives and leave home so she could invite them back now and then for dinner.

If she hadn't left her farm three months ago and stopped cooking their meals, they would have been happy to work around the place most days, then come in and drink beer while they watched football until she told them to go to bed. At twenty, neither of them had had a date that she knew about.

Elliot probably hired them out of self-defense. After the freezer emptied at home, they started dropping over to see their mother every day and stayed until she fed them.

As the men stood and walked out, Tye Franklin stayed behind long enough to thank her for the fine meal.

She saw the red in his eyes. The slight limp in his walk. The low rumble in his voice. He wasn't old. Probably in his early forties. But the last few years must have been hard on him.

Tye Franklin was a drifter. Maybe he'd stayed too long on the rodeo circuit. His dark blond hair was lightly salted with gray. He had well-worn clothes and scarred hands. If she was guessing, she'd say the once-handsome cowboy had been down for a long while.

A man not worth knowing, her mother might have called him. A tumbleweed loner who blows with the wind.

Yet Dani couldn't stop staring at him. She felt a pull toward this man, even though she knew if they became friends, he'd probably leave her crying. At forty, she didn't need to welcome any sadness; she was already living knee-deep in regret.

Dani didn't know if she felt sorry for him or simply longed for someone near her age to talk to, but she said, "I'm making pies tomorrow. If you drop by after supper you can join me for a tasting."

"You got apple?" A smile touched one side of his mouth.

"I will have."

"Then I'll be over after dark tomorrow."

"Don't bother to knock. The door's always open and no one will be in the kitchen but me."

He stared right into her eyes, his gaze unwavering. She felt like this stranger was really seeing her. No one had done that for a long time. Maybe ever.

As he walked away, she almost laughed aloud. A worthless man and an invisible woman might just become friends.

CHAPTER EIGHT

December 15
Winter Valley

An hour after dawn, snow was still falling outside the shack overlooking Winter Valley. It might be late fall down near the headquarters, but on the northern most point of the ranch, winter had arrived.

Cooper finished up breakfast, kept the stove burning and waited for the kid to wake up. One question kept worrying him. How on earth could a boy not ten years old be so far away from anyone? He was not only miles from a town, but he was also miles from the headquarters. Tatum said he'd walked, but most of it would have been on rough roads and uneven ground without even a trail to follow. Cooper didn't come up to the shack often enough to leave much of a path, so it had been pure luck the kid had seen him on the hilltop.

The next thought that kept circling in his mind was what would have happened to Tatum if he hadn't seen him on the ridge.

Hell, even now the boy was still in danger. Living in the line shack wasn't an easy existence. There were half a dozen cliffs within fifty feet of the cabin that he could fall from and break his neck. Come spring, one bite from half a dozen species of snakes might kill him. Add the cold nights, bobcats, mountain lions, an occasional pack of dogs—and the list got longer.

All at once, blankets flew back and the boy ran for the door. "I got to pee!"

"Put your boots on first." Hell, Cooper sounded like a dad.

He couldn't hold back the grin as the kid hopped around, pulling on his boots, then shot out the door in his briefs.

"Snow!" Cooper shouted, a little too late for the news.

The kid hopped like a rabbit over the piles of snow until he made it to the outhouse. Cooper had already made the trip, so he'd cleared the path. The door would open easy.

A minute later the boy was bounding his way back. When he passed under Coop's arm at the open door, Tatum announced, "I got snow in my boots. Why'd you build the bathroom so far away? I was so cold I could barely pee."

"Pull your jeans over your boot tops next time."

"What jeans?" Tatum almost hugged the old potbellied stove.

Cooper closed the door. "Outhouses stink in summer, so better they stay away from the house. Stop stomping snow on the floor. Put your boots by the fire. They'll dry while you eat breakfast."

Tatum did as told, then sat down on the stool by the little table, but he was shivering.

Coop tossed him a blanket and two dry socks that came up to his knees.

"These don't match, Coop."

"So?"

The kid nodded once. "Right. So? Mountain men don't need socks that match."

"I'm not a mountain man and neither are you. I'm a rancher and you're a trespasser."

Cooper slid three fried eggs and half a dozen slices of burnt bacon onto the boy's tin plate. "I cooked breakfast. You get to do the dishes."

"My grandma's place was little, but she had inside water and a heater. You must be a very poor rancher, mister." He chewed on a piece of bacon, then asked, "Shouldn't we skip washing the dishes and head down?"

"We're not going down until the snow stops."

Tatum smiled. "It would be too dangerous, right?"

"Looks that way. We'd probably be fine, but I know enough not to try to ride horseback down. From the look of those clouds, we're in for another storm. If it snows three inches down on flat land, it'll snow a foot up here. The horses can handle the snow. It's the ice on downward slopes I'm worried about. So we wait until it's above freezing."

"How do you know what the temperature is?"

"There's a thermometer on the porch."

Tatum wiped his plate clean with the last of his bread. "That seems a dumb place to leave it. You have to get cold to go out and look at it. Then you don't need to see it because you already know you're cold."

They ate with Cooper answering one question after another. Tatum wanted to know how to catch fish, how to hunt. Was water from the river at the bottom of the canyon okay to drink? What would they do if they ran out of toilet paper?

"I'm taking you back to town, kid, before you have that problem," Cooper said at least a dozen times.

"If you gave me that box of matches, I could stay here. I could survive. I'd be a mountain man."

"You can't be a mountain man on a hill, and there's a lot

more to surviving. I'm taking you back as soon as we can get down safely."

"Will you teach me to shoot while we wait?"

"No."

A cloudy afternoon arrived, with the temperature never reaching high enough to melt the snow. When the wind died down, they walked out to feed Hector and the extra mount Cooper had brought along. They cracked the ice that had formed on the water buckets. Then, with walking sticks, they carefully maneuvered up to the ledge and looked down at the valley.

There, a half mile from the stream, Cooper caught his first sight of the wild horses. Mustangs, their coats dark against the white earth.

"How'd those horses get there?"

"No one knows," Cooper whispered, as if the horses might hear him. "There were no horses around here hundreds of years ago. The Spanish came through this area, exploring, and either lost a few horses or abandoned them when they headed home. The herds grew and roamed wild from deep in Mexico to the Rockies.

"Maybe a few of the horses came down looking for grass after a dry year. Or one of the tribes who roamed this area might have driven them down. Maybe they just got trapped here in the canyons and couldn't find their way out. Coronado's men rode across Texas looking for the City of Gold. They would have traveled with extra mounts and pack animals, just in case they found the gold."

Tatum looked up at Cooper. "I got a lot of questions about that explanation."

Cooper smiled. "I figured you would."

That night when Cooper finally said, "No more questions," the boy protested, but curled up in his blankets while Cooper turned out the lantern.

The low fire flashed shadows along the walls. The wind howled so loud it sounded like a wolf, and tumbling branches knocked at the door. The echo of a horse screaming in fear drifted through his mind and he knew sleep would be slow to come.

Before Cooper could settle, he heard Tatum counting... No, he was adding.

"One plus one is two. Two plus two is four. Four plus four is eight..."

Cooper decided it was just the kid's way of counting sheep.

A few minutes later the adding turned to multiplying. "One times one is one. Two times two is four. Three times three is nine. Four times four is sixteen." The door rattled and he started again. "One times one is one."

"What are you doing, kid?" Cooper asked over the wind.

"It's how I get to sleep. I add. I'm good at it. But when I'm scared, I multiply. It's harder, but my grandma taught me. I know all the way to my twelves. Only I forget some of the sevens."

"There's nothing to be afraid of. This shack has stood for a hundred years. It's not going to fall down tonight."

"What if something breaks in?"

Cooper stood up and took his rifle off the high shelf. "I've been coming here to take care of the horses since I could ride, and nothing's ever come through that door. In fact, I've only used this rifle a few times to put a dying horse down, and I shot into the clouds to scare a bear once." He set the rifle beside his bed. "If I ever get hurt, I might use it to signal, but there's a good chance no one would hear me."

Tatum sat up, crossed his legs, tented a blanket over his sandy hair and started asking questions. *How do you know when a horse is dying? Is it a kindness to shoot an animal that's dying? Are there many bears up here? How about wolves? Can animals flip the latch on the door? How far down to the road? Can you tame a wild horse? How does the vet doctor them if they are wild?*

"Lie down and I'll answer your questions," Cooper grumbled.

Tatum followed orders.

By the time Coop finished, the boy didn't need to add numbers. He was asleep.

But Cooper still couldn't sleep. The howl of the wind kept him awake. He wasn't worried about some wild animal coming to get them; he was far more worried about the horses. Now and then, on the storm's breath, he thought he heard the wild cry of a horse.

The last thing he wanted to see in the morning was a trail of blood. A predator could attack one of the mustangs while the wind howled during the night. Or, if the herd was running, one or more of the horses might have tumbled off a cliff.

The need to get to them gnawed at his gut. In an odd way, he could relate more to them than he could most people.

CHAPTER NINE

December 16
Maverick Ranch

Snow started falling outside Dani's kitchen window around midafternoon as she rolled out a dozen piecrusts. Some would be stacked in the cabinet for a few days before being filled, but six would be pies before she went to bed.

Lazy flakes splattered against the glass and melted into winter's tears as she watched. Nature's ever-changing days calmed her soul—they always had. Maybe that was why she rarely left her little farm. She liked watching things grow and the seasons marching by. Her boys were more into ranching with their horses and small herd of cattle. They didn't see the beauty like she did. The seasons and the holidays always made her smile. Being here felt like home, as well. It might be a much bigger operation at the Maverick, but they lived as she did, by the seasons, and they planned by the weather.

It was almost Christmas, she realized, and no one at the Maverick had noticed. Elliot had mentioned that Sunlan would decorate when she got back, but they'd stayed over in Washington longer than anyone had expected.

Elliot said when he stopped by the kitchen to pick up lunch that Sunlan's father was having some tests run at the hospital, and she and Griffin might stay a few days longer just to make sure all was well.

Dani understood why Christmas needed to wait a few days, but with no decorations where she worked and no time to go home to at least put up her little tree, Dani feared this snowfall might be the only hint of the holiday she'd have this year.

"Oh, well," she said aloud. "Enjoy what you got." Her boys were healthy and seemed happy. She was making good money and was surrounded by interesting people. Life was good. Maybe she'd at least have time to drive over to her place, get her little tree and bring it here. It would look grand in her room.

Speaking of interesting people, the cousins had kept her busy all morning, but she didn't mind. She'd helped them alter their new lingerie, made snacks to go with different colors of wine and caught herself giggling at the funny things they talked about. In an odd way, it made her glad she had sons, as girls seemed to have a great deal more drama in their lives.

She'd also giggled over their choice of nightwear. The dainty gowns were beautiful, but she'd never sleep in such things. Her body was too round. A plain cotton gown would do fine.

As the day passed, Dani baked long loaves of bread and muffins while a huge roast with all the trimmings of carrots, potatoes and onions cooked. At sunset she'd load up the bunkhouse meal and take it over in the ATV Elliot had said was just for her. Four nights a week she cooked for the hands, mostly stews and chili. One night per week, a dozen pizzas were delivered from town, and on the weekends, the men were on their own. Unless company was in the house, the Holloway family meal was the same as the bunkhouse menu. And if Elliot and Cooper were the only two home, they usually joined the hands for the evening meal, saving her time.

As Dani worked, she thought about Tye, of the things she'd talk about with this man she barely knew. They'd *have* to talk. He couldn't just drop by and eat pie.

Maybe she'd ask him where he'd lived, but then he might ask her the same and she'd have only two houses to describe.

She could tell him about her little farm, but he might think she was bragging. It might not be a big place, but it had been in her family for three generations.

All the subjects the cousins had discussed were off the table. So she kept busy and waited. Even if he didn't show up, he'd given her a pleasant afternoon of daydreaming.

By nightfall, pies lined the counter, and Dani called herself a fool for worrying about something as simple as having coffee with a stranger.

Then the back door opened, letting in the cold wind and a tall, lean figure of a man. Her stranger had come for pie.

From the moment he walked into her kitchen, there seemed a quiet peace settling between them. Something she hadn't expected.

The cowboy pulled out her chair, then grinned. "I've been looking forward to our visit."

"Me, too."

He had a gentlemanly way that drew her, and a low voice that pulled her closer. They talked about the weather and how he liked this part of Texas. As she served him slices of pie, she managed to think of a few things the cousins had said that were funny. She was happy Tye seemed as confused as she'd been over the way they thought.

He told her about how his grandfather must have died in prison sometime back and how the Texas Rangers took the time to deliver a notebook of drawings to him that his grand-father had left him.

"I have a feeling that my grandfather drew them from what he saw around here. When I look at the notebook and then at this land, I feel like I'm walking in his footprints."

"What was in the drawings?"

Tye shrugged. "One had a Texas county-road sign that had been shot up."

She laughed. "I can think of half a dozen of those within ten miles."

"There are drawings of tumbleweeds and windmills."

"A hopeless quest, Tye. But I'll be happy to show you the signs. There are less of them than tumbleweeds and windmills."

His gray eyes looked straight at her as he grinned. "Thanks for the offer. I might just take you up on that."

She nodded once and changed the subject.

Tye finally pushed away his almost-empty plate. "The cherry was great, Dani, but I think I still like the apple better."

She laughed. "Took you two pieces of each to figure it out."

"I can't help it if you're a great cook, darlin', and I'm a man who likes to take his time with the finer things of life. Pie is one of them." He took the last bite between his fingers, then added, as if talking to himself, "Just as being able to talk with a lady who's gentle on the eyes is mighty fine." He downed the last bit of pie without taking his eyes off her face.

She wanted to hold his last words in before addressing the compliment, so she focused on the pie. "Maybe you've been eating at diners too long, cowboy. I hear restaurants don't even make their own crusts anymore."

"You may be right." He did that thing again. He looked at her straight on, like there was no filter between them, only hon-esty. "For a while I've been into the bottle. Funny thing about whiskey. I hate the way it tastes, even hate how it smells, but I like the way it numbs everything inside."

"Are you looking for a slow way to commit suicide?"

"No." He laced his hands together as if praying his answer was true.

When she didn't say anything, he turned toward the window and she guessed he didn't want to talk about his drinking. "What's your full name, Dani?"

"Danielle, but no one's ever called me that, not even my mother."

He turned back to her. "You mind if I call you Danielle once in a while?"

"No." She smiled. "Where is your home?"

"Nowhere. My mom moved every time the rent was overdue. My father dropped by now and then. When I'm asked, I usually say Amarillo because it's as good a place as any to be from. It's small enough to have a small-town feel and big enough to get lost in. I've got an old friend there I visit now and then."

She refilled his coffee. They'd been talking for over an hour. First about horses, then life's changes, and finally, they discovered neither had any idea which way to go in this life and both felt like they were just drifting. He might be moving from town to town, but she was drifting in her mind, making up lives she could have lived.

"An old man I worked for told me once that we all need a mission in this life." Tye seemed to be looking into the past. "He said if you don't have one, you're riding a horse, but you're not holding the reins. I asked him what his mission was, and he told me after seventy it's just staying alive."

She smiled. "You know, I think I live on the other side of the coin. Seems I'm always trying not to do stuff. Not to let anyone hurt me. Not to lose my land. Not to mess up raising my boys. I never think about what I want to do."

Funny, she thought, how for years she'd fretted over what might happen if she wasn't careful. Only now, when she put those doubts into words, the fear seemed to fly out of some invisible worry box hidden away in the back of her brain.

"I feel like I'm halfway through living and I've run out of goals." He stared at his coffee as if it was a crystal ball gone dark. "Or maybe I just gave up on trying to reach the ones I'd always had. Maybe an old bronc rider is like a tarnished penny. At first it was shiny, but now no one can see it atop the dirt." He met her stare. "But I'm still here. There's worth in this tired body."

Dani felt a tear threatening to fall. Yeah, this guy was going to make her cry, she thought, but dang it if he wasn't the most interesting man she'd ever met. He was a stranger, but she couldn't remember talking so honestly with anyone.

He told her that when he was twenty, there were a dozen paths he'd wanted to turn down and explore, but now, drifting seemed easier than picking a direction. When he was one of the top riders in the world, he was always afraid of falling, and now he wasn't sure he was brave enough to start climbing again.

She talked about her boys and he was kind enough to compliment each of their skills. Evidently they'd worked with Tye a few hours before Creed pulled them away. Tye told her Patrick was so tired after a twelve-hour workday, he'd collapsed on one of the couches in the bunkhouse. Pete made it to his room after eating supper. Tye claimed they were snoring while everyone else watched football. It seemed there was a rule in the bunkhouse that if you fall asleep or pass out before you find your bed, you sleep where you fall.

"That's how they are pretty much every night." She shrugged. "It's been over ten years since they were small enough for me to carry to bed. When I took this job, I went home after a month to check on the place. The barn was fine, but the house… Pizza boxes were knee-deep, but the sheets on their beds still looked clean."

"They'll grow."

She shook her head. "I hope not. They're both over two hundred pounds. But I know what you mean. I think my running away from home was the best thing I could have done for them."

A comfortable silence settled between them as if they were old friends. She wished she'd taken the time to put on a little makeup or tie back her hair. A plain, plump woman like her would never be noticed by a good-looking man like him if they'd met in a bar. He'd probably go for the tall thin type with boots up to her knees and hair down to her butt. He'd go for the women who wore the nightgowns made of nothing but lace, not cotton.

Dani's hair was long, but it was just brown. Not curly or rich chocolate or auburn. Just straight brown. Her hands had never had a manicure and her clothes were always ordered from a catalog.

Only, tonight she felt pretty when she saw the way he looked at her. He stared at her as if she was unique. One of a kind.

He'd said she was gentle on the eyes. Imagine that.

"This house sure is quiet tonight," he said, finally breaking the silence. "Big old place like this probably has ghosts."

"No, I don't think so. And it's quiet now because Elliot took his company into Lubbock for dinner. He tries, but I don't think he speaks their language. I have a feeling all three are very proper women in their everyday lives, but here, they just want to let their hair down. Sunlan was supposed to fly in today, but her father's having some health issues. For the Holloway men, I don't think it will be Christmas until Sunlan is home.

"She and Griffin have a daughter named Jaci, who looks just like Sunlan. I swear when Jaci is here, her feet barely touch the ground. She's usually riding on her daddy's arm or one of her uncles' shoulders."

Dani realized she was rambling, but Tye didn't look like he minded. "The cousins should be home soon. I'm guessing Elliot will bore them to death talking about the stock market or how impossible his taxes are to do. That man should have a book-keeper. This ranch has doubled in worth in the past few years, and he's still doing the books alone."

Tye nodded. "One of the hands said he doesn't ride much, but he cares about those horses Sunlan breeds."

"I heard Elliot tell Creed that he hoped you'd stay around." She patted Tye's hand on the table. "Elliot claimed you might just know more about horses than Sunlan, and that's saying something."

"I plan to at least stay the winter, if the work holds up. Ranch work and the rodeo is all I've ever done or wanted to do. I liked working with those fine champions today, and tonight's been the best evening I've had in a long time." Tye stood. "I guess I need to go, though. We'll be starting work before dawn. This was the first day of real work that I've done in a while."

She walked him to the door. "Your eyes are clear tonight."

He didn't act like he didn't know what she meant. "Yeah, I told Creed I wouldn't drink while I'm on the ranch. Plan to dry out for a while."

"You're always welcome in my kitchen for coffee, but I don't want to see you if you're not sober, Tye. You understand that. I've got a few scars from trying to reason with a drunk, and I don't plan to repeat any part of that history."

"I understand. You're a good woman, Dani." He leaned down and kissed her cheek. "The man who walked out on you was a fool, and any man, drunk or sober, who'd hit a woman isn't worth knowing."

Something inside Dani cracked open. A part of her had always blamed herself that the man she'd married hadn't loved her enough not to hit her. She'd been nineteen when she'd left home and had hidden the marks her husband left when she'd come back. He'd told her every problem was her fault.

She fought back tears, remembering how he'd yelled at her. He'd called her his bad-luck charm and laughed when she'd cried.

Tye put a knuckle beneath her chin and tipped up her head so she could see his eyes. "It wasn't your fault," he persisted.

She wrapped her arms around his neck and pressed against the warmth of this man. For a while they just stood there, so close she could feel his breath. Then she kissed him.

For a moment, Tye didn't react. When he did, the kiss turned real, and wasn't just a friendly exchange. He held her tight and lifted her off the ground. This wasn't a flirtation but a need. Two lonely people wanting to feel something besides hollowness.

When he finally lowered her to the floor, he just smiled.

"I don't want to talk," she whispered. "I don't want to figure out what just happened. All I have to say is…don't leave tonight."

He slid his hand gently down her arm and took her hand. Then, knowing just what she wanted, she led him to her room behind the kitchen.

In her mind she wondered what he was thinking. Wondered if this was right. Wondered if she'd be sorry at dawn.

But tonight, a lifetime of loneliness won out over what was proper.

They didn't say a word. They didn't bother to turn on a light.

She sat on the bed. He knelt and tugged off her boots, then kicked off his own. Then they were lying side by side atop a quilt her grandmother had made fifty years ago. He lifted his arm and she rolled close. They simply held on to each other for a long while.

Finally, he kissed her more gently than any man had ever

kissed her. Both knew they were turning down an untraveled road. Having an adventure. Changing their lives, if only by adding one memory.

When he moved his hand beneath her shirt, he whispered, "I like the way you feel, Danielle. It takes a strong woman to do all you've done, but there is a softness to you that I sense."

His fingers brushed just below her bra and hesitated.

"Don't stop," she whispered. She felt suddenly young and shy and hungry for life.

"Which one, the touching or the talking?" he asked with laughter in his tone. "I want to get this right."

"The touching. We've talked enough."

He nodded in agreement and continued with the touching.

Silently, each knew they were feeling alive for the first time in a long while. She'd seen that his hands were scarred and rough, but they slid over her like silk. She knew she wasn't beautiful, but the way he touched her made her believe she was to him. She'd had passion a few times and sex she didn't want more than once, but she'd never had caring. He touched her as if she was a rare treasure.

Gentle on the eyes whispered through her mind like a melody. It might not be beauty, but it was enough.

Long after midnight, when he kissed her one last time at the back door, she whispered, "I'll put an extra biscuit on your plate at breakfast as an invitation to come back some night when I know the house will be quiet."

His hair was wild, making him seem younger, and his voice was low and rusty. "I hope to be fat by the New Year."

They were both laughing as he disappeared into the night.

CHAPTER TEN

December 17
Long before dawn
Maverick Ranch

Elliot fell asleep at his desk sometime after 2:00 a.m. He felt like he'd been playing catch-up with his work every night since Sunlan's cousins arrived. The trip to Lubbock should have taken two or three hours, with most of that driving time. But the cousins had decided to restaurant-hop. Drinks at one place near the Texas Tech campus, dinner out near the mall and dessert at an ice-cream shop just off Quaker. Halfway through the evening he'd given up trying to be part of the conversation, and in truth he didn't think any of the women noticed.

He knew how Cooper must have felt in Fort Worth. His brother had said he was just along as a driver and to carry the luggage. Elliot now understood why Cooper had run for the hills the minute he heard they were coming. He'd been planning the trip up to Winter Valley for a week, but the Uber van turning off the county road had made him panic. They'd be lucky to see him by Christmas. His little brother would want to make sure the house had settled after the cousins' visit. If they hung around much longer it might take weeks for the echoes of giggling and squeals to still.

As soon as Elliot had driven the girls back to the ranch after the longest dinner out he'd ever lived through, they'd vanished upstairs, along with two bottles of wine, and he'd sat down to work. With both his brothers gone, he felt like he was working three eight-hour shifts a day. At least it was Sunday, the only day the ranch worked a light crew, and most slept in.

But Elliot needed to work. Somehow, he had to catch up before the end of the year. He opened the window beside his desk, hoping the cold air would keep him awake.

At dawn, he stumbled to the coffeepot by the front windows in his office and pushed the button. Dani always made sure the pot was ready to run. Five minutes later he was downing his first cup and watching the sun rise.

These few early, quiet minutes were his favorite time of the day. Before worries flooded over him, he simply relaxed and counted himself lucky to look at such a beautiful view.

On a whim, he pulled out his cell phone and looked at Jessica Brantley's number. Her picture flashed on the screen, and he smiled. She hadn't wanted him to snap the shot of her that day—almost a decade ago now. It had been her first and only visit to the ranch. They'd just announced their engagement, and none of his family seemed happy about it. They were too young. Still in school. Life was full of what-ifs. But Elliot didn't care. They thought they were forever in love. She'd be beside him until death parted them, and he'd never stop loving her, so they might as well make it official.

Only forever didn't last long for her. When he'd told her he had to leave school six months later, she'd refused to go with him. She didn't see why he was dropping out to help his brothers run the ranch. It wasn't a good enough reason to derail the life they'd planned. Elliot could have gone home on weekends to help. That was enough. His brothers could just hang on, then after he'd graduated, Elliot could go back home for a while.

As he'd packed, they were taking turns. First arguing, then not speaking. As he drove away, she'd stood silent on the steps of their apartment, her arms folded.

After he'd left, it took her a month to calm down. They talked over the phone. The engagement wasn't broken, just postponed. They'd still marry, only now it would be after she finished school, then after she had a free summer of traveling and finally after she got settled in a job. She'd promised she'd take some time off once she qualified for vacation, and they'd start over on planning the wedding and their life together.

But the starting-over part never happened.

At first, he'd called her every night, but she'd had excuses about having to study, then having work to do that she'd brought home from the office. She cut short their talks more often than not until he started calling once a week, then once a month, then never.

The second visit to the ranch to make plans never happened. She didn't want to talk about it and if Elliot pushed, she'd say she had to get up early or was going out with friends or simply couldn't talk now.

Two years after the picture on his phone had been taken, she was out of his life. Or, more accurately, he'd walked out of hers. He was needed at home, and she'd said she wouldn't wait forever. All the while he'd been waiting for her to come to him and she'd been waiting for him to care enough to come back to her. When he hadn't, she'd left to study international law in England.

He'd never forget her last words all those years ago. "See you," she'd said, as if they might be days or a few weeks apart. Then the phone had gone dead.

Elliot downed his coffee and, just for the hell of it, pressed her number. He'd done it before, probably a hundred times. No one ever answered, but in a small way he felt like he was still trying to reach out.

Somehow the number was still live, but no answering machine clicked on. It just rang and rang until an automated voice announced her message box was full.

If she was on the other end looking at the caller ID, she didn't want to talk to him. And, after all, that was all he needed to know.

Elliot flipped back to her picture. "Still mad, Jess?" he said aloud as he leaned back in his chair and remembered how it had been between them. People used to say that he grounded her and she woke him up to life.

They'd almost been the perfect couple. Almost. Was she flying high without him? Who knew, maybe he was dead without her and didn't even realize it.

He pulled back his mind from the past as he heard footsteps in the hallway. *Pat, pat, stumble, pat.*

The redheaded cousin walked in, leaning sideways as if the room had shifted overnight. "Elliot," she whined.

"How can I help you, Dallas?"

She scratched her flaming-tumbleweed hair. "I think I have an overhang."

He stood and wrapped his arm around her shoulder. "Dani, our cook, will fix you up. She told me, thanks to her two sons, she's become an expert at hangovers, or in your case, overhangs."

"The cook is up? It's not even daylight."

As they passed the foyer, he grabbed one of Cooper's sweatshirts and helped her put it on. "Now you'll be warm," he said, wanting to add that she'd also be out of the R-rated category now that her nightgown was covered up.

He walked her to the kitchen. The tall drunk looked startled to see Dani rolling out biscuits.

The cook took one look at them as Elliot sat the redhead down. "I've got it, boss. We'll start with coffee."

Elliot thought of running back to his office, then reminded himself he had to play host.

Dallas was on her second cup of coffee as she waited for the cure. The kitchen door opened, letting in blowing snow. She complained to Elliot as she pulled her long legs up under Cooper's big sweatshirt.

As usual, Creed showed up for breakfast early; the guy didn't seem to believe in weekends. He hesitated when he saw one of the cousins at the kitchen table. His frown showed what he'd never say: guests belonged in the dining room, not here at the round table.

Dallas waved her hand as if shooing away a bee. "Just pretend I'm not here, Mr. Creed."

Elliot fought down a laugh. Dallas would never be a woman people didn't notice, even with her makeup gone and her hair crazy.

Creed slowly sat down across from her and stared as Dani brought the woman a tray with three glasses lined up. Pear juice, ice-cold. Water with two Alka-Seltzers bubbling in it. And hot ginger tea.

"Start on these three, dear," Dani ordered. "I'll bring you toast as soon as it's burnt."

Elliot raised an eyebrow. "Does this work, Dani?"

The cook stepped out of Dallas's sight and shrugged.

Creed leaned low so he could see Dallas's face. "How old are you?"

"Old enough to drink." She threw back the pear juice like it was a shot of whiskey. "How old are you?"

Creed thought for a minute, then said, "Old enough to not drink like you do."

She made a face and Creed smiled as if they'd just agreed to silently ignore each other.

Dallas never looked up again as she worked her way down the line of drinks. The two men talked about what had to be done. Creed suggested the few men scheduled to work the Sunday shift start repairs in one of the barns. It wouldn't be warm, but at least they'd be out of the snow and the wind.

"Good idea, but make sure Tye works in Sunlan's barn." Elliot passed Dallas another cup of coffee—her fourth round. "I watched him working with that mare about to foal yesterday. I've never seen a man who can handle a horse better."

"Me, either. He told me he's worked with everything from rough stock for the rodeos to racehorses."

"We're lucky to have him."

"Yeah, but I heard one of the men say he'd worked with him on a big ranch in Oklahoma a few winters ago. Said he just packed his gear and drove off one day. He's not a stay-around guy."

Elliot shrugged. "I figured that. A man like him could be making ten times the money as a trainer."

Creed glanced over at Dallas. "With the snow still falling, I doubt any of your guests will be leaving today, unfortunately."

"Right. Maybe they'll sleep in. It seems a good day for it."

"All but one is sleeping in." The foreman pointed his thumb at her.

Dallas raised her head just enough to stick her tongue out at him.

Creed did a rare thing. He laughed.

As Dani began setting food on the table, Miss Dallas stood slowly and walked out of the room, her body still slanting like the Leaning Tower of Pisa.

Creed frowned. "Should I go help her make it up the stairs?"

"Yeah," Elliot answered. "She's now officially your responsibility."

The foreman was gone before Elliot could tell him that it was a joke.

Dallas's voice echoed throughout the house as she told him how to find the stairs. Then she asked him why his name was a tribe, and he asked her why her name was a city.

Elliot poured one more cup of coffee and headed back to the office. He was a man of routine. Every morning, no matter how much he had to do or how late he'd been up, he checked his email.

It was Sunday. The markets were closed. He'd probably have nothing.

But when he clicked on, Griffin's note came through.

Hope all is going well. We're staying over another week to make sure Sunlan's dad is okay. But don't worry. I hired you a tax accountant who's agreed to fly out and help you for a few days. Hoping to lighten your load. Grif

Elliot read it again before deleting the message. A tax accountant, good. Another guest in the house, bad. With Elliot's luck, he'd be nearing retirement and hard of hearing. Elliot could use the help.

Creed walked past the open office door. "Anything else, boss?"

"No. Did you get Dallas settled in?"

"Nope, she's changing. Claims she wants to see the horse that's about to have a baby."

"Did you talk her out of it?"

Creed shrugged. "You ever talk a woman out of anything, boss?"

"I don't think I ever have." Elliot shrugged. "I usually avoid them altogether. Only sane way to live." Before Creed could leave, he added, "Tell Dani to have that girl who comes in to help with the cleaning tomorrow to dust out another bedroom— we've got an accountant coming."

"Third floor?"

"No, better put him on the second. He'll probably be old and nearsighted. Two flights of stairs might be too much."

"Will do, but then he'll be next door to the girls."

"Correction. Put the old guy on three. We don't want him having a heart attack if the girls stay longer."

"You hoping they'll leave today?"

"I've been hoping for that every day for a week."

CHAPTER ELEVEN

December 17
Winter Valley

Dawn came in clear over Winter Valley with the air perfectly still, almost as if the sun hadn't awakened it yet.

Cooper pulled on a few layers and took his coffee outside to watch the sunrise while the boy slept. If the wind didn't kick up, it might be a good day to take Tatum back to the headquarters. The boy was not his problem. The sheriff in Crossroads would know what to do.

Another day of delay in caring for the wild horses, but it couldn't be helped. A boy didn't belong up here. Coop smiled. Correction—a normal kid would hate it up here. But Tatum was like him, half-wild. Maybe he thought if he asked enough questions, he'd figure out how to stay and live off the land.

Damn, he must have been treated terribly.

Tossing the last of his coffee out over the snow, Coop half wished he could keep the kid, but that wasn't the way it worked.

The sheriff would call the right people, and they'd see he got to a safe place.

Remembering his dream, Cooper decided to walk up the ridge and have a look at the valley. If a horse was down, he might be able to see it, maybe even help. The nightmare that one of the mustangs was in trouble had haunted his sleep all night.

Going up to the top of the hill was harder than he thought it would be. The thick layer of snow had melted just enough to add an ice coating overnight. He should have brought his hiking boots, but he'd left in such a hurry he only had his Western boots, and they weren't made for walking over ice.

When he reached the top, the sun was fully up and promised a warming, but the temperature still felt like it was below thirty degrees.

Cooper dusted off crystals frozen solid as spiked marbles from a rock and sat watching the river below. The banks were iced over, but water still flowed swiftly in the middle. The mustangs had probably found shelter in the overhangs and shallow caves.

No blood. All the snow sparkled in the valley. Maybe it was cold enough last night that not even the predators were hunting.

Slowly, Cooper started down off the ridge, thinking he'd feed Hector and saddle him before he went back to the cabin. In another hour or two it would be warm enough to start down. They'd have to ride double and move between the trees until they finally met a road that was little more than tire tracks. But from there, the ride would be easier. Another mile and a better road. It would take them 'til noon to make it to the opening of the pass, where Creed had dropped off the supplies. Once out of the trees, he might get a cell signal and be able to call someone at the headquarters to come collect him and the boy. Riding in the pickup would be warmer for the kid, and Hector wouldn't mind having a trailer to travel in, either.

He looked down and saw the shack about forty feet below.

The thermometer flashed in the sun, and Cooper laughed about how Tatum worried about it being left out in the cold.

A rabbit darted in front of him, not three feet away. Solid white, it almost looked like a ripple in the snow.

Cooper twisted and lost his footing. Both feet were sliding, but in different directions. He waved, feeling boneless, out of control, then he fell forward, slamming his face hard.

All at once he was rolling, bouncing off ice and rocks, fighting to grab hold of something that would break his fall. He tumbled and picked up speed before he reached a ledge, then dropped about ten feet down onto rocky ground covered in ice.

The blow knocked the wind out of his lungs, and for a few minutes, Cooper simply fought to draw a breath. When he finally gulped in cold air, every part of his body screamed in pain.

His next breath was slower as he began to move one part of his body at a time. Hands worked. Arms were bruised but fine. Wrist hurt—probably badly bruised or sprained. Neck hurt, but nothing damaged. He shifted to his left leg.

It didn't move. He couldn't feel anything in his left leg.

He moved the right leg. It hurt like hell, but it moved.

Cooper lay very still and stared up at the sun. He'd broken his leg. He'd broken bones before and he knew one fact: at any moment it was going to start hurting. Irrationally, he thought maybe if he was just perfectly still, the pain might not come.

He felt hot and cold at the same time. Sweat dripped from his forehead and froze as it slid down his neck.

"Mister!" Tatum called from the rock steps. "Coop, you all right?"

Cooper didn't move, but he heard the kid running toward him. As Tatum drew closer, the sun began to dim. Then there was silence and the whole world faded.

He tried to fight his way back. He thought he heard the boy yelling, but he couldn't open his eyes. The pain was crawling up his leg now. The boy screamed again, but he barely heard him. His head was pounding, as if he was reliving the fall over and over again.

Then, a moment before he gave in to the blackness, Cooper heard a rifle fire and he wondered if the bullet was heading for the sky or would do him a kindness.

CHAPTER TWELVE

December 17
Maverick Ranch

Tye dusted the snow off his shoulders when he stepped into the kitchen. He smiled and nodded at Dani, but he didn't speak to her. What was between them was private. No one else. The last thing he wanted was folks gossiping about them.

Elliot was filling the coffee cups while Dani passed plates and bowls across the bar. This was Sunday—no full breakfast. "You sleeping all right in the bunkhouse, Tye?" the boss asked.

"I am. The snoring lulled me right to sleep," he lied. In truth, he hadn't gone back to bed after he'd left Dani. The newly carved memory had been too fresh in his mind and he'd needed to live there for a while.

Tye forced himself not to look at her as he took his seat. "I've already checked on that mare you've got in the third stall in the white barn. She's not doing well. It's her first, and all she wants to do is run away. I hung blankets on the walls so not even wind will bother her, but she's pacing, restless and afraid."

"We call it Sunny Barn after my sister-in-law. My brother gave it to her as a wedding gift two years ago." Elliot sat across the table from Tye, guessing he'd already heard the story.

Elliot's words were calm, but his face twisted with worry. "I wish Cooper was here. I thought both my brothers were out having fun and I was left alone to take over the worrying. Turns out Coop is probably dealing with more snow than he needs and Griffin's father-in-law has had quite a time of it. Now he's getting better, Sunlan is probably smothering him."

Creed leaned forward from his usual place at the table. "You think we should put a twenty-four-hour watch on her?"

Elliot grinned. "The horse, or the redhead you just helped up the stairs?"

"The horse. Dallas told me after she changes, she wants to help with the delivery. So, Tye, be sure and slow the birthing down." The foreman laughed at his own joke. "I'm guessing her nap will run the clock around. Then she'll probably forget about the horse and want to head home."

"Not likely." Elliot scrubbed his face as if he could wear away the worry. "Looks like they're here for a little longer. They were planning on Sunlan flying them home and if she doesn't make it in, they'll have to fly standby out of Lubbock. But the university has about thirty thousand students finishing up the fall semester and heading home. Add that exit with the holidays coming up, and the airport won't be easy to navigate."

Creed looked like someone had just pumped a few rounds of buckshot into his chest, and he could feel the pain even though he hadn't heard the blast.

Tye didn't know what was going on with the redheaded cousin and didn't care. "I'll check on the mare now, and off and on all day while I work out there, then I'll take the first shift tonight." He glanced up at Dani as she passed out hot biscuits.

He only got one. No invitation tonight. He already had a date with a mare.

Creed shook his head. "Now you mention it, what about the cousins?" He looked from Elliot to Tye. "Someone's got to keep an eye on them."

"Right." The last thing Tye needed was one of those nutty cousins hanging around the barn.

While Elliot and Creed tried to come up with ideas, Tye took the time to study Dani. When she finally glanced up, she smiled shyly.

He smiled back, remembering. There would be other nights, just like there had once been other chances when he flew off a wild horse at the rodeo. In truth, he'd slept with more women than he could count. Most of them passed through his hotel room while he was in his early days on the circuit. With some, he was too drunk to remember their names come morning. Some he forgot by the next season. Only a few he could recall.

Dani would be one he'd never forget. She made him wish he'd been a better man. A man who could settle down, make something of himself, grow old with her. He had nothing to offer a good woman like her. He'd be doing her a favor if he stepped away now. But it had felt so right to be holding her last night.

She trusted him, and it seemed like a lifetime since anyone had believed in him.

He remembered that she'd silently cried, late in the night—she must have thought he was asleep—but he'd felt the tears on his shoulder. He hoped they were tears of joy and not regret. He'd only said a few words when he'd left her room. He guessed she'd be one of those women who'd take years to really know.

The idea of doing what was right for her worried him. Much as he hated to admit it, he'd spent his life thinking mostly of himself. Doing the right thing with Dani would mean a hell of a lot more than having a one-night stand.

When he left the kitchen, Tye took the time to thank her for the breakfast. He mustered the courage to look at her directly, praying he didn't see regret. To his surprise, he saw a twinkle of laughter in her eyes.

Tye walked all the way to the barn before he noticed he'd left his coat by the door. Thoughts of another night with Dani warmed him.

A little after nine, Pete and Patrick wandered into the pristine barn, which had been built to hold racehorses.

Tye studied the boys and swore he couldn't see an ounce of their mother in them. They were both built wide and low to the ground like bulls. They might be twins, but they weren't identical. Pete was two inches taller, and his eyes were more black than brown.

Pete's hair was shaggy while Patrick's was cut short. Pete laughed easily, but his brother never smiled.

"We're here to help," Pete said. "Just tell us what to do, Mr. Franklin."

"Call me Tye, for starters."

They both nodded, but Pete added, "We saw you ride once. Our granddad took us to the rodeo over in Fort Worth. Man, you were good."

"Another lifetime," Tye answered. "Right now I could use some help with this mare. I think she's about to drop her foal and it's not near time. We're going to work slowly when near her. Talk low. The last thing we want to do is make her nervous."

The boys did exactly as Tye directed. In an hour, the place was set for an emergency birth. As the wind howled outside the barn, each man took a turn calming the mare.

"Will it live, born this early?" Pete whispered.

"I don't know, but I'll do all I can. Elliot said the only vet for fifty miles was heading up the hills to help Cooper with the mustangs."

Three inches of snow had fallen during the night, then melted just enough to freeze when clouds rolled in. Now a layer of ice covered the earth outside the barn. The two Garrett brothers were happy to work in the barn. There was little to do for the mare but wait now, so they took on their share of the worrying.

Tye heard the side door to the barn open, but he didn't look up. Cowhands had been coming and going all morning. They cared about the mare, but Tye had no doubt that they also cared about Sunlan. Every one of the hands stopped by to talk about how much Sunlan loved her horses. Some said she wouldn't have married Griffin Holloway two years ago if he hadn't given her the fancy barn his father had built to house racehorses.

Everyone on the ranch watched over Sunlan's herd. And every man stopped to watch her ride when she was on the property. Dani told him it must be like seeing a prima ballerina on a New York stage. Poetry in motion, one man said.

Tye hadn't met the lady, but he admired her horses and considered himself lucky to be working with them.

The clang of tin caught his attention. He turned to see Dani dressed in his coat, two sizes too big, and mud boots to her knees.

She set down her load on a bench just outside the stall. "I brought you boys brunch since you two didn't make it in for breakfast."

Pete looked at her as if he smelled a trick and not fresh banana bread. "Do we eat brunch?"

"You do when I make five loaves for the houseguests along with two dozen blueberry muffins, and they turn their noses up and say they've all sworn off sweets. I delivered four loaves and most of the muffins to the bunkhouse, but I thought you men in the barn would like a treat."

Patrick passed Pete and tapped him on the head. "I'll eat yours. I don't think you'd like brunch."

To their credit, the boys exited slowly out of the stall, then rushed for the basket of food.

Dani moved near the stall gate and whispered, "How's it going?"

Tye placed his hand over hers. "I'd rather be with you."

"I wish you were. It's quiet at the big house."

Tye brushed his hand over her warm skin. "From the moment I touched you, I felt like I've been waiting for you. Like I've been working my way back to you, but we've never met."

"I know." She blushed, as though she'd never talked of such things. "Maybe we met a few lifetimes ago."

He grinned. "I'd remember you."

When she looked away, he worried that he'd said too much. They were still more strangers than friends.

She glanced at her sons. They were too busy eating to even look up. "Are they making a hand?"

It occurred to Tye that some people would have no idea what she meant, but he did. "They are. Patrick has a real way with the horses. I watched him working with half a dozen other mares today. Pete does what he's told, but I'm guessing he had more fun building the new stall in the back than working with the stock."

They were silent for a few minutes, only communicating by touch.

"I'm glad you came out here," he said, so quietly he wondered if she'd heard him.

She looked down but didn't pull away.

"I don't say much, Tye, but that don't mean I don't feel. I've spent most of my days alone." She wasn't apologizing, simply stating facts. "I don't want to go out, and don't bother to buy me anything. I don't need compliments or flattery, or even to talk more than necessary. It's enough to have you near now and then."

Tye nodded, as if agreeing to a contract. He pulled away his hand as Pete walked toward the stall.

"We left you a few slices, Tye. You don't want to miss tasting Mom's banana-nut bread."

"I'm hungry. Thanks." He was looking at her, not the food. She had no idea how cute she looked in her mud boots and his big coat. There was something so down-home about her, something so natural.

Tye stepped out of the stall and Pete moved in. "Did your mother bring any biscuits?" He might be talking to her son, but he was still looking at Dani.

"Nope, just muffins and bread," Pete answered.

Dani fussed with the a napkin as she said, "I only make biscuits in the mornings. I'll make sure you get an extra one tomorrow."

"That would be nice," Tye said politely. He ate a thick slice of the bread while she talked to her boys, then he stood and lifted the thermos. "If you men can stay a little longer, I'd like to catch a ride back to the kitchen in your mother's ATV and refill my coffee."

"No problem." Pete nodded his head as if he was glad to do Tye a favor.

Dani didn't say a word as she headed out of the barn with Tye walking beside her.

He climbed into the passenger side of her ATV, which had its back made for carrying groceries and meals from one building to another.

They headed toward the headquarters in silence, with her driving and Tye's hand on her knee.

She parked at the kitchen door. He followed her in. The little entrance was lined with hooks for hats and coats. The air was cold there and the overhead light wasn't on.

Dani pulled off his heavy coat and hung it on the first peg. Her hand straightened out the wrinkles of the jacket with a gentle brush, almost as if she was touching him.

When she didn't turn around, Tye moved closer, pressing his body against her back as he wrapped her in his arms. He kissed the spot beneath her ear and whispered, "You smell like cinnamon."

She laughed. "You smell more like horse."

He nudged her like a horse might. "I like how you're shy in daylight and not so shy in darkness. You fascinate me."

"I'm not that complicated."

"Then I'll keep trying to figure you out."

He guessed there were probably a thousand words that needed to be said between them. There was so much they didn't know about each other. But right now, in the shadows, all he wanted to do was to be close to her.

"I liked wearing your coat. It almost felt like you were holding me."

He rocked her in his arms. "I've been around, Dani. More than most, I'm guessing, but there's something about you that makes me feel like we're just starting out. Just learning to be truly alive."

She turned in his arms.

After one long kiss, he heard a door open in the main part of the house and knew their time was up. She moved away, and he didn't try to stop her. Dani refilled his coffee while he just stared at her. It had been so long since anyone had done something for him that her simple gesture felt like a gift.

He could hear voices now coming from the front foyer. One of the cousins said she wanted to ride, and Elliot said he was expecting an accountant and didn't have time to take her.

Tye wasn't surprised when the redhead huffed her way into the kitchen. When Dallas saw him, she switched to all sunshine smiles. "Tye, right? The cowboy who can dance."

"Yep."

"Would you take me riding this morning? I assume I slept thought the birthing of the baby."

"I'd love to, but I've still got a date with a pregnant mare. You didn't miss the birthing. Until she delivers, I'm living in her stall. You're welcome to watch if you promise to be quiet."

The sunshine smile vanished. "What else can I do around here? If it wasn't for the possibility of seeing the birth, I might as well go home. Even my parents aren't as boring as you people."

Dani must have been waiting days to present her idea. "I know something fun."

"Not baking. I hate cooking. In fact, when I get my own place in New York or wherever, I'm not even putting in a kitchen. All anyone needs is a phone and the food's delivered."

"Not baking." Dani held up one finger. "Decorating. We've an attic full of holiday stuff. Wouldn't Sunlan be tickled to come home and have the house covered in Christmas?"

Dallas's head ticked back and forth a few times before she smiled. "Might be interesting." She pulled Elliot out of the kitchen, demanding to see the attic.

Tye leaned across the counter and kissed Dani's nose. "You're brilliant."

She walked him to the back door and whispered, "I'm good at thinking of things to do." Her grin made him laugh.

CHAPTER THIRTEEN

December 17
Winter Valley

Cooper felt someone poking him. Short little stabs, like a porcupine was bumping against him. All he wanted to do was slide back into the silent blackness, but there was far too much yelling for that to happen.

"Mr. Holloway, you awake?" a woman yelled, as she patted him so hard it was basically a slap. "I've got your leg stabilized, but we need to get you in the house. It's too cold out here."

"Tell me about it," Coop muttered, but it came out as gibberish. "Go away, porcupine, and let me sleep." His rant didn't even sound like words, and he didn't care.

"It's a shack, miss. Not a house," Tatum said politely. "It don't even have a bathroom."

"Does it have heat?"

"Yes, ma'am. I know how to build up the fire."

"Then help me get him inside. He's been out in this cold far too long."

Cooper managed to open one eye. Seeing a dark coat and a floppy hat, he would have guessed that a man was kneeling near him, but a black braid hung over one shoulder and the voice was definitely female. In truth, she didn't look much bigger than Tatum. He couldn't see her face and didn't really want to.

She slapped him again. "Mr. Holloway. Stay awake. We've got to get you off these rocks." The next slap came full force.

Anger outweighed the pain. "I'm hurt, lady. I could have brain damage and you're only making it worse." He could have asked what she was doing on *his* hill overlooking *his* valley, but self-preservation outweighed curiosity.

Who knew, maybe the slaps had done him some good. At least his words were making sense.

"You probably do have brain damage, Mr. Holloway," the porcupine woman said, as if she thought he was deaf. "No one with any sense would be out walking in slick boots on the side of a snowy ridge, and only the brain-dead would bring a boy up here in this weather."

Coop thought of his father. He'd brought one of his sons up here every year since Cooper could remember. "It's hereditary. A lack of good sense runs in our family on my father's side. 'Course, my mother couldn't have been too smart. She married Dad and slept with him at least three times. My brothers and I are proof of that."

She wasn't listening, or maybe he was just talking inside his own head. The sun started to twinkle overhead like a huge star and the icy snow was winking back.

"Pull your daddy's boots off," she said to Tatum. Then she pulled off her coat and put it over Cooper. "We've got to get him somewhere warm. He'll have to help us some, do his part. Stay awake, Mr. Holloway."

When he didn't figure out an answer to her dumb order, she started rattling on to Tatum.

Cooper groaned. Apparently, she'd given up talking to him directly, and was now giving Tatum orders. That couldn't be a good sign.

Cooper stared at the lady's blue sweater. She appeared to be rather nicely rounded beneath the wool. "I'm not dead." He smiled. "Hope those nicely rounded things don't start twinkling."

If she heard him, she must have thought he was delusional.

She was looking at Tatum again. "I don't think we can carry your daddy. His socks will be less slippery than the boots, but we'll have to do most of the work, not him. Grab his arm from wrist to elbow and walk close to his left leg. I'll take his right side."

Tatum followed orders.

Before Cooper could veto the plan, she leaned close. The thought occurred to him that she smelled more like horse than woman. For all he knew she was wild. She must be. Why else would anyone be out here? This was Holloway land. People didn't just come out here to camp. Maybe Tatum should hang out with her. The kid was probably figuring out that she had more survival skills than he did.

"Now, Mr. Holloway, I want you to let us pull you up," she yelled, inches from his face, as if she thought him already bound for the hereafter. "As you stand, put all your weight on your right foot. I made a brace out of boards, so your left leg will be heavy. Try to keep it an inch off the ground. As soon as you can, put your arms around our shoulders and use us as crutches."

Cooper didn't like the idea of walking on ice in his socks, but he didn't argue. Her plan was better than his, which seemed to be to lie on the rocks until spring.

Slowly, one step at a time, they made it to the cabin. It wasn't easy, but they got him to the bunk. Cooper felt like he'd climbed

Mount Everest, but all the woman and Tatum did was complain about how hard the trip had been on them.

Coop eased back on the hard bed and tried to find a spot on his body that didn't hurt.

Tatum added wood to the fire.

The woman seemed to be taking inventory of the place, like she was a Realtor and had the worst listing ever.

Studying her, he couldn't find much to admire. Short. About his age. No makeup. Baggy pants. Hiking boots laced to her knees. Blue wool sweater with bumps in the right places. Nice round breasts.

Coop took a deep breath and decided he had to live because if he died he'd go straight to hell for what he was thinking.

CHAPTER FOURTEEN

December 17

Hayley Westland stared down at Cooper Holloway. All six feet of him. He was dirty, bloody and looked like he hadn't shaved in days. Surprisingly, he was exactly what she'd expected. Her grandfather had given her the map to this place overlooking Winter Valley and had described its owner as one-half wild and the other half crazy. This had to be the right man.

She'd heard about the youngest Holloway all her life. Her grandfather, whom she called Pops, used to tell stories about him growing up as untamed as a bobcat on one of the biggest ranches in Texas. Whenever he gave one of his don't-ever-do-this talks, Cooper was usually the bad example.

Until she'd reached her teens, she'd thought that he was some kind of myth, like Paul Bunyan or Pecos Bill.

Now, looking at him all bruised and broken, he didn't seem like a legend. She might be a vet, but since he was half-wild, he could fit in her jurisdiction boundaries of patient. His vitals were strong, but even if they hadn't been, no ambulance would make it up that hill. She'd spent hours cleaning his wounds and washing away blood.

Apparently, she was the only cavalry coming to the rescue, and he was a one-man battlefield.

Hayley would do what she could for his leg and tape up a few places on his head with homemade butterfly patches, but he needed X-rays, a hospital, a specialist, antibiotics and a tetanus shot.

In full disclosure, she was a very new veterinarian. She had her diploma on the wall of her office and a partnership with Pops. He said he'd take a year, working less and less, helping her get to know her way around, then he planned to go fishing and only come back to check in now and then.

It seemed a simple plan, but last week he'd called in sick. He'd complained of a terrible cold and asked her to take his calls. She'd said yes before she'd known one call would have her hiking up the tallest hill overlooking Winter Valley.

But that was yesterday's problem. Today Hayley had a real emergency on her hands, and she wished Pops was beside her. A dozen things could be going wrong with Cooper, and without X-rays, she couldn't be sure she was doing the right thing.

The winter sun would be setting soon and there was no way she'd find her way back to her Jeep, drive to the pass entrance and manage to get back by dark.

They'd have to stay the night. Warm and safe. She'd have to do what she could to keep him warm.

No bones sticking out. That was a good sign. He was bleeding from scrapes on both hands, one knee and several places on his chest. He had cuts on his face and his bottom lip. If he'd been in the emergency room, Cooper would have had a specialist working on him. But up here, miles from nowhere, all he had was her, a vet with no supplies to help a human.

"Is he going to live?" the sandy-headed boy whispered. Tears were running unchecked down his face, and he was shivering in the crisp air. "You got to tell me, lady. I was starting to like him. It's all my fault he's going to die. I'm a death carrier."

Hayley put her hand on the kid's shoulder. As they'd half carried, half dragged Cooper inside, he'd told her his name was Tatum and that Cooper was not his father. "He's going to live if I have anything to do with it, but whatever happens, you didn't cause it. Holloway stepped out on an icy slope. That's his fault, not yours. If he'd rolled a few feet closer to the edge, he wouldn't have stopped until he'd hit water at the bottom of the valley."

Tatum didn't look like he believed a word, but he made no argument.

She tried for the fourth time to get a signal on her cell. She had to do more and think fast. "At first light can you saddle one of the horses in the corral and ride for help?"

Tatum shook his head. "I watched Coop saddle up, but I don't think I can do it. I'm not even sure where the ranch house is. I came into the valley by following the stream. Coop says I'm a trespasser on his land, but he didn't say anything about having a house other than this one. I thought he was the first person I ever met poorer than my grandma."

"If you can't ride, you'll have to be the one to stay with him. I'll ride down to the pass and call someone to come help as soon as I get a signal." She tried to smile and look like everything was going to be fine. "I'm a doctor, Tatum. A horse doctor. My grandfather comes up here every year to help with the mustangs. But he's getting old, so I took his place this year. I had a map, but if I hadn't heard your signal shot, it would have taken me longer to find you. If Cooper had stayed out much longer, he might have frozen, so you may have saved his life."

The kid seemed to relax a bit as she talked.

"My grandfather said he'd sent up all the supplies I'd need with Cooper, so I decided to park my Jeep down the hill and walk up. It'd take me an hour to walk back, but on horseback I'd make it in less than half the time. You think Cooper would mind if I borrowed his horse?"

"I don't think he'd care if you took the black mare. The other horse is Hector, and Coop talks to him like he's one of the family."

"I'm not surprised. I'll saddle the mare as soon as I have enough light at dawn."

She touched Tatum's shoulder. "Can you stay right beside him until I get back? Keep him warm. Give him water if he asks and a few swallows of whiskey if he's in pain. As long as he doesn't move his broken leg, he should be fine."

Glancing at Cooper, she fought the urge to shake him and ask what kind of idiot came up here without a stocked first-aid kit. One flask of whiskey and a few Band-Aids were not sufficient supplies. Maybe the cowboy thought he was invincible.

Tatum's blue eyes filled with fear. "He won't go cold on me, will he? He won't die?"

"No," she answered. "I'll be back as fast as I can. He may be in pain, but Cooper Holloway won't die. My grandfather says he's too stubborn."

Tatum nodded once. "I'm like that. I'm stubborn. We're part of the wolf people, me and Coop. We can survive in the wild." He looked up and set his jaw as if he was a grown man. "We howl good-night to the wind. We don't wear socks that match, and we eat our beans right out of the can."

The boy didn't say another word, but he didn't sleep. Like her, he waited.

At first light Hayley grabbed her coat. "I'll be back as fast as I can. Now, remember, keep it warm in here and keep him calm."

Within minutes she was heading down the hill on one of the best cutting horses she'd ever ridden. The black mare sensed her commands. Once they hit level ground, she felt like they were flying over the snowy pastures.

She'd parked her Jeep a mile up from the pass entrance. A car might have had trouble making it that far, but her Jeep was part mule.

After what seemed like an hour, she rode past the Jeep and down toward the pass. Two huge rock formations formed the only entrance into the hills that surrounded Winter Valley. A boy might be able to walk in from the north if the water was low in the river, but her pops said he doubted an ATV could make it. The hills were spotted with snow, and she wished she had the time to stop and enjoy the view.

Whoever had driven the mustangs into the valley must have known the lay of the land. With plenty of grass and water, the horses weren't ever likely to leave this hideaway.

As soon as she got through the pass, she heard the ping of her cell phone and stopped.

On her way onto Maverick property earlier in the day, she'd stopped and met Elliot Holloway. He'd been polite but distant. One of those men so absorbed in his work he didn't really relate to anyone. It'd been early, but the ranch was alive and Elliot already appeared to be working.

He had insisted that she enter not just the headquarters' phone number into her cell, but his own cell number, as well. To her surprise, he seemed far more worried that she'd get lost than something might happen to Cooper. He'd asked her twice if she needed his foreman to take her in. She'd assured him her grandfather had drawn a detailed map. Pops had told her if she did get lost, simply climb to the highest ridge and look down. She'd see the roof of Cooper's shack.

When she tapped Elliot's number, he answered on the first ring. "Lost?" was all he said. "Hope you didn't have to sleep in your Jeep last night."

"No," she answered just as formally. "Your brother had an accident."

She heard what sounded like a chair tumbling, then boots storming across a tile floor. Elliot was already on his way.

"Details!" he snapped.

"Broken leg. Possible concussion. Three cuts on his head and one on his hand. Bruises and scrapes from a ten-foot fall on rocks. I think he's stable, but the boy and I can't get him down the hill, and my Jeep wouldn't transfer him comfortably."

"What boy? What do you mean 'possible' concussion? You're a doctor. You should know. Is he talking out of his head? Oh, never mind, he does that on a regular day. I'm on my way. Do I need to call an ambulance?"

Now Elliot sounded like he was running across gravel.

Hayley reminded herself to keep calm. She was a professional. "I'm a vet, Mr. Holloway. Cooper brought up supplies to treat horses, not humans. I'm dealing with the patient as best as I can. You can have an ambulance meet us at the headquarters. He'll need to be transferred to a hospital, but I think we'll get him off the mountain faster, easier, with a truck and enough people to carry him through the trees on a stretcher."

"One moment, Doc, hang on," Elliot said.

Hayley could hear him yelling, "Creed, load up a bail of hay in Cooper's pickup. Throw in as many blankets as you can grab. Pete, pull that old stretcher from the barn. It's behind where we keep the extra saddles. Creed and I are heading up to bring Cooper down off the hill. He's hurt."

She swore it sounded like an army moving around on the other end of the phone. "I'm on my way, Doc. I'll be at the pass as fast as I can. We'll hike up from there."

The racket on Elliot's end was loud, so she shouted her answer. "Meet me at the cabin, not the pass, and bring straps for the stretcher. I'm going back to help the boy keep Cooper calm until you arrive."

She disconnected just as she heard him yell again, "What boy?"

Swinging onto the mare, she rode back toward the cabin. This journey was harder and took longer, but the horse again seemed to feel her panic. All she'd wanted to do was to come up for a day or two and help out with the mustangs. She'd thought the mission would take her mind off the troubles that seemed to have followed her home from college.

She'd think about that another day. Right now she had all she could handle. This was rough country, and it would take all her energy to handle this crisis.

She reminded herself that it was the wild horses that had brought her. When this was over, she'd still have them to work with. Then she'd be in her element. It wasn't just the unknown, but was also the unpredictability of something untamed that she loved. It was the kinship she felt. To work with horses that had little or no dealings with humans was exciting. She had to be careful—no, she knew it was more than that. She had to be totally alive when she moved among them. There was no room for worries, no room for anything except helping a wild being survive.

Hayley shook her head. That kind of total concentration had worked for her before. It was working now with trying to treat Cooper. She hadn't worried about her own life since she'd heard Tatum's gunshot. She hadn't slept a minute last night and now she had to get him off the mountain before something happened and he died.

Maybe, for her survival, all she had to do was worry about someone else.

CHAPTER FIFTEEN

December 18

Elliot went back to the house to grab his heavy boots and a coat. He didn't have a clear picture of what he would find up at the shack, but he needed to be prepared. His little brother lived life in a full-out run, and trips to the emergency room were not unusual, but every time Coop got hurt, Elliot played the same what-if game in his mind.

He didn't have much family left, and he didn't know if he could face losing a brother. Griffin could handle it if death visited them again at the ranch; after all, he had Sunlan and the baby. Grif had always been a rock. But Elliot had no one except his brothers. He told himself he didn't have time to keep up with friends, but in truth, he'd grown comfortable with his small circle of family around.

He'd decided he liked it that way, but deep down, he simply couldn't face being hurt again. He'd loved one woman with all his heart, and she hadn't loved him enough to stay around.

Maybe he just didn't have enough heart left to try loving again.

The memory of Jessica walking away flashed in his mind. Hell, he couldn't even get rid of one old heartache. Maybe he did have a problem with moving on. Even after ten years, he sometimes walked into the kitchen and expected to hear his mother singing as she cooked. Part of him wished he could be brave like Cooper and rush in no matter the odds. Or strong like Griffin, who fought his way through any problem.

But Elliot wasn't made that way. Logic ruled his every action. And logic told him he had to get Cooper to the hospital as fast as possible. Not think about it. Not reason anything out. He had to move fast. His brother's life might depend on it.

Forget his feelings. Shove Jess far back in the shadows of his mind. Just do what had to be done. Right now, Elliot knew he had to respond, not think about it, not weigh the choices, just act.

He tugged on his winter boots as he yelled at Dani, "If the accountant shows up, put him in the room on the third floor and tell him I'll be back as soon as possible. He's welcome to start on the books I left on my desk."

"Will do," Dani answered. "Do you want me to feed him? I've heard tell if you feed an accountant, they'll never leave."

Elliot grinned at her humor. "Make him feel like family. I'm afraid we may have him as a guest for a while."

"Oh, all right, I'll feed him and put him on the third floor, but I hate to do that to an unsuspecting stranger. He'll be right over the cousins if they don't start packing soon. It just doesn't seem fair."

Elliot walked past her. "The skunk-striped cousin, Apple, said they were thinking of leaving today. Find one of the hands to drive them into the Lubbock before they change their minds."

Dani's tone grew serious as she followed Elliot out to the

waiting pickup. "I packed in extra pillows atop the hay. You bring Cooper back in one piece, you hear? I'll make sure the ambulance is waiting. It'll probably take you several hours to get him down."

She handed Elliot a thermos, a first-aid kit as big as a carry-on bag and a plastic basket of muffins. "If Cooper's conscious, he'll be hungry for sweets."

Elliot wasn't surprised that Dani babied Cooper. Everyone pampered him. Must be that stray-dog syndrome, or maybe women saw him as a project. He was never surprised at how women reacted to Cooper.

But he was surprised when he opened the door of Creed's pickup and found the redheaded cousin sitting in the middle, her knees on either side of the gearshift.

"What are you doing here, Dallas?" Elliot didn't even bother to be polite. He didn't have time. "I thought you girls were heading home today."

"Creed promised to take me riding. I'm tired of waiting on a horse to drop a baby. And I want to help get all the Christmas decorations up and…"

"Her folks aren't home, so she's stuck here." Creed joined the conversation as he opened the driver's-side door.

"That's not the reason." Dallas slapped Creed's shoulder. "Stop listening to my phone conversations."

"That's not easy when you're yelling."

Elliot felt like he'd just stepped into a kids' show and some clown in the background was singing, "Which of these things is not like the others?" He found it hard to believe that two people who were so different could find something to talk about, much less argue about.

He stepped back. "Get out of the truck, Dallas. This isn't a tour bus."

To his surprise, she simply folded her arms. "No. Cooper is

my cousin-in-law, and I'm not leaving him in the woods for the wolves to eat. I'm part of the rescue squad."

Elliot didn't have time to argue. He shoved the first-aid kit at her and climbed in.

Creed smiled at him like the first man out in a poker game would grin at the second loser.

"All right. You can go, but you may have to ride in the back with Cooper on the way back. There may be blood."

"I know there may be blood. I took human anatomy twice."

Elliot tried to fight against using sarcasm, but then asked, "Loved it that much, did you?"

"No, failed it the first time. Who knew all the bones had their own names. Couldn't we just call them leg bones or arm bones? Oh, no. They have to have their own funny little name and it's always something you'd never name a kid. Like ulna or phalanges. And muscles, don't get me started on them."

The foreman turned on the radio to get the weather report.

Dallas simply talked louder as she critiqued every class she'd ever failed.

When they finally shot through the pass, the road was so rough she stopped talking and started screaming.

Creed pushed the truck to its limit, but he only dared to go a few yards beyond where the doc had parked her Jeep. The wind was kicking up, and snow blew in swirls at the tree line. They needed to get to Cooper as fast as possible.

The men were out of the truck and packed to climb the hill while Dallas looked for her glove.

Leaning near Elliot, Creed whispered, "I liked her better drunk."

"Me, too," Elliot answered, then yelled at Dallas, "We're heading up. If you can't keep up, stay here. You should be safe from the wolves in the cab of the truck. Just honk the horn if they figure out how to open the doors. We'll come running to help, if we hear the horn."

Creed's low tone held laughter. "You do know there are no wolves up here, don't you, boss?"

"I do."

Both men were loaded down as they headed up the hill. Dallas carried the basket of muffins and complained.

Creed had grown up running these hills with Cooper. The boys were best friends, so the foreman wasn't slowing down for anyone. He was on a mission.

Elliot felt the burn in his legs, but he kept up with Creed.

Dallas, surprisingly, figured out she could breathe more if she talked less. Her long legs and agile body took to climbing. Or maybe she simply believed that Elliot would leave her behind if she couldn't keep up.

They saw the smoke of the shack's chimney first, and Elliot broke into a run, not caring about the uneven ground or the icy slopes.

Fifty feet out, they saw a kid sitting at the corner of the steps crying. Elliot slowed as he neared. "You all right?"

"I'm sorry, mister. It's all my fault. I liked Cooper and that's what killed him."

Elliot felt his own heart stop. Before he could breathe, the little doctor he'd met yesterday opened the door.

"You didn't kill him, Tatum. He's still alive."

The kid shook his head. "He won't be for long. He'll turn cold soon, and once they turn cold, they never say another word."

Both Creed and Elliot bumped into the doc as they rushed the door. Elliot didn't care who the boy was or what the doc thought. He had to see his brother.

Cooper was lying across a bunk too short for his long legs. He was muddy and bruised, but he was looking straight at them.

"Took you long enough to get here. If the doc would have made me a cane, I would have started searching for you."

Creed reacted first. "What in the hell is that on your leg, Coop? It's like you're turning into part of the roof."

"I think the doc pulled off boards from the house to make me a splint. But don't mention it. She's touchy about her work. The kid thinks he's killing me because someone told him he carries death, and the doc keeps threatening to kill me if I don't do what she says. I'm glad you got here. I don't know how long I can hold the Grim Reaper off."

His voice was a bit weak and pain reflected from his eyes, but he was alive.

Elliot breathed, really breathed for the first time since he'd gotten the call that Cooper was hurt. His brother wasn't dying, and if he was complaining...well, all was going to be fine.

He moved close and locked right hands with his brother, their hands forming a tight fist. "We need to get you out of here, Coop. You think you can make the journey?"

Cooper glanced at the little doctor. "I can make it. But what about the mustangs?"

"I'll stay here," Dr. Hayley Westland said in a very professional manner. "I can manage by myself."

"No!" both brothers said at once.

Elliot added, in as kind of a tone as he could muster, "It's too dangerous."

Creed stepped up. "I'll stay to help her. I know what to do."

"Well, if you're staying, Creed, I'm staying, too." Dallas barged into the shack as if she'd been invited.

"No," all three men shouted.

Cooper cussed. "Hell, I don't care who stays or goes. All I care about is getting out of here. This place is busier than the Driskill Hotel in downtown Austin. I'm hoping they put me in the hospital so I can get some rest."

Coop focused on Dallas, but his words sounded weaker. "I fig-ured the cousins would have left the headquarters by now. You must be really bored, Dallas, to follow the rescue team all the way up here." His eyes closed tightly as pain overtook his body.

She moved closer, having to push Creed over a few inches with her hip. "I was worried about you, Coop. I'm here to help you."

"Yeah, right." Cooper looked at Creed. "You're the only man I trust to take care of the mustangs. The doc's downright bossy, but she'll help. The boy stays with me. I promised him I wouldn't die. I have to prove I'm a man of my word before I figure out where he belongs."

Hayley straightened as if she could be as tall as every other adult in the room. "If Creed is staying with the horses, I'll see Cooper to safety, then I'll return when I can to help with the herd. I've covered the path from the pass to the shack twice today and I can do it again. Let's get him down, then worry about the horses."

Elliot agreed with the plan. He could see the pain growing in his little brother's eyes. They needed to get him to the hos-pital, fast.

Within minutes, Elliot managed to organize everyone. He and Creed took the two ends of the stretcher with Cooper wrapped like a burrito inside. The boy walked on one side, the doc on the other. Dallas followed, leading the mare. Once they reached the pass, Creed would have a horse to ride back and complete Cooper's original mission.

The journey down was slow. Elliot didn't miss that Hayley and Tatum did their share of holding Cooper level on uneven ground, and Dallas held branches back so they could pass. It took everyone giving their all to make the hike down.

Cooper groaned a few times and then closed his eyes. No one knew if he'd passed out or was simply trying to ignore the pain.

The weak sun above offered little warmth, and the north wind blew cold, as if pushing them along their way. Another few hours and the temperature would be well below freezing again.

When they reached the pickup, everyone was exhausted. Creed and Elliot carefully lifted Coop into the bed of the truck, and Hayley climbed in to cover him. As she sat beside him and lifted his head into her lap, everyone waited.

"His breathing is regular. One of my stitches on his hairline has come loose and it's dripping blood." She slid her hand between the buttons of his shirt. "He feels very warm. As the only doctor here, I feel like I'd better stay with him until we have him in hospital care." She looked up at Creed. "Weather permitting, I'll be back in a few days to help with the horses."

Creed nodded.

Elliot didn't argue with the plan. There was no one who could be of more help getting Cooper to the hospital than the little doc right now.

As she gathered up blankets and pillows, she took charge. "Tatum, sit close to his leg and pack blankets along his side so the brace won't move. That will be a big help. Creed, put the first-aid kit at his feet so he won't move down during the ride. Elliot, drive as fast as you can without being unsafe. We've got to get him to the headquarters in one piece."

"Will do, Doc." Elliot climbed into the truck. His job now was to get his brother to the ambulance. "Get in, Dallas!" he yelled.

"I'm staying to help Creed." She crossed her arms and took a step backward, silently telling him that she would allow no argument.

He threw the truck in gear and took off, ignoring Creed's cussing.

CHAPTER SIXTEEN

December 18
Maverick Ranch

A few hours after Elliot left for Winter Valley, Dani noticed everyone on the ranch seemed to be slowing down. With the Holloway men gone and Creed, the foreman, rushing to help Cooper, no one seemed to be in charge. The men were standing around talking, worrying, guessing how bad Cooper was hurt.

Only her sons and Tye Franklin were not among the men. It didn't take her long to figure out where they were. She packed up half a dozen fried pies and headed to the white barn.

Sure enough, her boys were on their knees rubbing down a newborn colt and Tye was working with the new momma. All three looked like they'd been rolled in mud and blood, then powdered with hay.

She couldn't help but smile. Her boys might have their faults, but they had big hearts. Pete had tears dripping down his face, and Patrick was smiling as if he was the proud father of the newborn.

"Look, Mom, we birthed a horse," Pete announced.

"I've felt like I've done that a few times." She giggled and caught Tye's grin. He was the only one in the stall who got the joke.

"Your boys were a great help. I couldn't have done it without them." Tye winked at her.

Dani looked at the mess. "You three been right here all night?"

They all nodded.

"Then you don't know what's going on." She set down the basket and told them what she knew about Cooper as Tye coached the colt to stand and have his first meal. The cowboy seemed far more interested in the mare than the owner breaking a leg.

"She'll be fine now." Tye wiped the sweat from his face. "I think I'll go clean up and then come back and check on her."

"Can you spare my sons? I've got a chore Elliot asked me to find someone to do before he gets back and I think my boys would be perfect for the assignment."

"Sure, but they've earned some time off." Tye watched her, as if suspecting a twist. "Can it wait until they eat and sleep a few hours?"

Dani looked serious. "There's no time. You two get cleaned up. Wear your best pairs of jeans and your Sunday shirts." She handed them the lunch. "You can eat while you shave."

Before they could complain, she added, "I've got two young ladies who need you to drive them to the airport, and you need to leave before they bring Cooper back. Those two sweet girls don't need to see their almost cousin injured."

Both her boys looked confused. She doubted either one of them had been close enough to the girls to even say hello.

Dani marched on with her explanation. "I think Elliot would appreciate it if you stopped at a steak house in Lubbock and made sure they had a good meal before they head home. He'll pick up the bill for you all, of course, plus gas. You can even take his Land Rover, but be careful."

Pete slapped Patrick on the back. "Come on. We've got a mission. I get to drive first."

"Fine with me, but I'm ordering the biggest steak on the menu. Lubbock has a dozen great steak houses. I get to choose which one."

They took off in a run when they reached the barn door, both laughing and talking about the desserts they'd order.

Tye leaned on the gate and watched them. "Did Elliot really say all that?"

"No, all he said was for me to help the cousins pack and make sure they get on their journey home any way I could."

"What about Dallas? That's the redhead who went with Elliot and Creed? If they left an hour ago, it'll be a while before she gets back."

"She wasn't planning to leave. I heard her talking to the other two. Apparently, her parents are delayed and may not make it home before Christmas. I think she'd rather be here than home alone."

Tye laughed. "In my world, *delayed* is usually code for *they're in jail.*"

"I doubt it. Dallas said she's been living away at schools since she was twelve, and now and then, she thinks her parents forget they have a child."

"Sad." Tye reached to touch her, then pulled back when he saw the dirt and dried blood on his fingers. "Too bad she didn't have a mom like you. Pete is going to love chauffeuring those girls around, and Patrick probably won't say a word. He'll just grin all evening. I wouldn't expect them back until late. There's a plane out of Lubbock heading to DFW every hour. They are probably all booked but the last one might take in a few stand-bys."

"I'll give them the kitchen credit card I use. Elliot won't care and the boys will show the girls the town. Lubbock's got the Buddy Holly Center and a museum that's nothing but wind-mills. Now, that's something to see."

"Maybe one afternoon we could go see the windmills and eat a meal you wouldn't have to cook." Tye's suggestion came easy as he brushed the mare.

Dani stiffened. "I don't want to go on a date, Tye. I didn't like it when I was young, and I don't think I'd like it now. If I go to see the windmills, I'll go by myself."

Like he always did, Tye studied her. Sometimes she swore he could see all the way to her soul with those wolf-gray eyes of his.

He didn't blink. "So you're serious. No dating. Nothing be-tween us but the night."

"You got a problem with that?" She'd never had an affair or a boyfriend since she divorced. She'd always had the farm to run and the twins to raise. She had no idea how this worked between two people, but she didn't plan on saying something she didn't mean. No promises come morning. No ties. That was the only way it could work between them. She'd had enough disappointment in this life.

Tye moved closer, his voice as low as it had been when he'd held her in the night. "No. I don't have any problem at all with you or how you want things to be between us. I think I'd better go over to the bunkhouse and clean up. Maybe shave and take a nap. It's going to be a long day." He grinned. "And maybe a long night."

She didn't say a word. Flirting was a skill she'd never learned. When she'd been seventeen, her ex had come to work on her parents' place. They'd talked, worked cattle together some. He'd kissed her on her eighteenth birthday, and three months later, he'd asked her to marry him. He'd talked of all the fun they'd have traveling, and Dani had wanted to see something besides the farm.

None of his promises had come true. In less than a year, she'd been pregnant, and all she saw was him leaving her for the open road. When he'd come back and seen how her belly had grown, he'd turned away from her as if she was nothing to him.

Dani had said she'd never let another man get close, but there was something about Tye Franklin. Something she couldn't turn her back on. She swore she could see gentleness in the hard man. It was a quality he probably let few people see. It was almost as if she'd been waiting for him all these years and simply no one else would do.

Her hopes were small. If he left her with a memory, that would be enough.

She watched as he walked all the way to the bunkhouse before he removed the lid of the lunch she'd brought him.

He looked back and waved. He must have noticed there were two biscuits on top of his chicken-fried steak.

Dani smiled, allowing herself, for just a moment, to think of what the night might bring. Then she pulled her mind back to reality. She had a bucketful of worries to deal with first. Cooper would be coming back in a few hours with a broken leg and who knew what else hurting. She had to get the cousins packed and gone. Elliot didn't have time to entertain right now *and* deal with his brother.

There were things that had to be done, things to be prepared for and things to worry about. She didn't have time to think of Tye today. But tonight, when all was in order, they would have midnight to live out a few fantasies.

Walking back to the house, she let herself remember how he'd touched her so softly. He was a man with a slow touch, and even with the cold wind blowing hard, she could almost feel the warmth of him.

Maybe they could have a kind-of date. Drive around one afternoon and look for one of the clues in his grandfather's book of drawings. The county-road sign with bullet holes in it wouldn't be hard to find. Maybe they'd count windmills. Maybe they'd pull over and explore one another in the sunset's light.

She shook her head for even thinking of doing such a romantic thing. Then giggled at the chance it might happen.

Just before she stepped inside, she watched a black Lexus pull up to the front porch. A stranger on Holloway land, and not one of the boys home to either welcome or turn him away.

The accountant...of course. Dani had forgotten all about him coming. Elliot said Griffin had hired an expert accounting firm to handle their taxes this year.

His room was ready. All she'd have to do was feed him at some point. She'd show him the work piled on Elliot's desk, and no one on the place would even notice he was around.

Dani headed toward the car. Might as well get him settled in on the third floor. The room was a fancy suite with its own bathroom, study and a huge bedroom with floor-to-ceiling windows that faced the morning sun. The third floor had been Sunlan's room before she'd married Griffin. After the wedding and as she grew with the pregnancy, she'd had a wing built on so she didn't have to climb the stairs, and the third floor became a guest room along with the old second floor the boys had used as bedrooms growing up. Sunlan had talked Cooper and Elliot into moving into the ground-floor master bedrooms. She'd said the second floor rooms had small closets, and the smaller the closet, the shorter the time the guest will stay.

Dani had almost reached the car before she looked up and froze when a woman, dressed in a black suit and heels four inches high, stepped gracefully out of the car.

With a quick smile, the woman turned and reached in for her briefcase. Her hair was short and stylish, like only the big-city salons could cut, and she looked a bit lost in the open country.

"May I help you, miss?" Dani asked.

"I'm with Moore, Brantley and Karter. I believe I'm expected."

"You're the accountant?"

"Yes. I'm Jessica Brantley. I believe Griffin Holloway is expecting me."

Dani offered to help the lady with her bag, but she shook her head slightly, so the cook waved her ahead. "Griffin Holloway is away at the moment. His father-in-law is ill. Elliot was told to expect an accountant, but he's not here right now, either." Dani had no idea how much she should tell this stranger. "If you'll come in, I'll show you to your room. We'll get you settled in while you wait."

"I suggest I pack the records and take them with me back to our offices. I can work faster from my home base. It's no trouble to fly back with my findings. I'll double-check to see that I have everything, consult with Mr. Holloway on his needs and be out of your hair by dark."

Dani might not know much about bookkeeping, but she'd heard Elliot say once that no document leaves the ranch unless it was in Holloway hands. "I'm sorry, Miss Brantley, but I thought there was an understanding you'd be working from here."

"There was, but I thought…"

Dani smiled and said simply, "You'll be working here."

The very proper lady looked agitated but not surprised.

"Well, I came to workx. The sooner I start, the sooner I'll be finished and gone from here. I'd like to get this done in as short a time as possible. I'm meeting my fiancé for the Christmas holiday."

"I understand." Dani couldn't figure out if she liked this accountant or not. She wanted to work and, after all, she wasn't a guest. She was just like Dani—hired help. "Mr. Holloway said the books are lying out on his desk if you'd like to look at them before he returns. There are two other desks in the office, but the other two brothers rarely use them. Feel free to spread out."

"And when will at least one of the Holloway men be back?"

"I have no idea. Elliot's gone to get his injured brother off a hill that has no road and a foot of snow. They had to hike up with enough gear to carry him down."

The accountant started up the steps to the main door. "I'm not surprised Cooper is hurt. He must be as wild as ever."

Dani followed her in. "You know Cooper?"

"I don't know him, but I saw him once." She stepped inside and walked toward the headquarters' office. "I'd like to go to work. You can show me where I'm staying later if I don't finish today."

A scream stopped her progress. Jessica and Dani both turned as Apple and Bethany rushed down the stairs in short robes and bare feet.

"Dani, Dani, Dani," Apple squealed. "Can you make us tequila sunrises while we pack? We just *must* have one for the road."

"Of course," Dani answered, thinking one drink might help with the shock of finding out that the Garrett boys would be driving them to Lubbock.

The girls thanked her and giggled their way back upstairs.

When Dani turned and saw the accountant's shocked face, she almost laughed. "Don't worry, Miss Brantley, they're leaving today. It's been a real party around here lately."

"Is it always like this? Half-dressed women running around ordering drinks before noon and injured men being carried down mountains?"

Dani couldn't help herself. "Yeah. It's just an ordinary day on the Maverick."

She should have been honest and said no, it was usually just dull, ordinary ranch work, but that would make it seem too sad. When Griffin and Sunlan were here, there were dinner parties. All fall, they'd hosted Texas Tech football evenings with everyone screaming at the TV. Then there was last month, when Cooper let two wild piglets into the house. Everyone had laughed 'til they cried.

"It's a wild time, miss, but you'll be sleeping on the third floor. It's usually quiet up there unless a bat flies in. If that happens, just ignore it and leave the windows open until it flies back out."

The accountant's face paled.

Dani grinned. The poor girl would probably work twenty hours a day so she could get out fast. "I'll make a pot of coffee for you to have in the study."

"No, tea. Herbal, if you have it. I'd like to get started right away."

The sound of sirens coming closer echoed throughout the house.

"What's that?" Miss Brantley looked like she'd gone from worried to panicked.

"Oh, it's only the ambulance and probably a fire truck. They usually come together in case they're both needed." Dani turned and headed to the kitchen. She didn't want to try to explain, and she knew nothing but rumors. "I need to go tell them to turn off the sirens and come in and have lunch. They'll have a while to wait before they bring Cooper down."

When Dani reached the foyer, she glanced back. The accountant had vanished into the study.

Dani didn't have time to worry about her. She had to make

drinks for the cousins and get them on their way, feed the ambulance drivers and the firemen, and try to find some herbal tea.

She was so busy she didn't have time to daydream of what she'd do to Tye tonight.

Maybe she'd just have to surprise him—and herself.

CHAPTER SEVENTEEN

December 18
Winter Valley

Cooper felt like someone had crammed him into a blender full of rocks. Every few seconds, Elliot ran over a hole in the dirt road, and he went spinning again.

The little doctor held his head as steady as she could, but she wasn't anchored in the bed of the truck. He tried to look up at her, but all he saw were those two nicely rounded blue bumps on her chest. Perfect, he thought.

He was going to hell for staring at her breasts. No doubt. Maybe it was the concussion? Women usually cuddled up to him, but the doc didn't even like him. She'd lectured him about walking on ice. Which he'd done. Then on bringing a kid up to the shack. Which he hadn't done. She'd even complained that whiskey was not considered a first-aid kit.

The doc obviously thought he had no positive qualities, and he wasn't about to mention the few he saw in her. It was possible that they might never have a normal conversation. Which was fine with him. She was too smart for him. Too short. And way too bossy.

He could hear Tatum crying. Even in a semidelirious state, Cooper thought he should reach out to help the kid. He lifted his scraped-up hand and said, "Take my hand, Tatum, and hold it tight."

The boy did as he was told.

"Now, hold it tighter. We're making a hard fist with our hands. If we lace our fingers, no one is going to break that hold. That's what my brothers and I do when we want to pass strength from one to the other."

The kid's hand reminded Cooper how his hand had once felt in Griffin's fist. Their mother had just died, and Cooper was losing it, but Grif's hold was strong.

"I'm going to need your strength to get through this, Tatum."

The kid sniffed and said, "I got you, Coop."

Cooper closed his eyes as the pain washed over him, but the boy's grip never lessened.

The sun was high, warming him, but Coop had lost track of time. Riding down on the stretcher seemed to have taken hours, and the ride in the pickup was endless, but over and over, he kept saying that he was heading home. He'd get through this like he'd gotten through other breaks. He'd mend.

Finally, he felt the pickup bump onto a better road, and knew he was close to the headquarters. Elliot sped up. Now the pickup was rocking him gently against the hay and blankets.

Cooper looked up at the doctor, who was sheltering him from the bumps. "Thanks, Doc. I owe you one. If you ever need me, I'll be there, I swear."

"I'll remember that, Mr. Holloway, but you've got to heal first before I can ask for a favor."

CHAPTER EIGHTEEN

December 18
Maverick Ranch

Elliot pulled the pickup close to the ambulance, jumped out and began yelling. Ranch hands came running, even though there was nothing for them to do except watch. The front drive of the ranch headquarters looked like a busy emergency way station with men running from every direction.

Even the weather seemed to feel the panic. Wind whipped in bursts of cold air and the sunny day turned cloudy.

The EMTs went to work even as the firemen were lifting Cooper out of the bed of hay. They seemed to be talking in a code Elliot couldn't understand. It reminded him of the night Cooper thought he'd try bull riding. He'd been eighteen. He and Creed were a calf-roping team. They'd even won a few prizes. But that night, no one could tell him what to do. Cooper had wanted to try his luck atop a thousand pounds of mean.

The only thing he'd ridden that night had a siren blaring. Cooper's only trophies were three broken ribs and a scar on his forehead. Elliot and Griffin had taken turns sitting up with him for two weeks to keep away the nightmare of his first, and only, seven-second thrill.

Still, even with the spills, Elliot had always wished he could be more like his little brother. Impulsive. Adventurous. Bold. But he didn't want the knocks that came with Cooper's wild life. With chance came falling now and then.

Elliot raised his hands and offered the doctor a lift down from the pickup after Cooper had been moved away. Like him, the boy and the doc wanted to stay with Cooper, but Elliot knew the routine.

"Only one passenger in the ambulance," the EMT yelled from the back door of the ambulance.

"You go," Elliot said to Hayley. "You know more about his condition. I'll follow right behind."

She nodded and climbed into the ambulance.

Elliot grabbed the boy just before he jumped in behind her. "You need to stay here."

Tatum reared up, ready to fight. "I'm going with Coop. I have to. You can't tell me what to do."

Great, Elliot thought, *I'm being bullied by a kid.* Tatum reminded him so much of Cooper. The wildness. The independence. "All right, but you ride with me. We'll figure out what to do with you later, but right now, you're part of the family if anyone asks. Keep your mouth shut and I'll bring you to whatever waiting room they send me to. Then, as soon as they're finished with him, you can go in with me."

Tatum nodded once.

Before Elliot could head toward the side of the house, where his Land Rover was parked, Dani stepped away from the crowd. "Take the pickup. Your car isn't back—Pete and Patrick are still delivering the cousins to the airport. And, Elliot, the accountant has arrived."

"Tell him I'll get to him when I have time." Elliot climbed back in the truck. The kid was already in the passenger seat, buckled in. He didn't say a word on the way to the hospital, and Elliot didn't feel like talking, either. Memories of other runs to the emergency room or the doctor traveled with him in the silence.

At the hospital, Elliot barged into the main waiting room with the boy one step behind him. Elliot filled out paperwork and made a few calls. He stared at the clock for a while, then finally seemed to notice the kid beside him.

"You hungry?"

"No."

"When did you eat today?"

"I haven't, but I'm not leaving."

Elliot rubbed his forehead and took on one more load. "See those machines? I'm going to walk over there and buy whatever looks good, and you're going to do the same. Deal?"

"Deal."

Tatum followed him over and picked out juice, two candy bars, a bag of chips and three packs of peanut-butter crackers. He stuffed all but the chips and drink in his pockets.

"Anything else?" Elliot asked. The kid must have been squirreling away food for winter.

"Nope. I'm not very hungry."

While the boy ate, Elliot watched the doors that barred visitors and drank a cup of coffee. It wasn't even dark, and he felt like he'd lived ten days in one. The waiting room seemed too hot after spending so much time in the cold.

He leaned back in the hard chair, rested his head against the wall and closed his eyes, but he knew he wouldn't sleep. An hour passed. Two. Three.

Hayley finally stepped through the double doors and hurried toward Elliot. "It's looking good. The leg was a clean break.

They're setting it now. He has a concussion but shows no sign of damage. They want to keep him for a few days, but all in all, I think he's very lucky."

Elliot hugged her, then the kid. He noticed that they both had cuts on their arms and faces from branches they'd fought while going through the trees. The blood had dried, darkening into scabs. He probably had them, too, but it didn't matter. They'd gotten Cooper out.

Hayley pointed to a cup beside Elliot's chair. "Coffee?"

She took a drink before he could tell her it was cold.

She made a cute, disgusted face and they both laughed.

While Tatum went to get her a hot cup of coffee, she continued her report to Elliot. "They are keeping him in ICU tonight under close watch. The surgeon said we might as well go home. We'll be able to see him tomorrow morning."

Elliot wanted to demand to see his brother, but in truth he was sleepwalking now, and he still had to drive home. "What about the kid?"

Hayley's dark eyes filled with tears. "It seems cruel to pass him off to strangers tonight. He's as worried about Cooper as I am. Would it matter if we wait one more day to call social services? Cooper told me no one is looking for him."

"I guess not. I'll call home and tell my housekeeper to have two rooms ready. One for you and one for him."

"I can drive home. I only live thirty minutes away from your place."

Elliot grinned. "Only your Jeep is miles away on dirt roads, and I don't think either of us has enough energy left to make the trip in the dark."

"Good point. I'll be your houseguest tonight, Mr. Holloway."

"You are welcome, Doctor. After all, you saved my brother's life today."

They were both smiling when Tatum got back with the coffee. "What did I miss?" he asked.

Hayley put her hand on his shoulder. "We're both going back to the Maverick Ranch. Elliot is putting us up for the night."

The kid turned to Elliot. "You got room for both of us?"

"I got room. You look like you could use a good bath, then I'll have a hot meal waiting for you both. You pulled your weight, son."

On the way home Tatum fell asleep between them. They were both too tired to talk. It was only half past nine when they pulled up at the headquarters, but it felt like midnight.

Elliot carried the kid in, and Dani took over from there. She stripped him and made him get in a bath, then she took all his clothes downstairs to wash. When she came back to his room, Tatum was wrapped in a towel as he ate the soup and sandwiches she'd left by his bed.

Elliot watched from the doorway as she tucked the kid in. "Tatum, when you wake, find the kitchen and Dani will have breakfast for you. She'll leave your clothes on this chair as soon as they're finished."

But the boy's eyes were already closed, and he still had half of a sandwich in his hand.

In the hallway, Elliot asked if they should check on the doc and Dani reminded him that Hayley could take care of herself. "I loaned her one of my nightgowns." The cook smiled. "It touched the floor on her. She's a little thing, but she did a big job today."

When they were almost to the bottom of the stairs, he asked if the cousins got off all right.

"Well. My boys took the girls to Lubbock and they wanted to see the sites." The cook hesitated, then added, "Seems they had so much fun seeing the town they missed their flight. All flights tonight, in fact, so the boys are driving them to DFW. They should be back with your car by dawn if they drive all night."

"Don't worry about it." He had too much on his plate right now. "Tell them to spend the night somewhere after they drop the girls off at the airport. It's the least I can do after they had to put up with those two all day."

"Will do. Do you need anything else? I'd like to turn in a bit earlier than usual. It's been a long day for us all."

"I think that is a good idea. Good night, Dani." He walked through the great room, turning out lights. When he glanced toward the kitchen, he saw she was doing the same thing. Tonight the household was closing down before the ten o'clock news.

As he passed the closed doors of his office, he saw a thin line of light shining out. He'd forgotten all about the accountant coming in today.

When he opened the door, all his senses came alive at once.

There, sitting in his chair, was Jessica Brantley. His Jess. Her short blond hair was a mess, the top two buttons of her very proper blouse were undone and she seemed to have lost her shoes.

For a moment, he thought it was simply a memory. A cruel end to a hell of a day. Then, he saw tiny changes in her. This wasn't the girl who'd walked out on him, who'd refused to skip a semester and come home with him to help keep his family ranch running. This was a woman now in her late twenties. A professional engrossed in her work.

This woman was polished to perfection. Her hair was a shade lighter thanks to highlights. Her delicate makeup helped to play up her eyes. As she stood, he noticed her clothes were cut to fit her exactly. She'd always had a model's figure, but now it looked more refined, more toned.

No words came. All these years he'd thought about what he'd say if he ever saw her again. How he'd yell or softly cut her to the quick. How he'd demand answers about how they could have loved so completely and broken so easily. But now nothing came. The memories of loving her when they were together slammed against the pain of hating her when she didn't love him enough.

She tapped her pencil on the desk and looked at him closely. Disapproval flashed in her green eyes before she hid it, and he realized how bad he must look.

He was exactly the picture of what she'd said he'd become if he stayed in a small town, from his muddy boots to his uncombed hair. Suddenly, he didn't want to see her. He just wanted to disappear. No—more accurately, he wanted *her* to disappear. She didn't belong here. Jess no longer belonged in his world.

Before he could turn around and make his tired muscles move, she faced him like an attorney presenting her case.

"When your brother called asking my firm to help out with taxes, I knew there was a chance I'd run into you again, Elliot. I just didn't think it would be this soon. While you've been running around the hills with your brother, I've been working and I think I can handle this mess within a week."

"Why'd you come?" He finally found his voice. Jess hadn't mellowed with age. She was still as sharp and to the point as always. "I'm sure you're one of the partners in that huge firm your daddy owns—surely there's someone who could handle this job."

In his mind he'd remembered only the good over the years, only the happy times, but now he saw what she was. No—what they had been. He'd been attracted to her beauty and her quick mind. From the time they'd met at eighteen, she'd made all the plans. She was the reason he'd majored in business. The reason they'd decided to wait until they graduated to get married. He'd loved her. He'd wanted to be together. But she'd insisted everything in their lives had to have an order.

It was never his way, or their way. It was always Jess's way. She set the pace. She set the rules. She set the goals.

They'd both wanted degrees in business. Hers in accounting and his in management. Of course, they'd planned to take jobs in Houston with her father's firm as soon as they graduated. In ten years, they'd either be running the place, or would have moved on to New York, to bigger things. She'd set the plan for their lives, and Elliot hadn't doubted for a moment that their dreams would come true.

The only thing she couldn't control was his father dying. She'd demanded he finish the semester before going home to straighten out the books at the ranch. Jess was still arguing when he'd packed.

He hadn't known it that day, but it was the end of them. At first, they talked often, then less and less. Maybe she simply got tired of asking when he'd be back. After she'd graduated without him, he'd call, and he knew she often didn't pick up or she was working on something, or just busy. When he'd ask when she was coming, she never gave him a date. Finally, he realized she was never coming to see him. She'd made other plans, and he was no longer part of the picture of her life. By the next fall, they'd drifted apart.

Elliot couldn't remember the last words they'd said to each other. He couldn't think of the last time they'd mentioned love. It had just drifted out of their conversations. Maybe that was why it had been so hard to forget Jess. He didn't know when the last thread that held them together had broken.

Maybe it never had.

He took a step toward her. "Why'd you come, Jess?"

She held up her chin slightly, like she always had when she was afraid or felt she was outnumbered. "I wanted to make sure."

"Sure of what?"

"That it's over between us. I'm getting married this spring, and I don't want the ghost of a past love hanging around. In truth, Richard insisted I settle anything that might remain between us."

"I see. We work together a few days, make sure there are no sparks and then we can finally know that whatever we have is dead."

"Right."

Elliot was too tired to argue. He was torn between tossing her out tonight and grabbing her and kissing her hard. Both seemed the improper thing to do.

He took a step backward. "You settled in with a room?"

"Yes." Her eyes told him she was expecting some kind of trap to fall closed around her. "Your housekeeper was very helpful."

"Good." He took another backward step. "I'll see you in the morning. Breakfast is at sunup. An hour later I'll be on my way to the hospital. If you have questions you'll have to work them in while I eat."

He turned and was almost out the door when she asked, "How is your brother?"

"He's hurt pretty bad, but he's going to pull through. Thank you for asking." He knew she didn't care. She'd never cared about his family. When he'd mentioned them, she'd always turn the conversation to what their lives would be like when they lived in the big city and had endless places to go.

Walking out of the room, he didn't bother to say good-night. After all, farewells weren't their thing.

When he reached the darkness of the hallway leading to his room, he turned back and saw her working in the circle of light around his desk. She looked so out of place there. In all these years, he'd never thought she would one day be in this house. Maybe that was part of their trouble. She wanted him in her world, but she wanted no part of his.

He showered, feeling numb all over. Maybe it was all that

had happened today, but he almost felt like he was walking outside his skin.

As he stared out at a moon peeping through clouds, he remembered an old Apache legend about a warrior who fought long and hard in battle with his enemies. When he finally swam in the river to wash off all the blood and war paint, he accidentally twisted out of his own skin as the current flowed around him. He was a warrior, honored by his people, but once he looked back at himself, he didn't want to go back inside his own skin.

Elliot had done what was right. He wouldn't change a thing. But tonight, he felt like the warrior. He was looking at himself outside his skin. Only when he'd seen Jess, all that was wrong with them came back, and he realized he didn't want to go back to who he'd been with her, either.

Maybe the part of them he hated wasn't her, but himself.

He dropped onto his bed. He'd think about his life tomorrow. Right now, he just wanted to sleep. He was too tired to even dream.

CHAPTER NINETEEN

December 18

Dani took her time getting ready for bed. She showered and even put powder on from a fancy jar the boys had bought her one year at Walmart. Her room behind the kitchen smelled of fresh-baked bread, and she'd opened the top of the curtains so light from the moon shone in.

Funny how she felt more nervous tonight than the first time she and Tye were together.

Maybe tonight she'd think before she acted. The first time it had simply been a need deep down inside her.

When she looked up and saw Tye standing at her door, she felt the urge to run. How could tonight be as magical as the first time? What if he thought she was too inexperienced, too dull, too ordinary? She didn't even watch R-rated movies. What did she know of sex, or loving a man, for that matter?

He didn't say a word as he set his hat and coat atop the yellow bedspread covering the chest. Walking across the room, he never took his eyes off her face. Then, when he was close enough to touch her, he smiled down at her and kissed her softly with cold lips.

She laughed. "You're freezing."

"You'll warm me up." Cold hands cupped her face. "I've been waiting all day to touch you. Have I ever told you I love the way you feel?"

"Several times." His hands were warming as he slid his fingers along the cotton nightgown.

"We'd better close and lock the door, darlin'. I don't want to be interrupted tonight."

She walked over, following his suggestion, while he sat on the bed and removed his boots. The low light of the lamp by her bed was all they needed. When she returned he pulled her in front of him and rested his head against her middle.

Dani placed her hands on his shoulders and stood still as he seemed to breathe her in. His touch was so gentle as his hands moved beneath the cotton. She leaned back her head and tried to remember every moment. The feel of his cheek pressing against her ribs. The way his hands covered her hips and pulled her closer as his legs held her tightly in place in front of him.

"Breathe, darlin', just breathe. We've got a long night ahead of us and I plan to take my time getting to know you. Any objection?"

"No," she whispered as his hand pushed her gown up so he could kiss the valley between her breasts. Then he stood slowly, his clothed body sliding over her bare skin as he removed her gown.

He turned and lifted the quilt. "Climb into bed, Danielle. I've been thinking about seeing you there all day." He winked. "Wearing just what you are now."

When she did as he asked, he didn't cover her, but stood staring at her as he undressed.

She reached for the quilt, but he stopped her. "No. Let me see you. I want to remember how you look tonight."

Dani blushed, but she let the cover fall away. She felt she could read his thoughts. No matter how many others there had been in his past, he was her onetime lover and she'd be the memory he'd carry to his grave. She'd be the one he longed for when he was alone.

And he'd be hers. The fantasies she'd dreamed had always been faceless mixtures of movie-star lovers. Now they'd all be Tye.

When he lowered onto the bed, he didn't lie down beside her, but gently moved on top of her, warming her completely. For a while they were still, feeling one another breathe, learning every inch they touched. Then, without words, they made love.

When she shook with passion, he held her close as if he'd never let her go. In that moment, Dani felt as if they'd changed hearts. They might never speak of love or forever, but she knew she'd felt it completely, if only one time in her life.

Deep in the night, when they were both spent, she smiled as she realized she was too tired to move. She was lying on her back as he pressed against her side. He whispered near her ear as his hand moved slowly over her.

"I love being with you," he said, his voice so low it almost seemed like a thought passing between them. "I always will."

She drifted into sleep smiling, knowing she was finally living in the perfect moment of her life.

CHAPTER TWENTY

December 19
Maverick Ranch

A little before dawn, Elliot walked toward the dining room and saw Jess sitting all by herself at the long formal dining table. A cup of coffee was in her hand but she seemed to have forgotten it as she turned the pages of a book.

Boxes of Christmas decorations, marked for the room, were stacked on the far end of the table. With a week left until Christmas, the odds were not good that they'd be put up.

Griffin had texted yesterday that they were keeping a close eye over the recovery of Sunlan's father. Sunlan's mother had flown in from Europe, causing more trouble than help. It seemed every time she got divorced, she came back to husband number one. Like he was the only real one she'd ever had.

Griffin ended the message by saying he'd love to be home, surrounded by the calm of the ranch.

Elliot had texted back, Me, too. The calm had been shattered and there was no sign of tranquility coming back.

He had to leave soon for the hospital. Right now, no one was running the ranch. Who knew what Creed and Dallas were up to at Winter Valley, all alone in a shack? They'd probably killed each other by now. Two people so different had never walked the earth.

Murder was a possibility if Dallas didn't get her way, and Creed wasn't a man to be pushed. Elliot decided he'd probably have to lug the shovel up there and bury them both.

But this morning, as first light sliced into the room, he studied Jess. She continued reading, either totally ignoring him or so lost in the book she didn't even know he was there. She was his biggest problem of all. If he fired her, the taxes would never get done. If he worked with her, it would be self-inflicted torture. If he didn't work with her, she'd be in his house twice as long.

The sound of Dani and Tye laughing in the kitchen drew his attention.

But before he could slip away, Jess looked up, saw him and opened her mouth.

"Wait." Elliot held up one finger. "I have to get coffee before we talk."

He turned and almost ran into the kitchen. He wasn't quite ready to deal with his ex-fiancée.

Dani poured his coffee and said simply, "The accountant doesn't eat much. Must be on a bird diet." She glanced at Tye and smiled. "Not much of a crowd to cook for this morning. Creed and that redhead are gone. The doc and the kid you brought home are still asleep. My boys haven't returned from Dallas. The way things are going, I'll be out of a job in no time."

"I'll eat double," Tye offered as he took an extra biscuit.

Elliot nodded at Tye. "Morning."

"Morning," the former rodeo star answered. "How is your brother?"

"I called a few minutes ago. He made it through the night

fine, and the duty nurse said he's complaining about being hungry, so I'm thinking he's on his way to recovering. I'll be headed there as soon as the doc is up."

"What about the kid?"

"He told me he doesn't have a home. Wanted to know if I'd hire him on as a hand. After I talk to Coop, we'll figure out who to call. Surely someone's looking for him. He's way too young to be on his own."

"If you like, I'll watch over him today," Tye offered.

"Good idea. Tell him visiting hours are not until later. If Coop's up to it, I'll take the boy back this afternoon, but I'm checking in with the sheriff this morning to make sure we're not breaking any laws with Tatum."

Dani offered to call her boys and have them pick up the kid some clothes. "I wouldn't even bother to use the outfit he had on as cleaning rags."

When she set down his plate on the kitchen table, Elliot picked it up and carried it to the dining room. "Fix the accountant a plate. She might as well eat while we talk."

"Will do," Dani answered as he closed the swinging door to the dining room to offer them a bit of privacy.

For a moment, Elliot stared at Jess. He had a hard time believing she was in his house, even though the proof was there. She was still dressed for the office, her blond curls neatly brushed back from her face, her makeup perfection. But he remembered her in jeans and her face scrubbed clean.

He took the seat across from her. Close enough to study her. Far enough to remember this was today, not a yesterday in his past.

Before Jess could start talking, the cook swung through the door and set a plate of pancakes and sausage in front of her.

"I—"

Dani interrupted, "Just eat what you can. Boss told me to feed the accountant, and that's what I plan to do. You could carry a few more pounds. You could blow away in this open country."

Elliot fought down a grin. His cook couldn't have been more obvious about what she thought of Jess.

When the door finally clicked to a stop, he realized he was alone with a woman he'd been talking to in his head for years. The thousand things he'd wanted to say to her drifted away as he took the time to really look at her.

She was thinner than she'd been in college. Her eyes looked bigger in her slim face. *Sad velvet eyes*, he thought. He'd known Jess better than he'd ever known any girl or woman, but he couldn't read her now.

"I must say before we begin that it was not my idea to come here." She picked up her fork and poked at the stack of pancakes.

"Your name's on the firm, Jess. I'm guessing near a hundred accountants work for you. You could have simply passed me along. The Maverick Ranch has to be one of your firm's smallest accounts."

"It's not that simple. I'm engaged to another partner's son who also works in the firm. Richard Moore. When your brother hired us, Richard thought I should come and maybe get closure on what was between us. In fact, he insisted I do just that."

"I find it hard to believe that any man is bossing you around, Jess."

"I go by Jessica now. He was not bossing. Richard thinks everything through. I've known him all my life. His father and my father have been partners since we were born. But they never thought we'd get together. He's twelve years older than me. Plus, he said he needed some time to tie up a few ends. Richard seems to do that a lot lately."

"You love him?" Elliot considered slamming his head into the plate of pancakes even before the last word was out.

"That is none of your business. But, of course, I love him. We have everything in common. We like the same things. We both love Paris. We both believe we can grow Moore and Brantley to be a national contender in the accounting world."

"Sounds good. What about Karter? You remember, the third partner."

She waved her hand as if brushing away one partner's name from the marquee. "Oh, he's older than our dads. Plus, he didn't have children. Richard figures in five years we'll buy him out."

"That's nice. I was afraid you were going to say 'kill him off.'"

She made a face he had once thought was cute. "Elliot, that sounds like something the Holloways would do. After all, you're still living out here in the wild, wild West."

"We're wearing shoes regularly. Keep our six-shooters locked away unless rustlers come around. Gave up making our own moonshine."

"Says the man who's dripping blood from his neck."

Elliot touched his throat, and his hand came away with red drops on it. "I thought it had scabbed over. I must have opened it when I dressed. We had to lug Cooper through a stand of trees with dried weeds up to our necks. We all took on a few wounds."

She leaned over and patted the tiny wound with her napkin. "Spare me the details. I tried to domesticate you, but I failed. How could I expect anything less?"

He managed a smile. Too many years had passed to argue over dead topics. He didn't want to walk through that grave-yard. "How about we start work? I can show you a few things, answer questions until I have to go. The faster we get this done, the better." He tried to smile. "You don't want to be here, and I don't want you here. At least we'll start by agreeing to one fact. I'll dedicate every hour I can to getting this done."

She seemed to relax a bit. "All right. I have to say, you do have the books in good order. I had no idea how complicated a ranch could be." She tapped the book she'd been reading. "I think I've already found a few deductions you might not have considered."

She left her plate on the table with one bite out of one pancake. He carried his breakfast in the office and propped up on a file cabinet while she began her questions.

This, he could handle. Keeping it professional. He told himself he wasn't even attracted to her anymore, but he knew he was lying. Jess was exactly his type. Smart, beautiful, quick to fire up and quick to love. Only problem was, no heart beat inside her perfect body. No compassion flowed through that sharp mind. This Richard Moore guy would probably be perfect. It seemed he thought more about the business than he did her, and Elliot would bet a hundred dollars the loose ends he was tying up were other women in his life.

An hour later, Dr. Westland interrupted them. "I'm ready whenever you are, Elliot." Hayley had on a clean pair of baggy trousers and what he guessed was one of Sunlan's Western shirts. She filled it out more than his sister-in-law did, but Hayley looked cute. The leather jacket she wore had been one of the cousins'. He wasn't surprised they'd left clothes behind. Amazon boxes full of clothes followed them wherever they traveled.

He stood, politely introduced her to Jess, then put his arm around Hayley. "You look like you're going to the rodeo, Doc. You sure those physicians at the hospital will believe you're a real doctor?"

Hayley laughed. "I'm a vet, remember? Medical doctors don't talk to me unless they're holding a pet."

Elliot winked at Hayley. They'd been through a war together yesterday. They were soldiers after a battle, forever friends.

He walked out with her already laughing at a few of the mistakes they'd made yesterday while trying to get Coop out of the trees and down the hill. Like letting Dallas hold the keys.

When they'd reached the truck, they'd all yelled at her as she emptied every pocket.

Looking back at Jess sitting at his desk, he almost felt sorry that he was leaving her alone with the files. Maybe she'd gotten just the life she wanted. Looked like her dreams were coming true, only he wasn't in them.

Get over it, Elliot, he thought to himself. He could handle her here. Maybe old Richard was right—this could be good for them both.

When he opened the door to leave, a dozen men who worked on the ranch were waiting. Elliot thought they might have questions about the work, but all they wanted to do was talk to the little vet. Three or four thanked her for saving Cooper's life. Two said they'd go up and get her Jeep with her anytime she wanted. One said she was a hero. And Charlie Daily, the ranch's oldest hand, asked her right out for a date. If they could have carried her to the pickup, they would have.

Elliot felt like the invisible man standing next to her.

Once they were headed toward town, Elliot whispered, "You're a hero, Doc."

"I just did what anyone would have done."

"No. You did much more. This family will count you as one of us from now on."

She was silent for a moment, then asked shyly, "Is there any way I can spend another night at your place? Tomorrow morning I'd like to head up and help with the horses at Winter Valley if the snow's melted some. If another storm comes in later this week, we may not have time to check each horse before winter pushes the mustangs farther into the canyon."

"Of course. Stay as long as you like. Your grandfather often stayed over when he came out and worked until dark. We tried to get him to stay in the house, but he liked sleeping over in the bunkhouse. Said he liked swapping lies."

"That's Pops. He loves animals, but he loves people more. I miss him, but he won't be back until after the New Year, if then."

"I'll bet you missed him when you went away to school."

"I did. I think I've spent every summer with him since I was ten." She stared out the window as they passed under the ranch gate. "Until I left for college, I thought all men were like Pops and my dad. I had to learn the hard way that they weren't."

Elliot had a feeling there was an untold story on her tongue, but they weren't close enough friends yet for her to open up.

They rode in silence for a few miles before she changed the subject. "After we check on Cooper and talk to the doctors, I'd like to sit with him. I know you've got your hands full—you're one man doing the job of three at the ranch. If he's able, maybe he'll talk to me about the mustangs so I'll be more prepared when I go up tomorrow."

"Four. I have to take over Creed's job, too. Dani told me most of the men stood around all afternoon waiting for orders yesterday, so we're a day's work behind. If you'd sit with him, I'll work today and pick you up tonight when I bring Tatum in to see him. Plus, I got an accountant in my office. Not sure how I feel about that, but I need to deal with her."

"Then it's settled. If Cooper is on the mend, I'll sit with him and we'll trade out when you bring Tatum up."

"All right. I'll have one of the hands come pick you up if you get ready to head back to the ranch before I return. But it won't be Charlie Daily. He'll think he's engaged to you if he drives you home. He's a good man, but don't talk to him. He'll scare you."

"Why would he scare me?"

Elliot grinned. "Last year a girl smiled at him at church and he wrote her at note saying he'd like to take all her teeth out so he could take them home and see her smile all the time."

Hayley took a playful swing at him. "You're lying."

Laughing, he added, "Maybe I am, but you'll never know for sure, and I'm betting you'll never smile at him again."

Elliot liked the easy way they talked. It made the trip to the hospital pass faster. Once they reached Cooper's room, he and Hayley had moved from being polite strangers to friends.

Cooper frowned at them both. "I'd rather go through the trees and roll down the hill again than stay in this torture chamber," he announced before they could get out a greeting. "You are not going to believe what they serve as food around here."

To Elliot's surprise, Hayley stepped right up like she was in charge of the hospital and needed to tell his little brother what to do. An hour later, they were still arguing when he headed out to go home. He grinned. Nothing would make Cooper get well faster than having a cute little doc picking on him.

Now he could stop worrying about Coop and handle everything else he had to do today.

By noon, he'd set up his desk to work with Jess on the taxes, but men kept coming in with ranch business, his broker called twice and Dani was banging around in the next room trying to decorate for Christmas.

Jess made an impatient little sound for about the tenth time. "Is it ever quiet around here? I've added this one column three times."

"No." He was trying to concentrate, too, but at least he wasn't complaining.

Before they could settle back into work, Dani brought in scones to go with the coffee and stayed to give a report on the twins. They'd dropped off the girls for their 5:00 a.m. flight to Boston this morning, after staying out all night showing them Fort Worth and Dallas. They'd closed the bars in the Fort Worth Stockyards district and eaten an early breakfast in the Warwick Melrose Hotel in downtown Dallas. An hour later, as her boys were checking into a hotel to sleep a few hours before driving back, Bethany called to say they'd fallen asleep waiting and had missed their flight. Since their luggage was heading home, they wanted to go shopping before trying to catch another flight.

Dani cleared her throat. "Her exact words were 'I cannot fly all day in clothes I partied in last night. That is simply not done.'"

Elliot broke into the cook's story. "The boys picked them up from DFW Airport and are shopping now, right?"

She nodded.

He shrugged. "You may never see your sons again."

"I'm not the one who should be worried. They've got your credit card."

He glanced over at Jessica, lowered his voice and whispered to Dani, "At least someone is having fun."

The cook giggled and left the room.

Elliot stood and looked out the window. Then he turned and, for a moment, simply watched Jess work. Part of him wished he could walk over and touch her. Maybe rub her shoulders. She'd been working since dawn.

But touching her wasn't going to happen. Whatever had been between them was gone, washed away by years of heartache.

As he walked over to his desk, she leaned back in her chair and looked at him. "Is it always this busy? You seem to wear a great many hats."

"No, sometimes it's worse. If fire breaks out on the grasslands, or a hundred-thousand-dollar bull gets out, or one of the men gets hurt, it can get real busy around here. Today is one of the calm days."

She smiled. "And I always thought ranching was a boring job. Just sit around and watch the grass grow, then watch the cows eat it."

"If you want to see what we do, we could take a break later and I'll show you around."

"No, thanks. I have a job to do, and a fiancé to get back to."

"Right."

An hour later, when Elliot headed out to talk to the men building a new corral, Jess told him to remind the cook that she didn't want anything to eat.

When he passed on the order, Dani just shrugged. "I'll set her a place at supper. We're having ribs and baked potatoes. If she doesn't eat, I'll feed it to the chickens."

"Good, sounds great. I'm not sure she's ever eaten either." As he put on his coat, he remembered a call he'd made between two others. "Set a place for Tatum. The sheriff called. Found a kid Tatum's age tagged as missing in Altus, Oklahoma. Tatum was honest—he has no living relatives that they can find. His grandmother died weeks ago. Sheriff talked to the authorities in both Jackson County and Lubbock County. When he told them what had happened, they agreed the kid could stay at the ranch until they could get a social worker out here. They could move him to a temporary group home, but the sheriff convinced them to let him stay with us for a few days."

"So, we keep him?" Dani asked.

"No, but he's better off here for the time being." Elliot looked around. "Where is he, anyway?" He fought to keep panic from his voice. The kid had run away once before; maybe he'd decided to hit the road again.

"He's out helping Tye with the new colt. Tye said he plans to teach him to ride if it warms up."

"Good."

She read his mind. "I'll keep an eye on him, don't you worry. He won't miss a meal."

"Tye or Tatum?" he asked.

The cook grinned. "Both."

CHAPTER TWENTY-ONE

December 19

The morning passed with rounds of tests on Cooper Holloway until Hayley wondered how he was taking all the poking and moving and blood drawing without going mad.

He barely seemed to notice her sitting in the corner of every room he was wheeled to.

The nurses finally got tired of his demanding to leave. They gave him a sedative mixed in with his IV.

As he relaxed he finally looked over at her. "Hi, Doc. You're downright cute. I've been meaning to tell you that."

She grinned. "Hi, Coop. You hang in there. They'll run out of tests eventually. How about you take a nap?"

"They think I have brain damage. Would you please tell them I wasn't all that bright to start with? Both of my brothers will verify that."

"I'll tell them. I'll also tell them that you remind me of a wild mustang. I have a feeling you'd heal if they just turned you loose."

"Thanks for the compliment, but I'm thinking of settling down. My roaming days are over. Elliot told me last night that if he had to follow the ambulance all the way to the hospital one more time, he'd kill me himself."

"Maybe you should settle down and marry, like your big brother did. Raise a dozen kids as wild as you are. That would keep you busy."

"I'm not wild. Trouble just follows me like a homeless pup, and I'm dumb enough to feed it now and then."

"I believe you." She'd seen the way he helped Tatum when the kid was so scared. Cooper might have scrambled brains, but he had a good heart.

His eyelids were starting to lower. "Any chance you'll marry me, Doc?"

"I have seen quite a lot of you in the past few hours, but no, Coop, I will not marry you. I want a man who'll stand by me until we're old. Like my grandfather did my grandmother, and my dad does with my mom. I have a feeling you'd be off on some adventure if I ever needed help."

"You don't think much of me, do you, Doc?"

"I've heard too many stories about you. You'd be a great guy to watch my back in a fight, but I'm not sure you'd be around for the day-to-day."

"If you ever get in a fight..." His words began to slur. "I'll be there. I like watching your back... I wouldn't mind watching your front, too."

Hayley pushed her chair close to his bed, cuddled up in one of the extra blankets and almost fell asleep beside him.

When he mumbled in his sleep, she patted his hand, and Cooper closed his fingers around hers as he settled.

She felt like she'd known him for a long time. They were both raised on the land, they both loved horses, they both hated being told what to do. If they'd met somewhere else, who knew, they might have been friends. She could use a friend.

When she'd been in school, she'd worked two jobs most of the time and fought to keep up with her studies. There was no time for friends, or money to travel—just work.

Once she'd come back home, the town had changed. She'd changed. So she did what she always did. She worked. Working ten hours a day, organizing the clinic, redoing Pop's bookkeeping, meeting all Pop's patients and their owners.

On weekends, she rebuilt corrals that had been neglected and studied up on new techniques and medicines. The friends she'd had in high school were settled with families, and those she'd had veterinary classes with were scattered across the country. Like her, they were starting their careers and didn't have time to catch up.

So she'd simply worked. She'd been alone so long it had become her normal.

Maybe she was just tired or worried or feeling very much isolated, but Hayley began to cry as she held Cooper's hand. He was touching her, almost caring that she was there.

She'd lied to Elliot when she'd asked to stay one more night at the ranch. She couldn't tell him that she didn't want to go home. Her pops had gone to visit one of his daughters in Dallas two weeks ago. His youngest child, now sixty, wanted him to move there as soon as Hayley took over. He wasn't sick or off fishing these days. He was planning to retire and leave, but he hadn't told anyone but her.

Every week since she'd started working, he'd cut his hours a little. First, he'd take off early to fish or come in late after having breakfast with a friend. Then he started calling, saying he'd be in after lunch. The week before he'd left, he'd worked four hours total, then he'd told her he was going to Dallas and had no idea when he'd be back. Maybe he wanted her to start her own life, and she didn't have the courage to tell him that she didn't have one beyond the clinic.

He'd made up that he had a cold to keep from going to church with her. He said he had car trouble to push her out on calls alone. He even said he had an emergency a county over. The fact was, he was ready to retire, and she suspected he'd kept the clinic open longer than he'd planned so she'd have somewhere to come.

As Hayley drifted to sleep, she daydreamed about the life she wanted. She had a big family—two older sisters, grandparents, parents, nieces and nephews—but they'd all drifted away.

She only had a few friends left in the area, plus one ex-boy-friend from her first year of vet school who thought they still had a chance. He'd call now and then to see if she wanted to pick up where they'd left off.

She had no one close. Nobody to relax with or go out to eat with. No one to celebrate Christmas with, unless she drove a few hundred miles.

She was living in the place she'd always wanted to come back to, doing what she wanted to do, but she wasn't living the life she'd planned.

CHAPTER TWENTY-TWO

December 19

It was late when Elliot drove Hayley and Tatum home from the hospital. Tatum hadn't wanted to leave Cooper. They'd ordered pizza and all sat on Cooper's hospital bed while they helped him eat, like he couldn't do anything by himself.

They talked and laughed, not so much to cheer up Cooper, but to set Tatum at ease. Just before they left, Coop and Tatum had Hayley open the window so they could howl good-night.

The hospital did not think that was funny.

Elliot noticed a difference in Cooper when the boy was around. His little brother was more patient, more easygoing.

On the way home Tatum fell asleep between them, and Hayley told Elliot all about her day following Cooper around. When they arrived back at the headquarters, the three simply waved their good-nights.

As they headed upstairs, Elliot walked across the great room and noticed one thin ribbon of light that told him someone was still in the study.

He slowly opened the door and saw Jess sound asleep. Her head was propped on her notes and there was a plate of rib bones by her elbow.

Jess managed to straighten and open one eye.

Elliot smiled. Her hair was out of place and she had barbecue stains on her blouse, and she mumbled something he couldn't make out. She was adorable.

"I told the cook not to bring you food," he said as he reached her.

"She only brought in a little plate. I raided the fridge for this plate. Who knew ribs were so good?"

"Pretty much everybody in Texas."

Her elbow slipped off the desk and she almost hit her head on a book. "Dani, your cook, told me ribs went with beer. I think I drank a little too much."

"Come on, princess, I'll put you to bed. You're in no shape to climb two flights of stairs."

She didn't protest as he lifted her up. "I decided to sleep down here." Her head rested on his shoulder as he walked across the silent house and headed up. "I've got to work harder. I have to prove my worth to the partners. Richard said I'm only a maybe partner and he's not interested in marrying a maybe."

Jess was asleep by the time Elliot reached the third floor. He put her in the middle of the big bed and covered her up. Then he pulled the drapes closed across the huge window. Tomorrow she didn't need to see the sunrise.

As he stood in the pale glow coming from the landing, he studied her. The need to touch her just once overwhelmed him. With a featherlight brush of his hand, he moved her hair away from her face and kissed her cheek. Part of him still loved the woman he thought she was.

"Good night, Jess," he whispered, then turned and left the room.

This "seeing each other again so they could get over a long-dead love" didn't seem to be working for him, and it appeared not to be working for her, either. If she was over him, she would have simply stepped in and done the job, not tried to kill herself working so she could get away as soon as possible.

He lay awake for a while, attempting to figure out if he was sad or happy that she still felt something. One thing he sensed: she wanted to get away from him more than she seemed to want to get back to Richard.

The next morning he got up at dawn, trying not to think about how Jess had felt in his arms all those years ago. No matter how tired they were, she'd always slept in his arms. Even if they'd had a fight and weren't speaking, she'd curl close and he'd hug her all night. It was more than touching. Elliot felt like his heart had to hear her heart beating as he slept.

Hayley joined him at breakfast with a dozen questions, not just about Cooper's care, but about the workings of the ranch.

Dani circled around them, refilling coffee cups and setting food on the table.

Since they hadn't heard from Creed and Dallas, the two must be still at Winter Valley. If they'd worked two days with the horses, maybe they'd isolated the mustangs who needed doctoring.

"I need to get up there as soon as possible," Hayley said.

"I'd feel better if one of the men went with you. Creed and Cooper are the only two who've climbed to the top in years, except maybe your grandfather. To tell the truth, I've worried about him the past few years." He laughed. "He brought this mule along last year. I don't know if he rode the mule up or just hung on to his tail and let the mule pull him up."

"I've seen that mule in the back corral at the clinic. I thought he belonged to someone else."

"Nope. Your grandpa told me that mule was his best friend." Elliot shrugged. "Wish you'd brought him along."

"The mule or Pops?"

"Either. They both know the way."

Hayley laughed. "I've already made the journey twice. I think I could simply follow the broken branches and find the place again."

"I should take you up," Elliot concluded, more to himself than Hayley.

Tye came in the kitchen door. As he removed his coat and hat, Dani placed his breakfast on the table across from Elliot.

Hayley nodded at Tye and continued arguing with Elliot. "No. You'll just have to turn around and go back down. It'll take you most of the day, and you've got a brother in the hospital, a ranch to run and an accountant in your office." Hayley glanced at the empty chairs on either side of her as if she might have missed something. "Where is the accountant, anyway?"

Elliot saw no reason for lying. "I found her drunk last night and helped her up the stairs. My guess is she'll be doing good if she makes it down by lunch."

"That settles it. I go up alone."

Tye took his seat and thanked the cook. "I could haul a couple of good horses up to your Jeep. We could ride up, and then, when we come back down, I could load the horses and you could drive your Jeep back. That would make the hike easier and I could help with the mustangs."

Elliot saw his point. Part of him was worried about Hayley making the trip alone with the weather so unpredictable. Tye would make her journey much easier and safer. They both knew how to ride. On horseback, they'd cut the time in half.

"If you go up with Hayley and then help, it'll save everyone time. If there's trouble and Hayley stays, I'm guessing you'll have to lead Dallas out when you start down. I'm sure she's ready for a salon day after two days at the shack."

"I don't need a babysitter." Hayley's dark eyes flashed. "But with three of us the work will go faster. I'm afraid I can't count Dallas."

"Then you can take care of Tye." Elliot laughed, guessing Hayley wouldn't stand for taking a keeper along. "He has no idea where the place is, and I doubt Dallas could find her way back alone. Add the fact that he knows horses. Trust me, Doc, he'll be a great help."

"Good point," Hayley said, surrendering.

As they ate, they made plans. They'd wait until the sun had started to warm the air and then they'd head up. They'd pack in a lunch and hope to be in Winter Valley in time to eat it with Creed and Dallas. Tye would ride down with the ladies before dark. Creed would stay a few days longer to make sure all the horses were healing. Then the foreman would ride his horse across open pasture all the way home, just as Cooper would have done.

Elliot gave the cowhands their orders for the day, then disappeared into his office. He had calls to make, and the first one was to the hospital. As Cooper told him how great he felt and how he needed to come home as soon as possible, Elliot looked over the work Jess had done.

"Coop, you're not leaving until they tell you to go," Elliot said as he raised his eyebrows, impressed at how much she'd accomplished in one day.

"Elliot, are you listening to me?" Coop asked again. "I'm well. Come get me."

"I can't. I have to work with the accountant this morning."

"Then send the doc. She can pick me up."

"I can't. She's heading up to Winter Valley. She has a job to do."

Elliot ignored Coop's rant for the next ten minutes. His fingers were sliding down the list of numbers, but in his mind, he was touching Jess's cheek.

When Coop finally took a break, Elliot got a word in. "I'll

talk to the doctor this afternoon. I'll tell him how you're needed here."

"Good, you talk to him. He talks to me like I'm senile. And if that nurse wiggles the straw in my face trying to get me to take a drink one more time, I swear I'm breaking out."

"All right. I'll head your way as soon as the accountant wakes up and I talk to her."

"The accountant is a her? It's ten o'clock. Why is she still asleep?"

"She got drunk last night on beer and ribs." Elliot kept his voice level.

"Hell, brother, things are falling apart. I got to get home."

"You may not be in such a hurry when you hear that the accountant Griffin sent is Jessica Brantley."

"Your Jess?" Coop whispered the question.

"*Was* my Jess. She hasn't been mine for years."

"Double hell." Cooper was silent for a minute and then he moaned, "Maybe I am sick. Maybe I should stay here for a while. Jess didn't mention that time she saw me in the hallway. I didn't know she was around, or I would have at least had underwear on."

Elliot laughed. "How long are you planning to hide out in the hospital?"

"Until your Jess leaves."

CHAPTER TWENTY-THREE

December 20
Maverick Ranch

Dani had just loaded the breakfast dishes when Tye walked into the kitchen.

He winked with mischief in his gray eyes and said, "I got to leave, but I must have forgotten my hat at breakfast."

"It's in your hand, cowboy." She couldn't stop smiling.

"Then maybe I forgot to say goodbye to my girl. I have to head up to Winter Valley."

She dried her hands and moved to the short hallway that led to her bedroom. It was in shadows and out of sight from anyone walking in. "So, I'm your girl, am I?"

He followed. "You are, Danielle. Should we repeat last night to prove it?"

"Definitely."

"I agree. It's always good to research the facts. You're my girl."

She turned to face him, laughing. He made her feel young

and cared for. "Well, if you didn't forget your hat, what exactly did you forget?"

He pushed her gently against the door of her room and pressed close. "This," he said against her lips, which were still tender from their night together.

Dani swore she felt her heart melting. In his eyes, she was special. She was the one thing he couldn't get enough of. In her mind she was already planning their afternoon together for one day in the future. She'd pick a sunny day even if it'd be cold. They'd search for his clues left by his grandfather's drawings, then they'd stop somewhere and have lunch. She'd pack a blanket so they could cuddle close and watch the sunset.

She loved dreaming up the future and knowing that Tye would make her dreams come true.

As he moved a few inches away, his hands still caressed her. "I won't be in until late tonight. I'm riding up to Winter Valley and helping Creed. I may not see you tonight or even tomorrow, but I want you to know that I'll be thinking of you."

"Be careful." She patted his cheek. "I'll be waiting." She almost added that she'd been waiting for him to come along for years.

He kissed her lightly. "I was hoping you'd say that."

Then the back door rattled open suddenly.

"Mom!" Pete yelled. "We're finally back. You wouldn't believe what those cousins talked us into doing in the city."

Dani stared up at Tye, panicked, but all she saw in his eyes was sadness, a deep sorrow, as if something was shattering and might never be the same again.

Two sets of footsteps were heading their way and there was no time to run.

Tye pushed away from her and turned to face her sons.

Pete saw him first, a look of confusion flashed across his face. "Hi, Tye. What are you doing here?"

Tye stood straight. "I was saying goodbye to your mother."

Patrick was just behind his brother. He was clearly figuring it out faster. "You ain't got no business back here. This is my mom's room." Patrick suddenly pushed past his brother. "Is this guy bothering you, Mom? I swear I'll beat him to a pulp if he's messing with you. I don't care if he is twice my age."

Pete finally seemed to figure out what Patrick was talking about. He puffed up like a balloon man, ready to fight. "He's taking advantage of her? Maybe he was gonna attack her? Why else would he be here?"

Patrick made fists. "We got here right in time."

Dani had never seen her boys like this. She'd always been the mother hen who took care of them. It made her proud that they were defending her honor, but she wasn't a woman who needed any protection from Tye.

Pete started cussing and claiming that somebody needed killing right now.

But Tye had obviously had enough; he shoved his way between the two men and shot out the door. "See you tomorrow night, darlin'," he said almost calmly.

"Like hell you will," Patrick yelled. "Stay away from our mother."

Dani rolled her eyes. A bit of protecting was flattering, but this was too much. Before she could sit her sons down and explain a few things to them, Elliot rushed in, demanding to know what was going on. Evidently the yelling had reached his office.

All three Garretts yelled, "Nothing!" They might be in crisis, but it was their crisis.

Elliot took a breath, looking like he didn't believe them, but said, "Good. Since nothing is going on and you two are used to driving my Rover, I want you boys to head into Lubbock immediately and check my brother out of the hospital."

The twins looked confused.

"Now," Elliot ordered and turned around.

Patrick looked at his mom. "We'll straighten this out when we get back. That drifter is not going to get away with this."

"Yeah, rodeo star or not, Tye Franklin is a dead man."

They were gone before Dani could say anything. She needed to reason it out, choose her words carefully. Telling her boys that she and Tye were friends didn't seem strong enough. Telling them that they were lovers was way too much. This was worse than when Bambi's mother died and she'd had to explain to her sons that it was only a movie.

Maybe she'd just wait until Tye got back from Winter Valley and they'd figure something out together. One thing she needed to do was talk to Tye. This wasn't the end. She'd seen the hurt in his gray eyes. He'd thought what they had would be over if anyone knew about them.

This misunderstanding with her boys could wait awhile. If Cooper was coming home from the hospital, she'd have to get ready. Tye wouldn't be in until late. They'd talk to the boys tomorrow.

CHAPTER TWENTY-FOUR

December 20

Hayley waited for Tye by the trailer. The horses were loaded. All was ready. But when she saw the cowboy storming toward her, she knew something was very wrong.

"What is it?"

"Nothing," he snapped. "Let's get on the road."

"I'm driving." She didn't give him time to argue. She climbed in and they headed toward the hills.

"The roads are wet," she said as they began their journey. "It'll take us longer to get there this time."

Glancing over at him, she could tell Tye couldn't care less about the roads. "At least it's turning out to be a clear day," she added.

Even less interest.

"Can you really handle wild mustangs?"

Finally, she'd caught his attention. "I can, but if one of them kicks me in the head, don't bother to save me. I'm a walking dead man."

"Want to talk about it?" She liked the idea of hearing about someone else's problem.

"No."

It took a few miles of silence, but he finally broke. "It won't do any good to talk. No matter what I do, it'll be the wrong thing. I finally find someone worth caring about, and it flies out the window in a blink. I don't blame the boys. I blame me for losing my hat. I should have left it on my head. If I fight, she'll hate me. If I don't, she'll hate me."

Hayley nodded. "I'm glad we're not talking about this."

"Good. You'd just kill brain cells conversing with me. If I wasn't already going with you I'd be headed to the nearest bar right now. This is a problem I'd rather see through a whiskey fog."

She shrugged. "I can feel a few brain cells dying right now just thinking about talking about it, whatever *it* is. Maybe we should change the subject?"

"I agree."

They were silent for ten minutes, and then he said, "Sorry. My problem, not yours."

"That thing we're not talking about?"

"Yes. I usually don't let things get to me."

"You got a friend you can call and talk to? I'll pretend I'm not listening. We've got a while before the signal dies. You could make a call."

"Nope. No friends."

She shrugged. "Me, either. I had friends when I was in high school, but they've changed, or I've changed. Maybe a little of both. Now all I talk about is my work, and all they talk about is breastfeeding. Apparently, it's not as easy as it looks. The friends I know who don't have babies talk about how terrible their husbands are."

Tye looked over at her and smiled. "I can see your problem, and I don't want to hear about it."

"I thought if I told you mine, you'd feel comfortable telling me yours."

"Not happening, Doc."

Hayley figured the only way to have a chance at a normal conversation with Tye was to change the subject. "You from around here?"

He looked at her like she'd just asked him to dance, but then he seemed to get the hint. "Not really. I think my dad grew up in the Panhandle. He circled through here, working the oil fields, after I was born."

Hayley smiled. Her plan was working.

"I noticed your drawing pad while I was waiting for you. You're sketching this area?"

Tye flipped the old notebook under the seat. "It's not mine. My grandfather liked to draw, I guess. The place where he stayed sent it to me after he died."

"I recognize a few of the places. The ranch gate with the Circle M brand looked familiar. Almost like the Maverick gate here."

"Yeah, but it's not just like the one over the Maverick entrance. I looked again the other day just to make sure."

"Right, but there's another entrance down by the south pasture. I don't think it was ever used, except for hauling cattle in and out, but it's got a bar over the cattle guard. Welded to the bar is a Circle M brand that looks just like the one in the picture. At one time it must have fallen off, and someone reattached it with barbed wire. Look in the book. You can even make the wire out."

Tye retrieved the book. After several pages, he found the drawing of a pasture. The dirt road. The entrance had three poles over the cattle guard as its gate. They were high enough that a truck might have passed. In the center of the cross pole was a rough symbol of the Holloways' brand. Hayley was right. As Tye looked closely, he saw a line of barbed wire holding it in place.

"When I get back, I'll go see if it's still there. If you're right, it means my grandfather came here in the nineties and must have drawn it from memory."

"Were you two close?"

"No, I barely remember him." Tye hesitated and then must have decided to be honest. "He died in prison, but the notebook only just made it to me. What about the other gate with the outline of a horse on his back legs? You ever see that?"

"I can't remember that, but I could ask Pops. He's driven down every back road for a hundred miles. If it's guarding the gate of a ranch around here, he's seen it."

"Only this notebook is at least thirty years old. What are the chances it's still there?"

She slowed just a little and looked at the ex–rodeo star. "I wouldn't think you'd be one to back down from a challenge, no matter the odds."

"You're right." He straightened in the seat and lowered his hat just the way a bronc rider did before the gate swung. "Come to think of it, I'm not."

Hayley had a feeling they were not talking about the lost ranch gates.

"If you need a friend to help find a few things in that book, I'll be happy to tag along. Two heads are better than one. Thanks to my pops, every ranch welcomes me in."

Tye was no fool. "You've got some time on your hands if you're making me that offer. I'm guessing you're about as low on friends as I am right now. I wouldn't mind having another set of eyes, but don't start up on that breastfeeding story again."

"Promise. We can start with an old map I have at the clinic."

As they reached her red Jeep, Tye turned all his attention to the job at hand. He let her guide him through the trees to the shack, then he looked after their horses while she climbed to the top of the hill.

From there she could see Winter Valley. The beauty of it took her breath away. No wonder Cooper came up here for almost a month every year. Nothing in her view had been touched by man. It was like she'd stepped back in time.

When she turned, she saw the roof of the shack and the little corral beside it. No one was around. The two horses that had been in the corral were gone. As she scanned the area, she could see the making of a crude corral tucked away just before the valley curved out of her sight.

That had to be where the mustangs were kept waiting for her. She rushed down to their horses. They loaded as much medicine as they could carry, and Tye even strapped the pack of food they'd brought to his back, and they started down to the valley.

Now it was Tye leading the way, picking the path, determining the speed. Hayley considered herself a good horsewoman, but Tye seemed almost one with his mount. About halfway down it occurred to her that he talked to the horses far more than he'd ever talked to her.

She understood. That was why she'd become a vet. Animals were easier to talk to. Easier to get close to. Easier to love.

They were almost to the water when they heard laughter. Hayley turned to see Dallas and Creed racing toward them on horseback. Both tall and lean, the couple looked like they were born to ride.

"About time you got back," Dallas shouted. "We've been working for days. How is Cooper? Did you bring something to eat? I don't do canned food."

Creed looked at Dallas, then grinned at Hayley. "She's been living on cookies for days. Sugar high most of the time. We ran out of cookies at breakfast, and I feared we may be living the Donner Party replay by dark."

"We brought lunch and we're here to help." Hayley swung from her saddle. "How about we eat and talk about all you've done so far? Then, I'm guessing we've got eight hours of daylight left. With four of us working, we should be able to help the mustangs."

As she helped Tye unload his pack of sandwiches and fruit, Dallas whined, "I was afraid you were going to say that. Creed seems to think a day's work is dawn to dark. I have got to teach him to tell time. No one starts before nine, and work should be over by happy hour." She squealed, "The bottom of your pack is lined with health bars. I'm going to live!"

They sat by the river and ate lunch. Dallas acted like it was a great feast and hinted that maybe they should make it an annual event. "Who knew that the outdoors could be so interesting?" she confessed. "I thought it was just something to pass through."

Creed talked about how they'd been able to round up almost all of the mustangs, but he'd still like a few days more to go deeper into the canyon. "Dallas was a great help. She'd close the gate while I herded them in."

Tye seemed to relax around Creed. Hayley decided the two men were very much alike. Both were loners.

As they rode toward the corral, Creed told Tye he'd built another holding pen in a small box canyon about a mile back. Thanks to Dallas's help, they had all the horses they'd found inside the corrals. Only they were so wild he hadn't been able to get within ten feet of them on foot, so none had shots or wounds doctored.

Tye nodded. "Mind if I give it a try?"

Creed waved him toward the corral. "We'll step back and stay quiet." Then, to Hayley's surprise, he circled his arm around

Dallas's waist and lifted her up on a huge rock. "If the horses stampede, you'll need to be up here."

Dallas didn't move. No matter what happened, she'd have the best seat in the house.

Hayley watched as Tye climbed down from his horse and stepped into the far end of the enclosure. The man truly must have a death wish. She thought she heard Tye humming, as if he was simply taking a walk, as he moved slowly toward the herd at the other end. Now and then, he stopped and stood as still as a post.

The mustangs began to circle, bunching up, kicking their hind legs like teenagers showing off. They might not like him so close, but they didn't see him as a threat.

Tye circled with them, drawing a foot closer with each round they made.

"I've never seen a man do that," Creed whispered, as he joined Dallas on the rock. "He's not challenging them. He's joining them."

Hayley stayed on her horse. She had faith that Tye knew what he was doing, but if the mustangs broke the barrier, she'd be safer joining the run.

As they circled, the mustangs began to slow. Now Tye was close enough to touch them, but he kept his arms close to his body. He wasn't advancing or threatening; he was linking, almost as if he was becoming part of the herd.

Finally, the horses stopped, but he continued to move slowly among them. A few butted him with their heads. Tye brushed them slightly with his shoulder. When he came close to Hayley, he said in a calm voice, "Get the shots ready and I'll do the job."

"No," she said as she slipped from her horse and crossed into the corral, following exactly how he moved. "I want to learn this."

Out of the corner of her vision, she saw Creed helping Dallas down. The threat of a stampede was over.

One by one, Creed handed Hayley the supplies as she and Tye moved among the beautiful animals. A few complained about the shot, but it seemed to bother them little more than a bug bite.

Once, Hayley took a nudge that knocked her down.

She stayed still and rolled in a ball as the animal's hooves came within inches of her. Tye moved gradually toward her, but she stayed calm; she knew she'd be in serious danger if either of them spooked the herd.

When he reached her, he didn't pull her up, but stood over her as she slowly got first to her knees, then to her feet.

"Thanks," she whispered.

"Anytime, Doc." He smiled at her. "Seven more to go, I think—then we move to the next corral."

He stayed closer to her after that. When they were finished, they smiled and ran for the fence. He swung her over, then jumped, laughing as he rolled.

Looking back at the mustangs, Tye said, "They're glad we're gone. They tolerated us because they didn't see us as a threat."

Creed was fascinated. "Next round, I'm going in. I've got to learn this. Last year it took Cooper and me hours to check five or six horses. We'd have to rope them first, then there was a real fight to settle them down."

Dallas was the only one who wouldn't get close to the horses, but she did pass the needed supplies through the fence.

"When we finish with the next corral, we'll take the fences down on both at the same time. Otherwise the free horses will rile the penned ones up, and a horse might get hurt breaking out." Tye nodded once to Creed.

"I agree, but before we let them free, I want to make sure Dallas and the doc are heading up."

"Sounds like a plan."

In the late afternoon, Tye opened the far corral. A moment later, Creed dropped the gate on the other. They both mounted up and raced back to the shack. When they got there, Dallas had dinner cooked. Canned chili and fruit left over from lunch. They all talked about the beauty of the place and the fun they'd had.

Creed stood as Tye and the doc packed up. "You sure you want to ride through the trees? It'll be dark soon."

"We know the way," Hayley said. "If I cover this ride many more times, it'll be a regular trail. If we hurry, we should just make open land by dark."

"I packed flashlights." Tye pitched one to the doc. "Once we get out of the trees, the rest will be easy. The moon will probably offer us enough light on a clear night like this. I got lights on my trailer, so loading up the horses will be no problem."

"I think I'll stay a few days." Creed looked around him. "This place grows on me. Tell Elliot I'll be down before the next snow hits."

Dallas frowned and looked straight at Creed. "Well, if you're staying, I'm staying. We'll be down when the health bars run out."

Creed's voice came quick and loud for once. "Great. I thought I'd get some peace and quiet."

Hayley didn't miss the smile on the foreman's face. It was obvious that Creed didn't mind at all if Dallas stayed.

She and Tye were picking their way through the trees as the last rays of the sun showed them the way. "Do you think there's something between those two?"

"No," he said too quickly. "What could they possibly have in common?"

"Love's a funny thing, I guess."

"No argument from me."

Whatever had been bothering him on the drive up had settled now. They talked all the way home. When they finally made it back to the headquarters, she kissed him on the cheek. "Thanks for saving my life out there."

"Anytime." He shifted. "And, Doc, if you ever need to talk, I'll listen, even if it's about breastfeeding."

"Thanks. If I see the outline of a horse on a gate, I'll let you know. You're close, Tye. Some of those scenes look like Crossroads."

"I might go into town and have a look. Then maybe I'll drive a few dusty roads and see what I find."

"You do that. Drop by the clinic when you do. The coffeepot is always on." She walked into the house and noticed he turned toward the barn. It had to be close to ten, but the cowboy planned to check on the mare and her colt before he turned in.

Hayley grinned. She'd made a friend today.

CHAPTER TWENTY-FIVE

December 20

Tye led the two horses they'd ridden all day into Sunny Barn. Though they were working horses, not the fancy show ones Sunlan bred, Tye thought they deserved a bit of pampering. He'd brush them down and make sure they had oats tonight.

A memory of his first job drifted into his mind. He'd been sixteen, and he'd talked his way into working on a ranch north of Amarillo. The rancher was a tough old guy but fair, and Tye had been as green as they came.

Every evening when they made it back from working cattle, the owner of the ranch did the same thing his men did before he called it a night. "You take care of your horse first, no matter what, and you never pass it off to someone else unless you're bleeding," he'd said.

The old guy had taught him a great deal that year, and not once had he ever raised his voice in anger.

Tye set his gear on one of the empty saddle racks as he worked.

About the time he finished checking their hooves, he heard footsteps coming from the main barn door.

In one easy movement, he stepped out of the stall and lifted the lariat from the saddle horn. Friends would just walk in. Strangers might tiptoe. But trouble thundered.

Whoever was coming his way was coming fast. The hammering of boots echoed across the open space.

The rope flowed as easy in Tye's hands as a saber blended into a fencer's grip.

"We've come to end this right now, Franklin!" Pete's words echoed off the tin wall as if a crowd followed him. "You'll give us your word you'll never go near our mother again, or we plan to beat the idea out of your head."

"Yeah!" Patrick said, looking a bit confused with their plan.

Tye stood relaxed, the lariat loose in his fingers. "You boys talk to Dani about this?"

"We don't need to. She's had a hard life and the last thing she needs is a drifter making promises he won't keep."

"Yeah," Patrick said again. "She said she wanted to talk to you before she talked to us, but we don't see there's any need for that."

Pete took a step forward. "Maybe it would be best if you just kept drifting on down the road. I'm thinking you should load up tonight. We'll pass on your goodbyes in the morning."

"I can't do that," Tye said slowly, as if they might need time to digest the words. "You see, I'm crazy about your mother. I figure if you two offspring don't frighten me off, nothing will."

Patrick scratched his head, but his younger brother, by five minutes, was ready to act. "Then we're going to have to beat the tar out of you. You'll be crawling around looking for your teeth when we get through with you."

Pete turned to his brother. "You ready?"

"I was born ready." Patrick hit his palm with his fist. "I'll pound him into the ground like he's a fence post."

Tye just waited, deciding these two were quoting lines from every Western gunfight they'd ever seen on TV. "If I was you, boys, I'd turn around while I'm able. I'm not going to fight you."

Pete laughed, and Patrick doubled up both fists, ready to charge. They bumped shoulders like football players just before kickoff.

The Garrett boys made it two steps toward Tye before the loop of the lariat circled overhead and dropped. One second later it tightened about knee level around them both.

Tye tossed the other end of the rope over a round log running the width of the barn and pulled. Both boys fell backward and before they could stand, their feet were where their heads should have been.

They weighed too much for Tye to pull them off the ground, but he had them upside down. They wiggled and screamed and cussed, but they couldn't bend enough to push the rope over their boots.

Tye tied the free end of the rope off against a thick beam, then walked closer to his catch. "I hope we don't have to have this talk again, boys."

They were still yelling and cussing as he walked out of the barn.

He made it three steps into the moonlight when Tatum caught up with him. The kid was hopping around him like one kernel of popcorn repopping. Tye was too tired to even be surprised to see him.

"That was something," the kid claimed. "Would you teach me to swing a rope like that?"

"What are you doing out here so late?"

"I heard Pete and Repete talking. I knew something was going to happen as soon as you and the doc got back. When I heard her come in, I snuck out to watch. I knew you'd go to the barn 'cause you told me a cowboy always takes care of his horse."

Tye leaned down. "You want to do me a few favors? First, forget about what you saw."

"Sure. I'll try, but it ain't going to be easy."

"It'll mean I owe you one. That's the cowboy way."

"I'll do whatever you say and never tell anyone," Tatum answered, as if swearing an oath. "My teacher said, 'Don't pass stories along unless you're talking to your mother or a judge.'"

"Good advice. Now, the other part of the favor. I want you to go in the barn. Take ahold of the end of the rope that is tied to the beam and pull as hard as you can. The knot will come away. Hold on as long as you can. When the Garrett brothers fall, they'll pull you off the ground from the other end."

Tatum thought about it for a moment, then said, "I'll do it, but you got to show me how to tie a knot like that."

"I will tomorrow. Right now, all I want to do is sleep." He turned toward the bunkhouse.

Tatum disappeared into the barn.

Tye didn't wait around to see the kid rescue the men. He felt like he was sleepwalking. Though he ached to see Dani, her room was the first place her sons would head when they got free, and he wasn't up to round two in a fight he figured would last forever. Tonight, he'd lock his door and simply sleep.

He was almost to the bunkhouse door when he heard a thud and guessed four hundred pounds of Garrett had just hit the barn floor.

CHAPTER TWENTY-SIX

December 20

Elliot watched Tye walk across the yard to the bunkhouse. His head was down, his limp more apparent than usual. It must have been a long day for the doc and him.

He knew the job was done at Winter Valley, or the cowboy wouldn't have come back. A door closed somewhere upstairs, and Elliot guessed the doc was calling it a day, too.

What he didn't hear was Dallas coming in. He had a feeling she wouldn't come in quietly like the doc had. Maybe she was riding home with Creed. A moonlit ride across the pastures, with windmills looking like skeletons walking the horizon and buffalo grass waving white in the breeze.

It would be romantic, but romance was wasted on Creed. He wouldn't know what to do with a woman like Dallas if you gave him the instruction booklet.

Still, Dallas would finally get that ride she'd wanted. Maybe she'd pack up and head home tomorrow after the long ride across empty pastures. He couldn't tell if she was just hungry for life or looking for a place to belong. All he knew was she hadn't found it yet.

Elliot glanced over at Jess, who was still working. Unlike Dallas, Jess knew exactly where she belonged and what she wanted. She'd told him her father had told all three of his children that they'd work at the firm when they grew up. Jess, apparently, was the only one who listened. One of her brothers was a soldier, and the other a struggling writer. Of course, with Brantley money, he probably wasn't struggling too much.

Even here, Jess worked around the clock. Elliot had taken time off to make sure Cooper was settled into the hospital bed Dani had set up in his room. By the time the Garrett boys had gotten him checked out and home, Cooper had been too tired to bother eating dinner.

Jessie had asked if all ranches stored beds, wheelchairs, crutches and walkers in their barn lofts. Elliot just shrugged. He'd never thought it unusual. Finally, he explained that a ranch was almost like a little town. They were isolated and couldn't just run to the store for what they needed.

Elliot made a final check on Cooper, then came back to the office. Jess was still there. He asked if she wanted to see Cooper, and she simply said she already had years ago, and apparently, he hadn't changed much.

They ate a light supper at their desks and went back to work without her asking one question about Cooper. Balancing the books seemed the only thing on her mind.

Dani brought in a late dessert and refilled the coffeepot. Tonight, as he looked out the window at his sleeping ranch, Elliot decided that as days go, this was about the most boring one of his life.

There was so much between him and Jess that neither would talk about. There were so many memories in his head. They might be in the same room, but an ocean flowed between them, and he had no idea how to cross it. Now and then, he swore he could hear the whispers of conversations they'd never had floating in the air.

"Want to call it a night?" he finally asked.

She looked at her watch. "I need to make a call."

"Make your call. I'll make drinks. Hot chocolate or beer?"

"Hot chocolate tonight. I had enough beer last night."

He left the room, guessing she'd like some privacy for her call, but he didn't go straight to the kitchen. After the light snow, the air had warmed, and tonight was clear and crisp. Elliot walked out on the long porch lined with white rockers and looked over his silent land. He loved this view. He had all his life.

When he'd been a kid, his father would sit out here at night. Everyone else in the house would be busy doing something, but his dad relaxed in silence at the end of the day.

Elliot would often join him. Some nights they didn't even talk, they just sat together. Tonight was a good night to just relax. He felt too tired to even bother to think.

"Hello."

He turned, and for a moment he thought Jess must have followed him out. Then he saw the window by his desk. He'd left it ajar.

"Yes, I'm still working, Richard. I'm finishing as fast as I can."

If Elliot moved, she might see him and think he was eavesdropping. If he didn't move, he *was* eavesdropping. He didn't move. Maybe she'd hang up soon.

"Of course I'm trying. Those books you packed for me are helping, but you do know this is not what I usually specialize in." She listened.

Elliot watched her. She closed her eyes and frowned.

Finally, she said, "I'll be home in time to catch the flight. I know both families are going. Stop worrying about it."

She was silent for a moment. From the darkness he could see

her twisting in her chair. She looked nervous now. "Are you alone tonight?"

She was silent, making no comment as she listened.

"Nothing has happened here. I'm simply doing what you insisted I do. I told you this was pointless. He doesn't want me here any more than I wanted to come. It's been too many years. We're strangers now."

She was silent for a while, then she said, "Don't bother to call me. I told you we'd talk about it later. I'm not moving the date up. In fact, I'm thinking of moving it back again."

She hung up her cell without saying goodbye.

Elliot sat still in the night as he listened to her crying softly. Jess wasn't happy. Her perfect life wasn't what it seemed to be.

He silently stood and walked back to the office. She'd moved to the window, her back to him.

For once in his life Elliot didn't reason out the problem or even think. He acted.

As he heard her continue to cry, he moved close. When she turned, he pulled her gently into his arms. She didn't step back or even say a word—she just let him hold her.

He knew he was holding the Jess he'd known years ago. Maybe a part of her was still in there, deep down, hidden beneath all the big-city, perfectly polished woman.

"You all right?" he finally asked.

"I'm just tired." She tried to smile. "I can't sleep out here. It's too quiet."

"I got just the cure. Grab your jacket."

"I can't... I don't..." He tugged her out the door.

"We're taking a break. We'll only lose an hour." He opened the door of his Land Rover, which disappeared now and then.

A few Coke cans fell out.

For a moment he thought she might turn around and run, but then she lifted her chin and climbed in.

Elliot circled the car, noticing how dirty it was. No telling how many miles the Garrett brothers had put on his car.

When they headed toward town, she shook her head. "Your car smells like old hamburgers and fries."

"I noticed. Don't look in the back seat. Garretts have been living back there."

"Where are we going?"

"I thought I'd show you the lights of Crossroads."

As they turned onto the county road, she seemed to relax. Ten minutes later, they were driving around the town square. The gazebo was decorated in tiny lights and garlands. This late, no one was around, and it looked like a Christmas card come to life.

"When did they evacuate the town?"

"Very funny. Folks go to bed early here." When Elliot passed the county offices, he noticed the sheriff's lights were still on. "Most, anyway. We have a few who stand guard."

They drove all the way out to the museum, which had cardboard cutouts of Santa's elves dancing on the second-floor balcony. Red and green lights shone on each one.

"Lovely," she commented.

Then they drove by the high school and through the streets, where every house was decorated in some way. One even had a blow-up Nativity scene with *Star Wars* characters.

Jess laughed. "I'll bet the kids love that."

"The Wilsons don't have kids. They're both retired teachers. They dress as Luke and Princess Leia to pass out candy on Halloween, and Stormtroopers with bunny ears at Easter."

A block later he turned into the drive-through at the Dairy Queen and ordered two ice creams, but he didn't pull over. "Now, for the fun," he announced, as he drove one more block and into an automatic car wash with faded "New" banners on three of its four corners. Ten dollars later, they were driving through, eating ice cream and watching rainbow-colored soap smear all over the windshield.

"I love it," she giggled.

He circled back and paid another ten bucks to do it again.

Somewhere between the ice cream and the laughter, his Jess came back.

They talked all the way home about the things they'd done in college and the crazy friends they'd had.

When they stepped out of the very clean car and walked across the gravel to the kitchen door, he took her hand as easily as he had all those years ago when they'd first met. Both knew they weren't freshmen in college walking back to the dorm, but for a moment, they wanted to forget today and live in yesterday.

As they reached the steps leading upstairs to her room, Jess took one step and turned to face him. "Thanks for the break. I needed that. I'll never forget seeing the lights of Crossroads."

"I'll never forget you." Elliot closed his eyes. He couldn't believe he'd said it aloud.

When he finally opened his eyes, she was gone. No goodbye, as usual.

CHAPTER TWENTY-SEVEN

December 21

Tye walked through the kitchen door just as dawn peeked over the horizon. He'd rather eat dirt than step into Dani's kitchen knowing she was probably going to be mad, but Elliot had been straight with him, and the least he could do was fill in the boss on the progress with the delicate mare before he left. And the chances were good he would be leaving.

Dani didn't look up when he sat down at the table.

"Mornin'," he said to everyone, but he stared at Dani. He thought that she was the kind of woman a man could sit across the table with for the rest of his life and never get tired.

"Morning, Tye." At least the doctor was speaking to him. "Elliot wants me to examine the mare and her new foal before I head home."

"All right. Right after breakfast." He could delay an hour or two more. After all, he wasn't going anywhere in particular from here.

Elliot set down his paper when Dani delivered breakfast. "Everything okay at Winter Valley, Tye? Seems to me you and the doc forgot a couple of people."

The doc laughed. "It went great. Creed and Dallas had the horses all rounded up and Tye, I swear, must be part mustang. You should have seen the way he handled those wild horses."

When Elliot didn't respond, she added, "We didn't forget the people. They just decided to stay a few days."

"Dallas can live up there for all I care, but I really need Creed here. I've got eight three-year-old fillies coming in from Sunlan's ranch in Colorado."

He turned to Tye. "Can you handle them by yourself? I could pull the Garrett brothers in from rounding up strays, but it's past time the pasture was cleared."

"I can handle them alone. They can't be as wild as the rough stock for the rodeo, and I usually take care of a dozen or more of them."

"Great. The driver said he'd be leaving at dawn and should be here by midafternoon. Have stalls ready." Elliot turned to Hayley. "I hate to ask, but I got two problems. One, when the horses get here, I'd like them checked out. They'll have papers to deal with also. Two, someone has to help me with Cooper until I finish the books. If you could take a shift, it would really help."

"I don't treat people." She leaned her head to the side as if considering the possibility that all Holloways were not quite normal. "You do know that?"

"Can't you just give him a horse-tranquilizer shot or something?"

"No, but I'll take him to the clinic with me if he's up for a ride. It'll take a couple of hours and probably distract him from the pain. He must love animals. All of you treat him like he is one."

"I like that clinic idea. Drive slowly. Maybe you can make it

three hours. And bring his medicine. If he gives you any trouble, lock him in the kennel."

"Will do, boss." She used the handle most of his men called
him. "Load a wheelchair and have a few men help him into the
car by ten. We'll manage once we're at the clinic. I have an assistant, Mary May, who comes in three days a week. I also have
a ramp. I'm only seeing pets today, so he can just sit and watch
the fun. By noon, he'll be tired and ready for a nap, and I'll make
sure I'm back in time to examine all the new fillies coming in."

Elliot grinned. "Take my Rover. It will be easier to get him
in and out of than that Jeep. Speaking of it, where is your Jeep?"

Tye and Hayley both laughed. "We forgot to stop and get it
last night," Hayley admitted, "I think we were both too tired
to think."

Elliot joined them in laughing. "This ranch is falling apart.
Doc, if you don't mind staying another day, I'll have a few men
go up tomorrow and get it. We're spread pretty thin today."

"I don't mind. I'll pick up a change of clothes at the clinic."

Tye knew Hayley now. The longer she stayed, the more laughter danced in her eyes. She must be very lonely, and he knew
from experience that Christmas was a hard time to get through
alone.

When Tye stood to leave, Hayley headed out with him. He
didn't get a chance to say a word to Dani. But he knew she was
mad at him. She hadn't even bothered to give him a biscuit at
breakfast, and there was no honey on the table.

Part of him wished he could just talk to her for five minutes.
Another part figured it probably wouldn't do any good. She
was a momma bear where her boys were concerned. She'd take
their side. He doubted he'd even get a chance to say goodbye.

When he shoved on his hat and stepped out the kitchen door,
he glanced back. She was cleaning off the table. She didn't even
look in his direction.

CHAPTER TWENTY-EIGHT

December 21

When Elliot walked into his office a little after dawn, he wasn't surprised to see Jess already at work. For a moment he just stood watching her. The girl who'd laughed at the car wash last night was gone. She was back to all business.

"I'm sorry," he said simply.

She looked up. "For what?"

"For last night."

"Forget it. It never happened."

That wasn't the answer he wanted to hear. "I'm not sorry I said the truth, Jess. I'm sorry I made you uncomfortable."

"I've moved on, Elliot. Whatever you say doesn't affect me."

The phone call he'd heard last night drifted through his mind. "Have you?" She hadn't said one enduring word to the man she planned to marry. In fact, they sounded more like partners in the firm than lovers. Partners rehashing unsolved problems. It seemed strange that she'd asked if Richard had been alone.

"Of course. Last night was simply a walk down memory lane.

Nothing more. I'm reaching my goals now. I'm on the path I've always wanted." She put down her pen as if being bothered to explain. "I'm achieving every dream I set out to meet. A long time ago, I thought those goals were our goals, but you left me." She didn't meet his eyes. "So I had to do it on my own."

Elliot set down his coffee cup. "I left you? You were the one who wouldn't come with me. Your goal was more important than what I wanted. More important than my family."

Finally, all the hurt and all the unsaid words were coming out. Not angry whispers to an empty room. Not cussing screams when he was alone. But calm, raw honesty between them in broad daylight.

She stood, braced her fists on the mound of paper on her desk and glared at him. "I knew if you went back home, you'd never finish school. You'd never work to make our dreams come true. And I was right. How long has it been, Elliot? Eight years since you gave up, or nine since you walked out on me, promising you'd come back?"

Elliot was yelling now. "You said you'd wait. You said you'd come see me, but you never took the time. You moved on. You must have been drawing up your new life plan while I was pulling out of the driveway. I didn't leave you."

"Yes, you did. You broke my heart. I finished school knowing a little more every day that you weren't coming back. Every time I called, you said you needed more time. There was always a crisis here. First three months, then six, then a year." She lowered her voice. "Then never."

A bit of the anger left his tone. "I waited for you to come here. We could have straightened everything out together. But when I asked, you always had other things to do. Not one weekend, Jess. Not one day did you come to see what I was facing."

She opened her mouth to answer, but the door slammed open

against the wall so hard it shook books off the wall. Cooper stood in the doorway on his crutches.

"Will you two stop yelling?" Cooper roared. "I'm dying two doors down. I had to crawl to my crutches to hobble down here and stop this before you two start slugging it out."

"Stay out of this, Coop!" His words were for his brother, but his stare never left Jess.

"Like hell I will. The whole ranch can hear you two."

Elliot, who never lost his temper, had never yelled at her like this. He gulped down his anger like poison. He took a step backward. He was the logical brother. The smart one. And he was losing his mind.

He straightened and walked away, past Cooper, across the great room, trying to hang on to his sanity. At the front door, he froze. He looked back, but he couldn't make himself let go of the doorknob.

Cooper just stood in the office, staring at Jess as if this was all her fault. Cooper's anger focused on her for a moment before he started wobbling, as if an invisible breeze might blow him down.

She recovered first. In an almost-professional voice, she said, "Nice to see you dressed, even if it is a hospital gown. And, Cooper, you look terrible, I must say."

Cooper cussed, and then Elliot heard his reply. "I was afraid I'd have to strip to get you to recognize me. I hate to ask someone who obviously hates me for a favor, but do you think you could help me back to my room? I figure I've got about one minute before I pass out."

Elliot thought of turning back, but he couldn't. Jess could handle this problem. She seemed to have solved all hers.

He grabbed his coat and stepped out the front door. He was almost to his car when he realized he'd given Hayley the key.

Without much thought, he went to the bunkhouse, where several of the ranch horses had already been saddled and were now waiting out front. He swung into the saddle of a fast three-year-old gelding called Lightning. For a moment, his boots felt strange in the stirrups, and then he took off for the open pasture.

The wind was chilly, stinging his face as the horse galloped. Never in his life had he run from a problem. He'd always done the right thing. Only now, he realized that Jess thought *he'd* let her down. All these years he'd blamed her, and she'd been blaming him.

He rode south, to where the land was flat. Muscles he hadn't used in months strained, but he didn't stop. He just gave Lightning his head and let him run. For once he didn't even want to think. He wanted to be like his little brother: free. To be wild and not think. To live off the land. To live on his own terms.

He couldn't see the beauty around him. In his mind, all he saw was the hurt and disappointment in Jess's face. Her pain must have mirrored his.

His college days had ended with a bang. One argument that lasted 'til he packed and drove away. A shot right to the heart that had never healed.

Finally, he slowed and let the horse walk. They stopped at a windmill for water. While the gelding grazed on green grass by the tank, Elliot lay down and stared up at the sky. The sun was just starting to warm, and it felt so good to just be. Not think, not plan, not take charge. Just be.

A hawk circled above him a few times, then flew off. Elliot closed his eyes and tried not to hear the echo of their argument bouncing off the corners of his mind. She'd blamed him? She thought *he'd* hurt *her*? He'd let her down.

When the horse nudged him, he opened his eyes. The sun was high and warm, though the breeze held winter's breath. Elliot had fallen asleep. After days of barely relaxing enough to get three or four hours of sleep a night, he'd drifted off in the middle of nowhere on dry grass.

He crossed his boots and put his hands behind his head as a pillow. "You ready to go back, boy?" he asked the horse.

The bay didn't answer.

"I'm not. I think I'll let 'Little Brother' handle things for a while."

Elliot closed his eyes and went back to sleep.

CHAPTER TWENTY-NINE

December 21

At ten o'clock Hayley was surprised to find Cooper still in bed. The accountant was sitting at the end of the hospital bed, laughing. They were playing poker on the sheets with peanuts as poker chips.

"Is everything all right?" Hayley asked. "I finally got the new little momma and her baby all checked out. I thought I'd head over to the clinic."

"Sure, everything is fine." Cooper smiled. "Jess was just keeping me company until you showed up to take me to the pound. We think Elliot ran off, so put an alert for the hands to round him up. He probably lost his mind and went to look for it."

Hayley took in everything he said, then started with corrections. "It's an animal clinic, not a pound, Cooper, and if your brother wants to go for a ride, the last thing he probably wants is people hunting him down."

"You're right, Doc." He winked at Jessie. "Thanks for straight-

ening me out on a few points. Must be the brain damage I suf-
fered."

Cooper started scooping up the peanuts, eating a few as he
worked, and then put the rest back in the jar. "I figure we're
about even right now, Jess. When I get back we'll finish the
game. Winner takes the whole jar."

"Sounds like a great plan, but I'm going to try to finish my
work today." Jess slipped off the end of the bed and straightened
her skirt. "One question, Coop—are you planning to go out
with the doctor in that hospital gown?"

He looked down. "Hell. What can I get over this brace?"

"Got jogging pants and a sweatshirt?" Hayley asked.

"Over there. I sleep in them on cold nights." He grinned at
Jess. "I sleep in nothing at all on hot nights."

"I'm aware of that." Jess grinned.

Hayley acted like she hadn't heard his confession. "Great.
We'll cut one leg off the sweats. Then, once you're in the chair,
I'll put a blanket over you. You'll be presentable enough."

He looked at the two ladies in his room. "Which one of you
plans on dressing me?"

"I will," Jess said matter-of-factly. "I've seen you naked. Won't
be anything new."

"One time in a dark hallway doesn't count," Coop countered.

"I'll dress you. I'm a doctor," Hayley offered. "I might be a
vet, but I've seen the human body alive and dead in a human
anatomy class."

Cooper grinned. "I'm flattered you both want to get your
hands on me, but not a chance, Doc. I'm building up my courage to ask you out. My success rate might go down if you see
all my scars."

"Cooper, I've seen most of you already. I spent an entire
morning with you at the hospital, and that gown was flopping
around as they worked on you."

Jess pulled the sweats from the drawer. "We'll both do it. You can keep the gown on until we get the pants on. Then I won't be reshocked at the sight of you, and there will be a chance that the doc would say yes to a date someday."

Hayley reached for the scissors on the bedside table and cut one leg off the pants. After a few tries, they managed to hold him up enough for him to pull on the pants. Both of them worked on the sweatshirt, bumping and brushing against him, but Cooper didn't complain.

When they stood back to admire their work, he asked for the crutches. "Now, I'm going to the bathroom by myself."

Neither argued, but both were waiting at the door with the wheelchair when he came out.

The Garrett twins ran up as soon as they saw them and offered to lift Cooper into the passenger seat. They managed to hit his broken leg twice while shoving him in. Cooper managed to thank them.

He reached for Jess's hand. "Come with us. I'm starting to like you, Jess."

"No. I really do need to finish up and get back to my life. But I promise I'll still be here when you finish your field trip. I'll roll you over to watch those fancy horses be unloaded if I have time.

"Then Elliot and I need to talk. When I saw how he shattered, I realized our breakup hurt him as much as it hurt me. Maybe now I can move on and so can he."

"I've never heard him yell like that. He doesn't even scream at me like that, so I guess you're right."

Her laughter had no humor. "I've never yelled at anyone like that, either. I guess we finally let out all the pain at once."

"Is there a possibility that you might give him another chance? If you both said you were sorry...if you gave it a second chance—"

"No. I'm on another path now. I'm where I want to be. Richard was probably right—it was smart for me to come here and end it for good." She leaned over and kissed Cooper on the cheek. "Coming here wasn't all bad. I got to know you. You're a good man." She leaned closer. "Ask the doc out."

"I will when I can dance with her. She's short and bossy, but dang if she isn't cute."

Hayley acted like she hadn't heard every word he'd said as she climbed into the driver's side of the Land Rover.

"Buckle up." Her seat was as far up as it would go, and his was as far back. She felt like he was in the back seat.

She wasn't surprised when he went to sleep as she drove the thirty miles to the clinic. Part of her hated to wake him up, but she couldn't just leave him in the car.

Her assistant, Mary May Canton, came out to help her get Cooper inside. She and her husband had worked at the clinic part-time since they'd retired. She helped with the calls and the billing. He checked the place every night and fed the animals that were staying over. They made sure everything was in order and took care of the boarded animals when Pops was out of the office, and now, when she was called out on emergencies.

"Hello, Cooper Holloway," Mary said in a teacher-like voice. "Did you finally get kicked out of a real hospital and have to come here?"

"No, Mrs. Canton, I'm just visiting."

"Well, you behave yourself."

Hayley decided Cooper would always be a kid to Mary May. After all, if her students all grew up, she'd have to admit to growing older.

For the first hour Hayley kept a close eye on Cooper each time she welcomed her next patient. He talked to everyone who came in. He probably knew all of them, except an old lady who brought in her cat. By the time Hayley said it was Fluffy's turn, Cooper could list all fourteen of the old lady's grandchildren in order.

Hayley realized folks really liked Cooper. Not for what he'd accomplished, but just for the way he was.

After an hour, he wheeled himself into her examining room and watched the show. No one seemed to mind. When someone finally asked why he was there, he said he was the doc's next patient.

She didn't mind having him near. Except for the snake, Cooper loved every animal that came in. But gradually, he started looking tired, and Hayley knew it was time to go.

Mary May gave her a stack of phone messages and mentioned that Pops had called in to check on her. "I told him you were a grown woman and could take care of yourself. He wants to retire, but he still wants to know what's going on."

"Right," Hayley said as she rolled Cooper's chair down the ramp. "And would you mind telling Cooper that I've been driving as long as he has, and I do not need advice?"

The assistant looked at Cooper. "You hear that?"

"Yep. I'm too tired to argue. Take me home or shoot me. I don't much care which."

Hayley drove and he slept. By the time they got back, it would be almost time to start with the new fillies.

"Coop, you awake?" she whispered as she slowed the car.

He didn't answer.

"If you ever do get around to asking me out, I might just say yes." Hayley smiled. It had been a long time since she'd gone out with a man, but this one might just be worth breaking her rule of never dating.

She'd had time for one boyfriend in vet school and he'd become overly possessive. He'd wanted to know where she was every minute. He'd even tried to convince her it was her fault that he worried about her.

But Cooper wouldn't be like that. He loved his freedom, so he wouldn't mind hers. If they ever had a date, of course.

When she drove up next to the headquarters, both Garrett brothers were sitting in the rockers on the front porch. The two of them looked like the largest yard gnomes she'd ever seen.

"You two waiting for me?" she asked.

"No," one said. "We're waiting for Mom to kill Tye Franklin, then we're going to bury the body."

"Is Tye in there?" Hayley pointed to the kitchen door.

"No, he's in the barn, but sometime today he's going to have to come try to talk to her, and when he does, he'll be breathing his last breath."

CHAPTER THIRTY

December 21

Dani had burned two batches of cookies. Then she'd forgotten to add the eggs to the chocolate pie. By the time she'd dropped them in the filling, it was already hot and now she had scrambled eggs floating on top of her pie.

Picking up the empty piecrust, she fought the urge to throw it across the room. She was so mad at Tye Franklin. First, he'd messed with her sons, and now, he was messing with her cooking.

Her boys had come in early and told her how he'd hog-tied them in the barn. It had embarrassed them. Here they were, finally trying to grow up and hold jobs, and now every cowhand on the place was making pig sounds when they passed him. Kidding them about how one man, twice their age, could capture them.

They were just trying to be protective of their mother, and he'd made fools out of them. They might have gone a bit far when they saw him standing in the hallway with her, but Tye was older; he should have been more understanding.

When she heard the kitchen door open, she didn't look up right away. She couldn't. She'd been fool enough to think she'd finally found a man to love, even for a short time, and he'd ruined it. He'd tumbled down her hope of a memory. She'd have to throw away those two loving nights because he'd spoiled them. Now, when she thought of him, she'd remember what he did to her boys.

"I smell cookies," Tatum yelled as he ran to the bar. He plopped down like it was happy hour in sugar town.

Dani looked down at the boy, remembering how dear her sons were at that age. Patrick had told her he loved her every night until he was about ten, and then he'd just say "Ditto, Mom" when he went to bed. He'd thought he was too cool to tell her he loved her, but he wanted her to know that he still did.

The memory calmed her. She winked at Tatum. "I have a few that are okay, but I burned most. How about you have some milk and eat the ones I saved? It wouldn't be fair to set them out. There's not enough to go around."

Tatum seemed to like that idea.

As he ate, she worked on another batch. At the rate she was going, there would be no dessert tonight, and the meal would be salads all around.

"I saw your sons sitting on the porch."

"They must be taking a break." She smiled, thinking about how hard they were working. Elliot had thanked them twice for delivering the two cousins to Dallas, like they'd really done him a great favor. But the boys had assured him it was no trouble at all.

"Nope," Tatum said around a mouthful of cookies. "They're not taking a break. They're not even working this afternoon. Told me they were just waiting for Tye to come over here to talk to you. They said you planned to kill him, and they were going to bury the body."

"I'm not going to kill Tye," Dani said, angry that her sons would say such a thing to the child.

"Good. I've been following him all day, worrying. He's a nice man. He's never yelled at me, and he takes the time to answer questions. I don't want them to hurt him. After I let your boys down last night, they were making dark plans."

"You were there?" Dani was shocked.

He looked down at his cookie.

"Tatum?"

"Tye said I wasn't supposed to tell anyone what I saw. He made me swear."

Dani could feel her blood boil. What the boys had told her was terrible, but what they hadn't said might be worse. If she hadn't asked Tye to stay that night, this would have never happened. If she'd never given him an extra biscuit. She'd started this entire feud.

Her dad always said "Scratch a mother and she'll bleed guilt." Well, that was true. This was all her fault.

"Tye told me I'd stay out of trouble if I always told the truth. He also said something about if I'm carrying somebody else's secret, I can only talk to a judge or a mom. I guess since you're a mom, I can tell you. Bad things were said last night. It hurt my ears to even hear them. Things I don't want to think about."

Before he could say more the kitchen door opened again, and Tye's figure stood there, silhouetted in the light.

After a long silence, he removed his hat and asked in his low voice, "All right if I come in?"

Dani reacted before she thought. She picked up the empty platter dusted in cookie crumbs and threw it straight at him.

He didn't bother to duck. It hit him hard in the chest and

bounced off. When it landed on the tile, it shattered in a million pieces.

She lifted a plate. "I don't want to ever set eyes on you again, Tye Franklin."

Pain filled his gray eyes, but she didn't care. He'd hurt her sons, and he must have threatened them.

When the second plate flew, Tye blocked it with his arm. It hit the wall before it joined the platter in pieces on the floor.

Dani raised the third plate and Tye vanished. She had so much anger built up in her veins. She slammed the plate against the counter.

Tatum ducked under the bar.

Dani stood there, another plate in hand as she tried to breathe. At the moment, her life seemed as shattered as the plates.

Finally, she heard someone crying. She came around the counter and pulled Tatum from under the bar. He fought, not wanting her to touch him, and his cries broke her heart.

The boy thought she was going to hurt him.

"It's all right, Tatum. I promise I won't throw any more plates."

"Did you hurt Tye?"

She'd seen the look Tye had given her, and she knew she had hurt him—not physically, but deep down inside. Like her, he wasn't a person who trusted easily, and she'd shattered his belief in her.

"I was just mad at Tye for hurting my boys," she explained. "That's all."

Tatum wiped his nose on his sleeve. "He didn't hurt them. They were coming at him, saying they were going to beat him up. Telling him to pack up and go away. Tye just stood there, watching your boys coming closer."

The kid gulped down a cry. "When they came at him, fists up like they both were going to pound on him, Tye swung his rope. I never seen anything like it. The rope caught them around their legs. He pulled them up until it looked like they were standing on their heads with their hats still on."

Dani cuddled the boy close. "Then what did he do?" She closed her eyes, wishing she didn't have to hear what happened next.

"He said something like 'I don't want to have this talk again.' Then he said he didn't plan on stopping seeing you, but he wouldn't fight them. Then he walked out of the barn.

"When I caught up to him, he told me to go pull the rope and let them down. He made me swear I wouldn't tell anyone."

Dani's voice was soft. "But how did everyone on the ranch find out?"

"Patrick told them. He thought the boys in the bunkhouse would side with him and Pete, but they just laughed and told your sons not to mess with Franklin."

Tears ran down Dani's face and she made no attempt to stop them.

"I shouldn't have yelled at him," she whispered.

"Or tried to whack him with a plate," Tatum added.

She kissed the boy's head. "Would you go tell him I promise not to throw anything if he'll come back? I'll even serve you both cookies."

"I'll go tell him, but I don't think he'll want any cookies. I can smell them burning from here."

Dani ran to the oven. Tatum was right. While she scraped the blackened cookies off the tray, she tried to think about what she'd say to Tye, and more important, what she'd say to her sons. Maybe Tye shouldn't have tied them up, but he'd told Tatum to get them down and he hadn't been the one to spread the story. Plus, he'd been outnumbered, and he'd done what he had to do to stop the fight from happening.

And what thanks did he get? She'd turned on him. Dani wouldn't be surprised if he never wanted to see her again.

More cookies were almost done when Tatum walked back into the kitchen, his head low.

"Where's Tye?" she asked, fearing that he wouldn't come.

Tatum looked up, his light blue eyes full of tears. "He's gone."

CHAPTER THIRTY-ONE

December 21
Maverick Ranch

Cooper followed Hayley across the great room and into the kitchen. They'd stopped by the office and talked Jess into taking a break to eat cookies. The smell of baking had drifted all over the house.

Both women fussed over him and Cooper didn't mind a bit. When they stepped into the kitchen, Tatum was sitting at the counter and shards of broken plates were all over the floor.

"What's happening here, kid?" Cooper asked as if it often rained porcelain in their kitchen. "I'd think it was a bar fight, except the whole place smells like cookies."

"I was sitting right here, but I don't understand nothing that's going on. I can tell you what happened, but I can't explain it."

Cooper slid onto the stool next to Tatum as Hayley started sweeping up the mess. "Start from the beginning."

"I came in for cookies, but Dani had been burning most of them. We talked about what happened in the barn last night."

Coop nodded. "Get to how the plates broke. We'll worry about what happened in the barn later."

"Okay. Dani threw the plates at Tye when he walked in. He just stood there, taking the blows. She kept it up until he left. Then, for no reason I know of, she broke a few more."

"Thanks for explaining. Are there any not-burnt cookies left?"

Tatum jumped off his stool. "I took the last batch out after Dani ran back to her room crying."

"Mind passing me a few?" Cooper reached for a glass and the milk jug, then began eating a cookie.

Jess had been silent, holding Coop's crutches and listening, but now she spoke up. "Let me get this straight, Cooper. You come into a kitchen with broken plates everywhere and the cook has left in tears and all you ask about is if there are any cookies that you can eat?"

Cooper finished his chewing and turned to face her. "I can't do anything about Dani crying. If she wanted to talk about it, she wouldn't have run to her room. As for the plates, if we worried every time a cook threw a few plates at someone around here, we'd never be able to keep any help."

Jess moved closer and glared at him. "While Elliot's gone, you're the only one in charge. Now, what are you going to do about it?"

"Order paper plates?" When she didn't smile, he said, "Some of those plastic ones they have at Walmart almost look real." When she shook her head, he added, "Come to think of it, those wouldn't kill a fly. It'd be a waste of time to use them as a weapon."

Jess huffed and marched off, and Hayley laughed. "Coop, a woman has to grow up around men like you to understand them."

He winked at her. "Jess doesn't know I'm kidding. Let's keep it to ourselves."

Cooper ate another cookie and asked Tatum to go get the wheelchair. "Doc, if you'll drive me to the door of the barn, I'd like to see the horses being unloaded."

"I'll do that if you're sure you're up to it."

"I've taken three naps today. I'm up for it. My leg only hurts when I move it."

Tatum helped Hayley get Cooper into the Land Rover this time. He claimed he might not survive another round with the Garrett brothers. "When we pass them on the porch, tell them to stay there until they receive further orders. I have a feeling they have some explaining to do, but I'm not sure about what. It's kind of like when you see some guy's arrest picture on TV and you know, just by looking, that he's guilty."

The doc jumped behind the wheel and drove him to Sunny Barn. The trailer hauling the fillies was just pulling up.

"Why do they call them fillies and not mares?" Tatum asked.

"Because they haven't spent any time with a stallion yet."

Cooper was worried about how he'd answer Tatum's next question, but the boy was pointing to Tye's pickup and trailer, which were parked on the far side of the barn. "Look! He hasn't left yet."

"He said he'd help with the unloading," Hayley said. "Maybe I'll get a chance to say goodbye to him." But she didn't sound too hopeful. "I wish he wasn't leaving. I think I could learn a lot from him."

"Yeah, me, too," Coop admitted.

Tatum held the chair while Cooper slid out of the car, Hayley steadying him. He was a man who took care of himself if possible, but he didn't mind her being close. She was one of those rare people who grew smarter and more beautiful with time. He had a feeling her kind heart had something to do with it.

One by one, the animals came out of the trailer, as if dancing. Ranch hands stood around, admiring them and talking to Cooper. Elliot might think he ran the ranch when Griffin was gone, but in truth, Cooper had figured out a long time ago that the workload was pretty evenly split. The hands who worked the ranch year-round reported to Cooper if there was a problem with the stock. He was the only brother riding out to check the pastures when trouble came, or helping with the branding, or loading stock for transport. He was there when a calf needed to be pulled and he was there when an animal had to be put down. Elliot might know the books, but Cooper knew the count of every horse or cow on the property.

When Tye walked up, Cooper didn't say a word about the mess in the kitchen. Judging from the kid's story, the cowboy had only played the part of target in the drama.

Tye stood next to Cooper's wheelchair and kept his voice low. "I think we need a man with each filly. We need to walk them awhile until they get used to the place. I'm guessing everything's different here. The air, the smells, the people."

"I agree. Make the assignments."

"Will do." Tye hesitated. "One more thing. I'm taking a few days off after this job is done. I'm not sure if I'll be back."

"We'll miss you if you don't, but I want you to know if you come back in two days or three years, you are always welcome here."

"Thanks. I might take you up on that."

Tye stepped away to do his job. Maybe his last job for them.

Coop kept watch over all around him. The excitement, the fresh air and the sounds almost made him believe he was cured.

As the afternoon wore on, he found his gaze going back again and again to Hayley. She was doing her job, working around the big horses without fear. He wished he could stand beside her, make the job a little easier on her. He could never remember admiring a woman so much.

Finally, she walked over to him, dirt on her cheek and pants muddy from the knees down. "Ready to call it a night, Coop? We've got them all checked out and logged in."

"Take me home, Doc," he said. "I'm all yours."

Five minutes later, she'd rolled him to his room, where Dani had made them a dinner for two on a card table next to his bed. The cook was a bit quiet, and she didn't say a word about the broken dishes or the rumor that she'd cried.

"Your boys still on the porch?" Cooper asked.

"They are."

"Tell them to go over to the bunkhouse for supper and I'll see them in the morning."

"You planning to send them after the doc's Jeep?"

"No. I'm going to talk her into staying another night. We need her help, and if she has to make any calls, I'd like to go with her. Be a fly on the barn wall while she works. I'm hoping to learn more about being a vet."

"I'm right here, Coop—you can talk to me. Of course, I'll stay if I'm needed."

He grinned, his eyes opening wide as if he hadn't seen her there right in front of him. "Oh, there you are. I didn't notice you."

She sighed. "Are you considering going back to school? Giving me a little competition in the vet department?"

"Nope, but I am thinking about dating a vet."

Dani stepped out of the room, probably aware that she was no longer part of the conversation.

"I don't know about that, Coop. You seem more of a talker than a man of action."

He pushed the card table a few feet away. "Come over here, Doc, and I'll show you."

She laughed. "No way. If you want me, Coop, you'll have to catch me."

"A challenge?"

"Nope, a promise. How about we eat dinner? I'm starving, but I can't enjoy a meal smelling like the barn." She tugged off her muddy, baggy pants and tossed them into the shower.

Her shirttail dropped halfway to her knees. Then, as if at a fancy restaurant, she sat down on the other side of the table and began her meal, seemingly unaware that he was staring at her and not the food.

"You've got legs," he finally said.

"Of course I've got legs." She leaned across the table and whispered, as if not wanting anyone to hear a secret, "Coop, sometimes you say the strangest things."

"I've noticed that lately. I'm not sure there's a cure."

CHAPTER THIRTY-TWO

December 21

Tye walked through the barn as the last watery rays of sunlight shone through the wide-open doors. All the three-year-olds were settled in their stalls. He'd thought he would have to sing the chestnut one to sleep before she'd stop pacing.

Smiling, he decided the fillies reminded him of the cousins who'd invaded the Holloway place. They were a lot of trouble to everyone, but now that the girls were gone, the house seemed too quiet.

Correction, he thought: the redheaded cousin was still up at the line shack at Winter Valley. A few of the men thought she might be keeping Creed, the foreman, captive up there. One man suggested she might be holding Creed as a sex toy, and all the other men volunteered to take his place.

Double-checking the last gate, Tye walked slowly out into a rainy sunset. He didn't look back. He never looked back. It was time to go. A man shouldn't come between a woman and her children. Even if he'd won this battle with the boys and Dani had agreed to keep seeing him, it would only be a while before she regretted it. He'd lose the war in the end. A clean cut now was better than a slow decay.

Walking out to his old pickup, he barely noticed tiny drops, half snow, half rain, tapping against the brim of his hat. He tossed his coat and gloves onto the passenger seat and climbed in. It was time to move on.

But where to? The bad thing about moving around while growing up was that he had no town or state to call home.

The notebook brushed against his leg as he rattled toward the county road. The ranch gate loomed in the evening light. The *M* blinked a moment in the headlights as he left the ranch, reminding him of the message in his grandpa's book.

Follow the lone star. Find Dusty Roads. My gift to you waits.

The handwriting had been shaky, as if Tye's grandpa had added it at the end of his life, but the message was there if he could just understand it.

What were the chances a gift his grandfather left somewhere years ago would still be out there to be found? But it must have taken him months to draw clues on every page. Why would he have spent the time? To play a joke? To daydream that he'd left Tye something? Or maybe to draw Tye a very unusual map to something worth finding?

It was a miracle the notebook had finally found its way to him.

But Tye knew from the drawings that he was close. The old Circle M brand on the back gate was proof. After that, there was nowhere else he could think to look. There were probably a hundred miles of dusty roads near the south entrance to the ranch.

The only gift he'd found here was Dani. A real woman. Down-to-earth. She wore no makeup and she didn't need any.

She was beautiful just the way she was. He'd guessed by a few things she'd said that she thought she was plump, but she was just right in his eyes. She thought she'd failed in raising her boys, but Tye hated to think how they would have turned out if she hadn't been there.

Only Tye didn't have Dani in his life anymore. He'd lost her, kind of like he'd lost most everything. The only thing he was truly good at was leaving.

As he turned onto the county road, he decided to head for Crossroads, where the doc had said she thought some of the drawings resembled buildings in town. He'd get a room if they had an it'll-do hotel, and walk around come daylight. It shouldn't take long. Maybe he'd drive a few dusty roads looking for a ranch with an outline of a horse as its brand.

He passed a café with a line of windows facing the road. Old blue-green booths were pushed close to the windows inside so everyone had a view of the traffic and the post office across the street.

He circled, then turned into the café and parked. He took a few minutes to flip through the drawings. There it was. A café with wide windows and the booths showing in every frame. Of course, it wasn't any great revelation. Probably every town had a café that looked pretty much like this one.

Tye decided to eat before he drove farther. He wasn't very hungry, but it was something to do, and he estimated he had about forty years left of looking for something to pass the time.

Inside, the waitress took his order without trying to make small talk. While Tye waited for his meal, he watched rain dripping down the windows, forming a hundred tiny streams. Cars passed, their lights blurred into starbursts.

Only a few people dotted the café. Loners like him, eating late. Tye leaned back and studied the notebook. If he could find one or two more clues, he might have some direction. So far all he had were maybes, nothing to anchor the book to this place. But the book was trying to tell him something.

When the waitress brought him his ticket for food he had barely tasted, Tye debated asking about a hotel or where the nearest bar was. For once, the hotel won out.

"There's a motel just out of town, but it's closed for remodeling. Has been for almost a year now, and no one has seen any work going on out there."

"Thanks." Tye wasn't sure for what, but it seemed the right thing to say.

Just before she walked away, she added, "There's a bed-and-breakfast inn at the center of town. You can't miss it. Two stories, looks like it was built with the leftovers from *Gone with the Wind*."

"Thanks," he said again. "That's not really my style."

"Suit yourself, but you'll have to drive awhile to find another hotel, and this time of year, rooms book up the first sign of ice on the road. On flat roads like this, if you lose control and start to slide, you could be in Oklahoma before you bump into anything to stop you."

Tye grinned at her joke. "Maybe I'll try the bed-and-breakfast."

Ten minutes later, when he pulled in front of the old two-story house, he knew he was looking at one of his grandfather's drawings come to life. He parked across the street from a house that loomed like an ancient relic in a modern world. The trees were bigger than in the drawing. There were houses on either side of it now. But the pillars out front lined up the same. The windows, all the way up to a tiny triangle window in the attic, were exactly like the drawing.

He'd found another clue.

As he ran through the rain, he thought he saw *Franklin* on

the mailbox, but he didn't stop to make sure. He was wet and cold and tired. He'd check tomorrow.

From the moment he entered the house, it felt familiar. Like he'd walked into this parlor before, a long time ago. He remembered the smell of lemon polish and honey-wax candles, and the way the Tiffany-style lamp made a thousand tiny triangles of light on the ceiling. As he circled the room, he decided Christmas must have exploded in this place. Every corner was decorated.

A little lady, round as she was tall, hurried toward him. She had a red-and-green apron on and a necklace that jingled as she moved.

"'Evening, stranger. If you're in need of a room, we've only got one left. It's small, but you'll be out of this weather."

Tye removed his hat. "That's all I need. One room for a night or two."

As he said the words, he realized that *was* all he wanted at the moment. A dry place to sleep. Maybe, if he was lucky, he wouldn't even dream.

CHAPTER THIRTY-THREE

December 21

Elliot took his time riding home. He needed to think as he watched the sun fade, blanketed in clouds. Maybe he should have run away from home more often in his life. Nothing cleared the mind like stepping away.

When the wind from the north picked up, he knew he'd be racing a storm to headquarters. He shivered as he galloped over the dry grass, but he couldn't remember feeling so alive in years. Sometimes, all he saw was what was wrong with the ranch, but today he saw the beauty of it.

He made it back, cold and hungry and happy.

In the foyer, he dropped his coat and boots. As he walked through a silent house to his room, he really looked at the details of his home, for the first time in a long while. A hundred years of Holloways had lived here, worked here, loved here and died here. Some people needed to travel the world, but his world was right here.

It was so late, even the office light was off. Maybe Jess had finished and left. Back to her life. Back to her fiancé. She and Richard could go to Paris and live the rest of their lives as partners.

He felt strange not hating her anymore. The hate he'd carried so long had melted into sorrow. For him. For her. Even for poor old Richard, whom she probably didn't love, and the guy might never know it. If she had to ask if he was alone, that had to mean that she knew that he had someone else he spent the midnight hours with. They had a company to run, vacations to take with their families. Their world would be full of numbers, not passion.

It told him a great deal that there hadn't been one word of endearment in her phone conversation.

He made it to his room and went straight to the shower. The strange day had been a journey for him. A roller-coaster ride over emotions deeper than he'd thought he had. A part of him would always love Jess, and maybe a part would always be sorry it hadn't worked out with her. But he'd make it, though.

When he stepped out of the shower and wrapped a towel around his waist, his thoughts were trying to form words that he might say to her. Strangely, he wanted to part, if not as friends, at least not as enemies.

As he turned into his bedroom, the sight of her sitting on the corner of his bed hit him like a cattle prod shock. Still dressed in her very proper black suit and cream blouse, she reminded him of a judge about to hold court.

She didn't say a word as he crossed the room and pulled out underwear and a T-shirt. "Mind if I get dressed?"

"No. Would you like me to leave?"

"I don't care, Jess. In case you've forgotten, we were lovers for three years. One of which we lived together. I think you've already seen a lot of me."

She grinned. "College days. I remember. You never did your half of the housework."

He turned his back and began to dress. "From the mess in that two-room apartment that I remember, neither of us did. How about old Richard? Does he do his half of the housework?"

"I wouldn't know. We don't live together. He lives in a town house thirty minutes from the office. I live in a high-rise two blocks away from the firm. I walk to and from the office with no traffic."

"Let me guess—you live on the third floor."

"Fourth." She lifted her chin an inch. "It was the only apartment available that was close to my requirements."

"I know, high enough to be off the ground but nowhere near the clouds."

She nodded. "You remembered. But I've changed. Fear of floods doesn't bother me as much as it used to."

"That's good. Of course, they rarely reach the fourth floor. Surely there's room for old Richard."

Elliot glanced at her and raised an eyebrow. When she didn't answer, he figured it was none of his business. He pulled on a pair of jeans, even though he'd planned to go to sleep. But he wasn't about to ask her to leave.

"Want to go raid the refrigerator?"

"Sure. After you left, I just worked. I don't think I've had a meal since the ribs and beer. I ate enough of them to hibernate for the winter."

They moved through the silent house to the kitchen, and Elliot put out leftover coleslaw, green-bean salad and different kinds of cheese. He didn't look up when he asked, "Any chance you're going to tell me why you were in my room?"

"I wanted to say I'm sorry."

"For what?"

"For all of it. For not making an effort to come visit years ago. For not supporting you when you lost your dad. For hating you half my adult life."

He forgot about the food and came around the bar to stand in front of her. "I feel the same. I never meant to cause you pain, Jess. Never. You told me from the first how important your goals were, and I understood why. I remember thinking your dad might disown you if you didn't do everything just right. Is he still as overbearing as ever?"

"Not so much. He and my mother divorced a few years ago. He's remarried. She keeps him busy. I rarely see him outside the office."

He might have hugged her, but her back was ramrod straight. He had the feeling she'd shatter if he touched her. His Jess had been a fighter from the day he'd met her. She'd been valedictorian of her private high school, graduated with a four-point GPA from Texas Tech so she could have her pick of jobs and, of course, she'd picked her father's company. She'd known she would since she'd played in his office chair.

"So," she began with what he knew was probably a planned speech. "How do we end this? Shake hands and walk away? Toast to the rest of our lives apart? I have no idea how people like us say goodbye. Maybe that's why we didn't."

After all these years, he could still read her mind. "How about we finish with the books?"

She nodded. "I agree. The perfect ending. We'll have worked together, if only once."

"I'd like to add one other thing. When the books are finished, Jess, you stay one more day, and we figure out how to be friends. Like it or not, we are both a part of each other's past. Maybe we can get to a place where we can exchange Christmas cards, or maybe call now and then, maybe be friends online."

"I'd like that." She picked up her plate and suggested they move to the office. She had a few questions, and he might as well answer them while they ate.

Logical Jess, he thought. No wonder she'd been so easy to love.

She thought just like him. The work always came first. It had been the balance in his life.

She asked a few questions about the books, then a few about the ranch. He was surprised she was interested. Rain tapped on the windows as they talked, and he remembered how she used to be afraid of storms.

When he asked if she still was, she said that was what was great about living in downtown Houston. She was surrounded by buildings that seemed to protect her from the weather. "If I'm home, I barely notice when it rains, and I can't see enough to watch the sky."

He couldn't relate. As far as he knew, everyone on the ranch woke to the weather report. It was their partner, their enemy, their friend.

When lightning flashed outside, she jumped, and he realized her fear was still there.

"I remember how it stormed that weekend I visited here before. I feel so raw with the storms out here."

"I'd forgotten about that storm." Thunder rattled, and he doubted she was listening to him. When it calmed, he added, "I guess we'd better call it a night."

She nodded, as if trying to think of something positive about this frightening place. "I love the sunrise view from my room on the third floor, but I left the drapes open this morning. Would you close them for me?"

"Sure." He followed her up the stairs, but when they reached the third floor, the storm seemed so much closer. Rain pounded on the roof. The thunder was closer. The lightning flashed brighter. Sunlan had put in east-facing floor-to-ceiling windows, but now the storm was putting on a show only one pane of glass away.

If he'd been alone, he would have watched, but all he saw

now was her fear. "It's all right, Jess. This house has stood for a hundred years, and it'll stand tonight."

He pulled the drapes, plunging the room into darkness except for the one lamp by her bed. "It's all right," he said again. "It'll pass soon."

She sat on the bed, her hands laced together on her skirt. When she'd been five, her family had lost their roof to a tornado. Her house had flooded that night. Just a few inches, but she'd told him the cleaners had come in and thrown away all her toys. He remembered she'd coped by always having a windowless bedroom if possible.

He remembered that when they'd lived together, she'd always placed towels at every door, as if it would keep out any water.

This house was built to see the land, and those who lived in it would wake up to the sunrise and go to sleep with big enough windows to watch the moon from their beds. The thing he'd always loved about living in the country was now frightening her.

Elliot wasn't sure what to do. Maybe just being near would be enough. When he'd left school, he hadn't been there for her. All he'd thought about was his family. Now, if only for just this once, he'd stay. He'd help her however he could. She'd be his priority, his only concern.

Kneeling, he pulled off her high heels, wondering why she insisted on wearing them. Part of her armor, he guessed. Then, with tender care, he helped her remove her jacket.

He couldn't resist letting his hands brush over her leg, then touch her shoulders. There was a time when he knew every inch of her.

"It's after midnight, Jess. Any chance you can go to sleep?"

She shook her head.

"How about I move you to another room? You can have mine and I'll sleep up here."

Thunder shook the house.

"The storm would still be out there. I'll wait it out. Richard tells me it's mind over fear. He calls me a coward when I'm afraid."

He pulled back the bedspread. "Crawl in. I'll stay with you until the storm passes. We'll wait it out together." He almost added that he was starting to hate old Richard.

Elliot covered her with the spread, then lay on top a few feet away.

For a while neither said a word. Then, to his surprise, she took his hand. "Thanks for not calling me a coward."

"Why would I do that? Everyone's afraid of something."

She turned toward him. "What are you afraid of?"

He could barely see her face in the lamp's light. She didn't look so frightened as she gripped his hand.

"Praying mantises," he finally admitted. "I know they can't hurt me, but I swear they belong as characters in horror movie, not running around in the ivy. I used to have nightmares about them growing to be ten feet high and coming after me. Did you know they practice sexual cannibalism? The female has sex with her mate, then eats him. Creepy little bugs."

Jess laughed. "I had no idea you were afraid of a bug. Aren't they good for the environment, eating other bugs?"

"I don't care, and I imagine the female mantis's boyfriend doesn't, either. She bites off his head first. Probably his own fault. We should blame him for losing his head over a female."

Jess's laughter turned to uncontrolled giggles as she walked her fingertips over the bare skin of his arm.

He shivered and pushed it away.

A moment later, her bug-like touch was on his ribs. Suddenly, they were twenty again. Laughing and picking on each other.

When he finally pinned her arm to make her stop *bugging* him, his face was inches from hers. In shadows she was the girl—the only girl he'd ever fallen in love with.

Without much thought, he closed the space between them and kissed her lightly. He knew it was a mistake a moment later. Elliot rolled onto his back and let go of her arm, closing his eyes.

The yelling would start any minute. She'd call him every name in the book, and most of them would hit home.

She leaned on her elbow, as if waiting for him to open his eyes.

When he did, she asked calmly, "Why'd you do that?"

"I don't know. You can slap me if you want to. Loving you always felt so right, Jess. Maybe I just wanted to remember or pretend."

"Oh. That makes sense." She placed her hand on his chest and leaned over him, then kissed him back. Only her kiss was longer. That wasn't fair, but he decided not to complain.

He'd always loved the way she kissed around his mouth, as if she was a butterfly looking for the perfect place to land. And when she did land, her kiss was suddenly demanding.

Elliot pulled her onto his chest and gave her what she asked for. A real, passionate kiss, just the way she liked to be kissed.

When she finally pulled away, she was out of breath. "You always knew just how to kiss," she whispered.

"That's how you should always be kissed." He wanted to ask if Richard kissed her like that, but he knew the old guy didn't. If he had, they wouldn't be sleeping in beds thirty minutes apart.

Jess curled against his side. "In some ways, we were so right for one another."

He ran his fingers through her soft hair and tilted her face upward. When he lowered his mouth to her, she was ready for more. As the storm raged, a deep hunger stormed in him. He let his hand glide over her silk blouse, but he didn't unbutton one button. She wasn't his. His Jess was promised to another.

She seemed to understand the unspoken rules. Somehow, the night let them feel what they couldn't talk about. She might have moved on, made a life without him, but her body still needed his nearness.

Slowly, they drifted into sleep, both holding the other close, as dreams of yesterday played in his mind.

CHAPTER THIRTY-FOUR

December 22
Franklin Inn

Tye almost stumbled as he made his way down the narrow stairs at the bed-and-breakfast. It was past dawn. He'd overslept. He never missed a sunrise unless he was drunk. Last night he'd been stone sober, but he was exhausted. That, or he was getting old.

"Morning." The little round innkeeper popped out of the kitchen like an aging cuckoo clock. "I'm Daisy. We didn't get properly introduced last night." She raised and lowered her round shoulders a few times. "You're a little early for breakfast, but I've got coffee on. Come on along to the kitchen and you can help me roll out the cinnamon rolls."

Tye wouldn't have been surprised to see Santa and his reindeer in the kitchen. This had to be ground zero for strange decorations. Stuffed animals with antlers, teapots that looked like tiny Christmas trees, candlesticks in red and green.

As she poured him a cup of coffee in a Santa-head cup, Daisy gestured with her head to a slightly taller, and wider, woman cooking. "This is my sister, Rose."

The bigger woman turned around. "Welcome." Her smile was more of a twitch. "What's your name, stranger? You forgot to sign in last night." She looked at Daisy. "It's a rule around here. Everyone has to sign in."

"I'm Tye Franklin. Thanks for letting me in last..." He stopped. Both women had frozen and they were staring at him.

Fearing they might start screaming at any moment, Tye rushed on. "I work out at the Maverick Ranch for the Holloways. I'm in town, just looking around on my day off." There, that should be enough information to take him out of the serial-killer category.

Rose set down the fork she'd been flipping sausage patties with. "What's your full name?"

"Tyson Jefferson Franklin."

Daisy grinned. "You're Adam Franklin's grandson. He's our half brother. Don't you remember us? You came here once with Adam. We had breakfast out in the garden so you could play."

A faded memory drifted in his mind. "I do remember. Last night when I stepped inside, I had the feeling I'd been here before. I remembered the smells."

Rose cleared her throat. "We're your great-aunts."

"Half great-aunts, I think," Daisy said. "Adam was married twice, so we're half aunts to Tyson."

Tye almost laughed. Daisy had confirmed what he'd feared for a long time. Being nuts ran way back in his family tree for generations.

While he watched them, Rose tried to explain to Daisy that just because Adam married twice before he went to jail didn't make them half great-aunts.

An hour later they were telling him all about his second and third cousins here in town. Daisy started patting his hand as she said she was so sorry his grandfather had died in jail. If he'd been free, he might have lived to his nineties. He'd written them a letter every year to tell them the food was terrible.

When Tye tried to pull away, Daisy kept patting and telling all the bad news since he'd been for a visit all those years ago. Kin he'd never heard of had died of cancer and one of a heart attack...and no one had found him for three days. One Daisy mentioned was too dumb to come out of the cold...so he'd frozen to death. Another had died giving birth to her fourteenth child...and the family had thought about shooting the husband at the funeral. A cousin twice removed had disappeared in New York City...and no one had heard from him since. The sisters thought he was probably dead.

Finally, they had to stop logging dead relatives when the other guests at the inn began coming in for breakfast.

Tye was relieved. He'd had about all the "catching up" that he could take. He decided he liked the idea of having no one to call kin. He moved into the parlor while the half aunts served their guests. They were sweet ladies, but he needed to disappear so they could log him as one of the missing.

He was halfway up the stairs when Hayley walked through the front door.

"Don't you dare run, Tye. I've just spent an hour looking for you."

He smiled at the doc. "How'd you find me?"

"The waitress at Dorothy's told me you were staying at the inn. I drove down the street and there was your truck. I'm a great detective."

He came down the few steps he'd climbed. They moved back into the dining room and sat at the far end, away from the travelers who were keeping the sisters busy with questions about the town.

"So what do you need, Doc?" He handed her a cup of coffee. "Coffee's on the house. Turns out I'm a relative."

"I had to come to tell you Dani is looking for you. She says she needs to talk to you, and she's going to find a way to do it, even if she has to join the rodeo circuit."

"We don't have anything to say. I tried, and she almost flattened me with a platter."

"I heard about that." Hayley smiled. "I love staying at the ranch. Something is always happening. The foreman and Cooper's redheaded cousin haven't come down from Winter Valley. Some of the men want to go rescue him. But Cooper says Creed can take care of himself.

"Oh, and in other news, Elliot and the accountant came out of the same bedroom this morning. That was interesting. Tatum asked them if they were having a sleepover. Neither one said a word to the other at breakfast. Oh, and I almost forgot—Cooper likes me."

"Of course he does." Tye grinned.

"No. I mean he really likes me." She almost sounded like she was back in high school.

"How do you feel about that?"

"I think he's too wild for me, Tye. What do you think?"

"I think I'm the last person in the world you should ask for advice on dating or love. No, come to think about it, my two half great-aunts are. Have you met Rose and Daisy Franklin?"

"Of course I have. The whole town loves them." She jumped up. "I forgot why I came here. I talked to Pops last night and he gave me an idea of where to find a brand that looks like a cutout of a horse on his hind legs. You up for a road trip?"

"Sure. I'm not ready to face the Garretts again, and when I see Dani I'll probably make a fool of myself. That can wait. I'm ready to go."

He said goodbye to Daisy and kissed her chubby cheek, promising to be back by supper. She told him there would be no charge for the room because he was family, but he'd have to clean his own room when he left.

When Tye climbed into Elliot's Land Rover, he asked if the boss ever got to drive his own car.

Hayley shook her head. "He never goes anywhere, anyway, and I still had the keys. Oh, I forgot to tell you. We have to make a couple of stops on the way to your treasure hunt."

"That's fine." He relaxed. Hayley was a good vet, and he had a feeling if he stayed around, they'd always be friends. Over the past few years, he'd given up on making friends. He'd either let them down or they'd drifted in another direction.

It had been over a week since he'd had a drink. The world seemed clearer somehow, even if he still had no direction. If he could live a week without alcohol, maybe he'd try for two.

CHAPTER THIRTY-FIVE

December 22
Maverick Ranch

By the time Cooper was up, Hayley had already left on an emergency call.

He ate breakfast with Tatum and they talked about the storm last night. Finally, Cooper asked the kid how he liked living on the ranch.

"I love it. I can go wherever I want to and no one yells at me. I like going over to the barn and checking on the horses and eating lunch with the men in the bunkhouse and talking to Dani. Elliot had one of the men put a TV in my bedroom, but I haven't had time to watch it. There's too much to do around here."

Cooper kept his words easy. "I talked to the sheriff, and he's talked to case workers in both Lubbock and in Oklahoma. It took some doing, but they all agreed that you could stay with us until after Christmas."

The boy's smile almost touched his ears. "I'd like that." Then he went silent.

"What's the matter, Tatum?"

"Where will I go after Christmas?"

Cooper didn't want to talk about it, but he had to. "I don't know. They are looking for your kin. The sheriff said your grandmother's will mentioned having another daughter. They are searching for her. You might have an aunt somewhere."

Tatum shook his head. "Grandma said she had one dead daughter and another who was dead to her. When I asked about it, she told me I didn't need to know."

"If she's alive, the law will find her."

"You're my kin, Cooper. We're wolf people, remember? We howl at the wind. I don't want to go to some aunt whose own mother wishes she was dead."

Cooper was glad when Dani interrupted them. He had no answer for the kid.

She took the little boy's hand and said, "We got new chicks back in the henhouse. You want to come with me and help me count them?"

"Sure," Tatum answered.

When Tatum left, Cooper sat alone, thinking how empty the house would feel without the kid. He looked toward the kitchen door. Tatum had already headed out, but Dani was just closing the door behind her. For a moment, he saw her sad stare, and knew she didn't want the kid to go away, either.

She'd saved him from having to answer a hard question, but Cooper knew it would come around again. Maybe some family would adopt him, but chances were they'd live in town. Tatum belonged in a place where he could roam. Where he could howl at the north wind and people wouldn't think it was strange.

He belonged here.

CHAPTER THIRTY-SIX

December 22
Maverick Ranch

Elliot sat at the bar in the kitchen, watching Cooper pace with his crutches. He looked like some kind of broken windup toy, limping to the great room, through the dining room to the kitchen and then around again. Finally, he tossed one crutch away and started limping along on what seemed like a journey to wear out the tile.

"The doc is out working. She said Mary May called her before dawn," Elliot said for the tenth time. "She's just doing her job."

"Don't you see, Elliot, there is no telling what kind of emergency she's walking into? She could be trying to doctor a wild horse or a rabid dog and no one would be there to help her. Hell, that guy who loves snakes could have lost his pet last night and she could be out looking for a runaway snake. Or maybe someone called in an injured bear. I know her. She'd try to save the fellow. Probably march right up to him and start bossing him around."

"She's fine, Coop. She managed to stay alive as a vet without you around."

"I know, but she should have woken me this morning. I could have dressed by the time the car warmed up and gone out with her."

"Right, Coop, you're such a joy to be around. And your broken leg wouldn't slow her down. You know, just because she saved your life doesn't make you her bodyguard."

Elliot faced him. "Have you taken any of those pain pills the doctor in the emergency room gave you?"

"No. They make my brain fussy."

"You're not too clear on a normal day, little brother. Remember when you decided to swim in the horse trough on the east pasture? When you reached for your clothes, two rattlers had taken up residence on top. You rode home naked."

"No one I knew saw me."

Elliot laughed. "Maybe. But every car that went down the county road honked at you."

Cooper stopped and rested against the back of the leather couch. "I've matured since then. My wild days are over. I'm going to settle down and date one woman. She may not believe it yet, but she's the one."

"Does she know anything about your plan? There will be at least a few weeks between the first date and the honeymoon, I hope."

"I've told her, but I don't think she believes it."

Elliot knew the woman Coop talked about was the doc. Coop had been nuts about her since she'd helped him at Winter Valley. Like everything he did, he wanted to rush in when it might serve him well to go slow.

Coop looked at his brother. "Did we have a good year this year? The ranch made money, didn't it?"

"We did. Best one ever. Sunlan wants to go ahead and start the other two wings of the house. Maybe put in a pool out back."

"Well…" Coop pushed himself away from the back of the couch and limped over to the bar. "I've been thinking. You know how Griffin won Sunlan over by giving her the white barn? Well, I decided we could build a vet clinic on that square of land near the road. It's too rocky for grazing, and the clinic the doc's got is falling apart. I don't think her grandfather has done a repair since the sixties."

Elliot laughed. "You think she'd marry you for a clinic? I don't think it works that way."

"I was afraid you'd say that. I guess I'll have to do it the hard way. Ask her out, send her flowers, take her out somewhere expensive to eat a few dozen times. We'll go away places for the weekends, anywhere she wants. Then I'll buy a ring and we'll set the date. The wedding will cost a fortune. I'm telling you, Elliot, it would be cheaper to just build a clinic."

"That's right. In your case, tossing in a clinic might improve your odds."

Dani passed through the kitchen. "Have either of you seen Tatum?"

Both brothers headed out. Elliot to the barns and Cooper to the chickens. The kid was fascinated by anything newborn.

Coop found Tatum sitting on a bucket trying to get all the baby chicks in his lap. He was laughing as he talked to them.

When he saw Cooper leaning against the chicken-wire door, he said, "Look, Coop, they think I'm their daddy. I got to figure out names for them. How is the chicken going to nurse all of them?"

"Momma chickens don't feed like mares do."

The kid looked confused. "Why not? Chickens got breasts."

Cooper felt his heart turn over. "Tatum, promise me you'll never leave the headquarters area without letting me know. I was afraid you'd headed up to Winter Valley. If you left me, who would be around to ask the important questions?"

"I can't leave, Coop. I got too much to take care of around here. First, I got to watch you 'cause you might fall over again any minute. Then I had to watch Tye to make sure the Garrett brothers didn't kill him. The baby colt always needs brushing, and now the chickens."

He took a breath. "I haven't even got to the cows and the barn cats. Elliot said one is about to drop kittens. I probably should be following her around."

"That's right. We couldn't get along without you." As Cooper said the words, he realized how much he meant them.

He wondered if Hayley would mind if he picked out their first son before they married.

CHAPTER THIRTY-SEVEN

December 22

Hayley loved Tye Franklin making calls with her. It was like having a big brother. He knew horses and was more help than ten Mary Mays would be. They mostly talked about the calls she'd made. One had been an emergency: a colt had gotten caught in a roll of barbed wire, and he'd tried to fight his way out. The cuts were deep and plenty, but he'd pull through.

After a few routine calls, they turned south toward the back of the Holloways' ranch. Pops had told her there used to be a little ranch not far from the back gate and he thought he remembered a marking over the entrance had been the outline of a horse.

Tye got out his grandfather's notebook and watched for a clue as she drove.

Hayley told him that her pops had said an old guy who raised a few horses lived out on a dead-end road. He believed the world was about to end, so the only safe place was out that far from anyone. Pops commented that the old man was as crazy as the horse on his brand. He'd figured out how to survive, but once in a while his horses needed a doctor's care.

Three roads forked not far from the Maverick Ranch's back gate. Tye offered to drive while Hayley marked off their route. In this backcountry, most of the roads were not well marked. A few only had a sign on a post or a rock naming the pasture or the name of an owner from years ago. Ranches often changed hands without changing the names of the pastures, or even the ranch itself.

The third road they tried was so twisting, Tye had to slow down. The winding roads were dirt and had a few holes they had to go up against the wire fence to get around.

"I got a feeling about this one," Tye said. "Let's follow it until it ends."

Hayley felt like she was on a treasure hunt. She had no idea what would be at the end of the journey, but just finding the next clue would be exciting.

It was almost noon when they reached the last gate and the road ran out. Any mailboxes had vanished miles ago.

The ranch gate was leaning, but still standing above the entrance. And there, swinging in the wind, was a tin square with the outline of a horse on his back two legs. It fit somehow in this land—wild, untamed, alone.

"Should we go in?" Hayley asked. The dirt road turned into a path past the cattle guard.

"Might as well. I don't see any doorbell."

They made it half a mile driving on mostly grass. When they saw the barn and the house, both thought it looked abandoned.

But Hayley explained, "Pops said the old guy living here puts a letter in his neighbor's mailbox when he needs a vet. He doesn't even put a stamp on it, but the mailman drops it off at the clinic, anyway."

"We need to be careful. If this guy's crazy, he might come out shooting."

They parked a hundred feet from the house and began to walk slowly toward it. Hayley carried her medical bag, and Tye held the notebook.

When they were about twenty feet from the house, someone yelled, "You can stop right there."

"We mean no harm," Hayley yelled back. "I'm Dr. Westland's granddaughter."

The voice came again. "I figured that. Looks like you're carrying his bag. But I don't need no vet right now, so I figure you and that man you got with you don't have any reason to be here, unless the world finally blew itself up and we're the last people alive."

"The world is fine as far as I know. I just came out here to ask you a question."

"Ask, then leave. I ain't buying or selling anything."

Tye held open the worn notebook. "My grandfather willed me this book. He drew pictures in it of this area, and one looks like your gate."

"I don't want no picture."

Tye tried again. "My grandfather died in prison. He left me this for a reason, but I can't figure out what it is."

"What's your name?"

"Tyson Franklin."

The screen door hit the house as an old man stepped out. He lowered a rifle and moved into the sunshine. "Let me see that book."

Half an hour later, Tye and Hayley were still sitting on the porch as the old man flipped through the pages.

Tye tried for the third time to ask a question. "Do you know what he meant by *lone star* or *dusty roads* or a gift waiting?"

The old man nodded. "I know all about it. I've been waiting for you to drop by for over twenty years." He explained, "I'm Dustin Roads, and your grandfather was my best friend. He always called me Dusty, even when we were in the army together. He never talked about his son, but he mentioned you a few times." Dusty stood. "Come with me. I want to show you something."

They followed the old guy to the barn and then a corral that opened into a pasture. Several horses grazed.

Tye whispered to Hayley, "He's got some beautiful horses. From the markings, they've got Steel Dust bloodlines."

"They sure do." Dusty puffed out his chest. "Finest horses in the West. Your grandfather brought me a pair just before he went to prison. He said he won them in a poker game. Even had papers. He told me to save a colt and a filly for you. I said yes before I knew you'd take years to come pick them up."

Dusty looked at Hayley. "Your grandfather made sure to file the papers for me. Every time they bred I made sure it was recorded. I sold one now and then to pay for their keep, but I kept the best. I'd like to keep two pairs, but you can have the rest. Last count, I'd say that gift your grandfather talked about has multiplied to twenty-seven horses. They've never been ridden, but they're all gentle. Eat out my hand."

Tye moved slowly toward the animals. Within five minutes, they'd surrounded him, as if accepting him.

Dusty leaned close to Hayley. "He loves horses, don't he? I can tell. I don't know if I could have given them to him if he didn't. Adam told me once his only grandson loved them from the time he could walk."

Tye finally moved back to Dusty. "I don't know how to thank you."

"Don't thank me. I did it for a friend. I've thought about it, and decided if you ever showed up, I'd tell you I want you to leave the four oldest. They're past breeding years and they've lived here too long to be moved." Dusty grinned. "I figure four will be plenty to talk to. If they outlive me, I want you to take care of them. I'll draw up the paperwork so they'll be yours."

"All right. But from now on I'll pay any bills." Tye offered his hand. "Okay if I come check on you and them now and then?"

"I guess I won't mind that. But don't come too often. Don't want you wearing out the road."

He thought about it for a minute, then added, "The day you come to take them away, I'll walk them out to that mailbox a few miles back. You can pick them up there. They'll follow me and they'll take a rope if you're easy."

"I'll come back when I figure out where to move them to." Tye couldn't stop watching the beautiful animals. "If it's all right, I'd like to work with them awhile before I go, get them used to me."

Dusty's grin was toothless. "Shouldn't be too hard. I've been telling them you were coming for years."

"In a strange way, I feel like I've been getting ready for them. Thanks, Dusty. My grandfather had the best of friends."

"You just take care of them 'til the world ends. If death gets me before the bombs come, I want your word in writing that you'll come get the four left here. I'd hate to think of them out here hungry."

Hayley felt a tear falling as she watched them shake hands.

CHAPTER THIRTY-EIGHT

December 22
Maverick Ranch

Elliot was packing up all the files when Jess stepped into the office. They were almost finished with the last of the accounting. All the documents were stacked on his desk. She was right. Two hours' work was all it would take to wrap up the year's books if they worked together.

Elliot would enjoy the time now they'd stopped fighting. There was a peace between them.

To his surprise, she had on jeans and a Western shirt. She couldn't have looked more out of her element if she'd been wearing a Halloween costume. He'd gotten used to the very proper suits and the silk blouses.

She twirled. "I figured if I was going to spend the day on a ranch, I might as well look the part."

"We're not finished working on the books." He had to be the voice of reason, even if he could still feel her sleeping in his arms.

"We can finish up tonight or early in the morning. If I leave

by eleven tomorrow, I should drive into Houston long before
it's dark. It'll just give me time to pack before we head for Paris.
Now, it's just simple paperwork, Elliot. I'd rather start the day
with you." She moved closer and brushed her hand down his
shirtsleeve.

"Where'd you find the clothes?" He couldn't take his eyes
off her face. Somehow she looked younger.

"I ordered them a few days ago. Dani said FedEx knows the
route here well. When I got here, I felt so out of place. I thought
if I changed clothes maybe people would stop calling me 'the
accountant.'"

"You look great." He had to fight not to touch her.

One day, he thought. One day with his Jess and then she'd be
gone forever. He had to do everything right. One day to show
her why he'd stayed all those years ago.

"Thanks. I feel short in the boots. I'm too used to heels. Do
boots come with four-inch heels?"

Elliot had no idea if she was making a joke or being serious
so he asked a question. "Where do you want to start?"

"Show me your ranch. I was a self-absorbed kid when I came
before. Now I want to see it through your eyes."

He offered his hand and suddenly they were running. He
wanted her to remember this place for the rest of her life. They
might only have a day, but he planned to plant a memory in
her mind forever.

First, they spent an hour at the barn. Slowly she lost her fear
of the horses, and it turned out she loved petting the tiny colt.
Elliot explained far more than she needed to know. In the future, the only horses she'd see would be in parades.

Tatum joined them on a drive around the ranch, and when
they got back, he stole her away to see the chicks.

Elliot joined Cooper on the porch to wait for her to come

back. His brother seemed to think his new job was to worry about the doc.

"Strange thing happened a few minutes ago." Coop filled his brother in. "One of the Franklin sisters called Dani and mentioned that a long-lost relative had dropped by the inn. Turns out it's our Tye."

Elliot shrugged. Like Cooper, who'd missed all the drama from the kitchen, he was confused as to why Dani would care one way or the other where Tye was.

"Dani talking to the Franklins was nothing new," Coop explained. "They exchange recipes from time to time. But the sisters invited her to supper tonight."

Elliot frowned. "You know what that means?"

"What?"

"We're having pizza tonight. It's Jess's last night."

Coop grinned. "How about we have it in the bunkhouse? That'll add lots of atmosphere."

Elliot didn't want to take her off the ranch, but he wasn't sure about a bunkhouse supper. "Sure, but we won't stay long, and Doc has to come along. I don't want Jess to be the only woman at the table."

Coop nodded. "I'll plan the whole thing. Don't worry."

They rocked for a while watching the weather. Clouds were building.

"Elliot, we're turning into two old men visiting on the porch."

"Yeah, I know. Got any ideas of what I can show Jess? I thought I'd show her the west pasture at sunset, but that's hours away. I don't want to bore her or do anything to make her mad today."

"Why don't you marry her? Then you two could argue in your bedroom and not wake the whole house up. That accountant is growing on me."

Elliot was silent for a moment and then he said simply, "She's leaving in the morning. She has to be in Houston by dark to catch a plane to Paris."

"You sure?"

"Positive."

Coop shrugged. "Well, then, show her a good time today. The best. Then she'll always remember what she walked away from."

"I thought I'd take her riding, but I'm not sure she'd get on even our gentlest mount."

"Then pull out that old buggy in the barn. She might like that."

Thirty minutes later, Elliot had Jess and Tatum in the buggy. Tatum was driving, which had Jess laughing.

"We'll be back for lunch. I wish it was warm enough to have a picnic." Elliot waved goodbye over Tatum's laughing.

After a few minutes of wind, Jess opened Elliot's coat and cuddled against him as she settled in for the ride. He thought of having Tatum circle back to get her a jacket, but then he decided he kind of liked it the way it was.

When Jess spread her fingers over his heart, he could feel her warm touch through the cotton of his shirt, and he knew he was the one storing memories for a lifetime.

"This would be perfect if I had a cup of Starbucks coffee."

"I'll build you one if you stay."

Jess laughed. "I heard about Cooper's plan to build a clinic. Tell him just to ask her what she wants. I'm betting she'll say him. Nothing more. Just him."

Tatum followed directions as they moved along a path that headed toward the ribbon of hills that ran along the north border of the ranch.

"What's out here?" Jess asked.

"Nothing much. The Winter Valley, where Coop was, is over there, circled by those hills, but I'm taking you two to a very special place. When my dad was a little boy, he loved trees and wanted all kinds. He planted maybe a hundred in a small canyon over here so they'd be sheltered from the wind."

Elliot laughed. "I guess you could say all the men in my family have a thing for trees. My great-grandfather planted fruit trees, though in truth I think his love was more for fruit pies than trees."

As they rode into the canyon, the colors of late fall surrounded them. Some of the trees were still green, but others looked naked in the wind. The cottonwoods near a stream were the oldest. The evergreens were the tallest.

"It's beautiful." Jess stood up and Elliot had to hold her in the buggy until Tatum could stop. "I've never seen anything so lovely."

Elliot laughed. "Dad used to call this place his church. He buried Mom up above the tree line, and we put him beside her when he died. I kind of thought they'd like looking down on these sheltered trees, watching the colors change. The hills block most of the wind.

"The first Christmas after my folks died, we decided to cut one evergreen down for the house each year. It's kind of like having them near. Then, behind where they're buried, we plant ten new trees every spring. As the years go by, they'll become a part of the forest, surrounded by evergreens."

He climbed out of the buggy, secured the reins, then helped Jess down. "I thought you two could help me pick a tree out for the great room at headquarters. I'll tag it and have it moved. We'll need one about twenty feet high with wide branches."

Tatum took his assignment seriously, wandering around and examining every tree.

Jess simply walked around, smiling. Finally, she extended her arms and closed her eyes. "I know how your dad must have felt. There is a peace here."

As they walked, Elliot took her hand. "When Griffin and

Sunlan married, they made garlands from some of these branches for their wedding. They even cut mistletoe."

"It must have been grand, but I'd have moved the wedding here."

He wanted to kiss her, right here, right now, but that wasn't what the day was about. This was time for them to become friends, to mend a bit of the pain they'd caused each other.

But hell, he wanted to kiss her all the time. He wished he could get down on one knee and ask her to marry him. Only she'd already told him several times that she'd be marrying Richard. Then she'd have all she'd ever wanted. She'd be happy. She'd reach her goal.

As they continued walking, they didn't talk.

They picked a tree and Jess helped Tatum collect an armful of leaves. They walked back to the buggy with Tatum talking.

The boy was feeding the horse an apple when Elliot lifted Jess up. But he didn't put her in the buggy. He raised her above his head, then slowly lowered her close until her lips met his.

The kiss was so tender he felt a tremor, as if an earthquake was happening. She wrapped her arms around his neck and held on tight. They were silently saying goodbye again.

Tatum broke the mood when he jumped in the other side of the buggy. Elliot slowly lowered her inside. Neither said a word, but once Tatum had turned the buggy around and they were headed back, she opened the side of Elliot's coat and cuddled against him as if that was her place.

On the way home, he held her a bit tighter than he had before, and wondered how he'd ever let her go again.

CHAPTER THIRTY-NINE

December 22
Maverick Ranch

Cooper decided to sit on the porch another hour and worry. Maybe the doc would come back by then. It was either that or start drinking. If he did that, he'd never be able to handle the crutches.

The Garrett brothers came out to keep him company. They claimed their mother had told them to stay out of her personal life.

"I didn't even know she had one," Pete complained. "Isn't she too old to have a personal life? Seems to me she gave that up when she had us."

Patrick looked like he was thinking and it seemed a painful process to him. "I think maybe we should go away for a while. Give her some space. In a few months she'll be begging us to come home."

"I don't want to go home. It's no good without Mom to keep the place up and cook." Pete looked as miserable as his brother.

"I like living in the bunkhouse. Maybe that's where we belong while Mom's having her personal life."

Cooper thought it wiser not to comment. He switched the conversation to the two cousins they'd driven all over Texas. Apparently, the girls had been perfect ladies. Which surprised Cooper.

"How about you men take a trailer that will haul two horses and drive up to the pass at Winter Valley? You can leave it for Creed, if he ever decides to come down, and you can drive the doc's Jeep back. That will give you both time to think, maybe plan."

"It'll take half the day." Pete sounded like he was taking on a huge load.

"You men can handle it. Ask your mother to pack two coolers. One for you two to snack from, and the other to leave in the truck. I'm guessing Creed and Dallas will be hungry for something besides soup and power bars when they come down."

"Will do," Pete said, but he made no effort to get started on his journey.

Cooper realized the boys had changed lately. Maybe they were growing up. He wondered if he had the cousins to thank for that. Driving them all over, first Lubbock and then Dallas, would make any man want to seek the quiet life.

When a sports car turned off the county road, the brothers stayed around to see who was coming.

Cooper didn't try to stand as he watched the company coming. In his grandfather's day, uninvited people were welcomed with a shotgun in hand. Today, all he had was the Garrett brothers. They'd have to do.

When a stranger, dressed in a suit and tie, stepped out and started up the steps, Coop asked, "What d'you need, mister?"

The man looked bothered to have to talk to the help. "I'm

here to see Mr. Holloway. I was told Dr. Westland is staying here. If you could direct me, I'd like to talk to her."

Cooper decided it was time to stand. "I'm Mr. Holloway, and she's not here. In fact, I'm not sure where she is. Who are you?" The guy didn't look like a salesman or a relative. If he'd been family he'd have called her Hayley.

"I'm Johnson Sanders. I'm Hayley's fiancé, or I would be, if she ever comes to her senses."

The Garrett brothers growled. They didn't like the guy any better than Cooper did.

Cooper managed to keep his voice calm. "Is she expecting you?"

"No, but I told her I'd come around before the end of the year, and this time I'm not leaving until we set a date. It's been three years. She doesn't know her own mind. I'm the best offer of marriage that she'll ever have. Without me, she'll be stuck here in nowhere-land, living alone in that dump of a house her grandfather left her."

Cooper leaned on his crutch. "Let me get this straight, you're not dating her, but you've come to ask her to marry you?"

"Not that it's any of your business, Mr. Holloway, but if you must know, we were dating and she got the crazy idea that we take a break."

"How long ago was that?"

"Three years ago. I gave her some time. Like I said, she doesn't know her own mind. She needs someone to tell her what to do. Take care of her. Keep track of her. Put the brakes on when she gets one of her ideas or takes off on a mission to save some animal no one cares about, anyway."

"She saved my life," Cooper said. "I'm glad she took off on that mission."

"I'm sure she helped you, but I doubt Hayley has ever saved anyone's life. She's a vet. If she had any brains, she wouldn't have spent eight years of college becoming a vet to make only sixty thousand a year. If that much. She needs to be working with pets, not horses."

Johnson straightened. "Now, it's been nice talking to you, but I really am short on time. Tell me where she might be and I'll find her."

Cooper turned to the brothers. "You men want to show him the way to Winter Valley? She was up there last week. It's a clear day. He should have no trouble walking through the trees. She might be there."

Looking at the stranger, Coop added, "Just park your car next to her Jeep and head up the hill."

Johnson took one look at the two men behind Cooper and said, "Never mind, boys. I have GPS. I'll find it myself. How hard can it be? You can see a hundred miles in every direction in this godforsaken country."

Coop had to eat a few words before he managed to speak. "If you get lost, light a fire. We'll take on a mission to find you."

One of the Garrett boys tossed him a lighter.

"I never get lost." He looked insulted, but he pocketed the lighter.

Cooper sat back in his rocker and watched the red sports car drive off toward the hills, which were barely visible in the distance.

"Do you think you should have told him all cell service runs out at the pass?" Patrick asked.

Coop shook his head. "He'll figure it out. If you see him when you drop off the trailer, don't bring him back here. I don't care where you direct him to, but it better not be here."

Pete puffed up. "Can you believe he thought he was gonna tell our little doctor what to do? She's not some pet trained to come when he calls. She took charge when you were dying, practically carried you in to the shack by herself, yelled at you to keep breathing."

Raising an eyebrow, Coop asked, "How do you know all this? You weren't there."

"Tatum told the whole bunkhouse at dinner last night. That how it happened? He even said you asked her out while she was sewing up the gaps in your head."

"Yep." Coop shrugged. Tatum had been more awake than he was. Sounded like an eyewitness account.

All the words he'd mumbled to himself and Elliot this morning came back to Cooper. He never realized how wrong he'd been acting until some idiot in a suit held a mirror up to his face.

"Boys, pull your mother's ATV around. You're driving me to the barn before you leave. I've got work to do. I've sat around enough."

Five minutes later Cooper was back to work and had every man tackling new projects. In a few days, most of them would be heading home for Christmas, and the place needed to be in top shape.

CHAPTER FORTY

December 22

By the time the buggy made it back and they'd eaten lunch, decorating was in full swing. Elliot had a text telling him that Griffin and Sunlan were flying home with Jaci tomorrow morning. Sunlan's dad was out of any danger.

The house had to be ready. Elliot found men to go up to bring down the tree, and Jess helped with getting every neatly marked box down from the attic and placed in the right room.

Right in the middle of the mess, a tall woman with flaming red hair walked in on the arm of a lean cowboy with several days' growth of beard.

"Creed!" Elliot and Coop both yelled. "You're back." Both Holloways started patting the foreman on the back as if he might be choking.

The redhead looked bothered. "Well, what about me? I'm back, too."

Everyone watched Jess hug her awkwardly. "Welcome back.

Dallas, right? We haven't formally met, but I've heard a great deal about you."

"Yes, I'm Dallas, and you're the accountant. You've apparently gone native. Don't accountants usually wear suits? Personally, I wouldn't trust one who didn't."

Jess took no offense. "I'm glad you're back."

Elliot gave his almost cousin a one-armed hug. "Me, too. We need to help get this place ready. By nightfall, it's going to be nothing but Christmas around here."

Dallas straightened to her full six feet. "I must have a bath first. Then, while we decorate, I want to talk to you about putting a proper bathroom in the line shack. Maybe a kitchen, too. And windows so you can see the view. And a porch. Those rocks just don't work. Of course, it should be painted the color of the sky up there. I'll help you with the colors you'll need."

She whirled, hitting Elliot in the face with her wild hair, and headed upstairs to her room. "I'll be back when the hot water runs out."

Elliot turned to Creed. "How'd it go up there? Seems like you were gone forever."

"Fine. The mustangs were all treated. They'll be all right for another year, the doc said. Tye was a great help."

"No, not that." Elliot tried again as he looked toward the stairs. "I meant how did it go with Dallas?"

For once Creed acted like he didn't hear the boss's question. "I should inform you, I ran into a guy wandering around, looking for the doc. Told him he was heading in the wrong direction. He said some things about the doc and I corrected him." Creed grinned. "He didn't look like he planned to take my advice on which way to go."

"Good, but what about you and Dallas?"

"It was fine." Creed's face was blank.

"Anything else?"

"Her hair went curly when she washed it in the river."

Elliot gave up. Creed wasn't a talker. "After you clean up, go with the men to bring down an evergreen, would you?"

"No problem." Creed disappeared as silently as usual.

Five minutes later, Coop yelled from the front door, "That red sports car is back. The Garrett boys must have missed him. I told them not to invite him back here."

Elliot decided he'd better stand beside Cooper. From what he'd heard, Coop didn't like the stranger, but there didn't need to be a scene. Just telling him to get off their land would be enough. He lifted down his grandfather's old rifle from the mantel. It hadn't been fired in fifty years, but it'd probably scare off a man who was dumb enough to drive a back road in a sports car.

Cooper was watching the car pull up when Elliot stepped out.

The man in a wrinkled suit, with one pant leg ripped, stormed up the steps. When he saw Elliot standing behind Cooper he backed down one.

"Are you aware, Mr. Holloway, that you gave me the wrong directions?"

"I told you I didn't know where the doc is right now, but you didn't seem to like that answer. So I guessed." Cooper leaned down, looking at the stranger more carefully. "You got a black eye, Johnson?"

"That's another complaint I have. Are you aware that you have a mad cowboy riding around up there? I told him I was looking for the doc because she probably didn't have the sense to find her way home. Without a word the man slugged me. I can feel my eye swelling closed as we speak."

Coop looked back at Elliot, and they both mouthed, *Creed*.

Johnson jerked out his card. "I'll find her. If she comes by here, give her my card."

"Will do." Coop shoved the card in his pocket.

"Tell her to call me right away. Evidently she changed her

number and forgot to let me know. I swear she has butter for brains."

"Good day," Cooper said.

When the stranger hesitated, Elliot raised the rifle a few inches.

Johnson turned and walked to his car, but before he stepped in, he turned back. "It frightens me to think she even knows someone like you, Holloway."

Coop smiled. "I was having that very same thought."

The brothers watched him drive away.

"You going to give the doc that man's card?" Elliot whispered as he rested the rifle on his shoulder.

Coop nodded. "I will. It's her decision to make, not mine. Hayley is a woman who knows her own mind."

Elliot stared at his brother. "What blew through here since we talked this morning?"

"Johnson Sanders blew through, and the way he talked about the doc left a bad taste in my mouth."

"So you're not going to tell her what to do when she gets back?"

"Nope. I think I'll just listen."

CHAPTER FORTY-ONE

December 22
Crossroads, Texas

It was almost dark by the time Tye and the doc made it back to Crossroads. She'd invited him back to the ranch for supper, but he'd said he had plans. He knew she'd be welcomed to join him for dinner with the sisters, but she shook her head.

"Spend your days off with them. You'll enjoy it and so will they."

When she let him off, he shook her hand. "Thanks. I'd never have found those horses if you hadn't been with me. I feel like the old man gave me a fresh start and I aim to take advantage of it."

"You would have found Dusty on your own. Do you have any idea what you're going to do with them? They've got to be worth close to a million dollars, maybe more."

"I'm not going to sell them. It's like they're part of my family. I've got to find a way to take care of them. They're depending on me. I don't think Dusty will mind me keeping them there until I find the right place."

"Good luck, Tye."

"You, too, Doc. I'll see you around."

Tye walked up the winding sidewalk to the bed-and-breakfast, planning his next move. If he went back to work for the Holloways, he could pay for feed and still save most of his pay. A few evenings a week he'd go over and work with the horses. A few needed work on their hooves. All could use a good brushing.

He'd never been responsible for anyone but himself, and the weight on his shoulders somehow made him feel stronger. Twenty-seven horses. He owned a herd.

As he stepped into the Franklin sisters' old home, he smelled a pot roast cooking. He and Hayley hadn't stopped to eat lunch, and right now, home cooking smelled like heaven.

When he got to the kitchen door, he saw Dani sitting at the table, visiting with the sisters. She had on a shirt he'd never seen. It was green, like her eyes.

Eyes that no longer held anger.

Tye smiled. Things were looking up. She didn't have a plate in her hand or any offspring in sight.

Daisy bounced up and hugged him. "Finally, you're here. We invited another guest. She says she knows you."

Tye removed his hat. "Danielle."

"Tyson," she answered.

Even if they'd had anything else to say, neither guest could get a word in between the chatter of the sisters. As Daisy set food on the table and Rose poured tea, Daisy said, "Dani brought us a basket of biscuits and some honey. She told us she thought you once said you liked her biscuits."

Tye smiled, deciding this was about the best day of his life, and he was stone-cold sober. As they talked and ate, he couldn't take his eyes off Dani.

Finally, when the dishes were done and the sisters said goodnight, he walked Dani out to her car.

"Are you coming back to the ranch?" she whispered.

"I am. I'll even let your boys beat me up this time, but I'm not stopping seeing you until you tell me to go."

"I'm not doing that. Not ever, I think. You ate half a dozen of my biscuits tonight. You owe me several nights, so you best be thinking of taking naps."

He laughed and kissed her. His hands moved beneath her coat and touched her. "Did I ever tell you that I love the way you feel?"

"Many times. When you get back, I expect you to prove it."

"I'll be back tomorrow."

"I'll be waiting tomorrow night."

He stood in the dark and watched her drive away. She'd come after him, he decided. He liked that she was so brave. No one had ever cared that much for him.

Tye walked slowly up to his room. He doubted he'd sleep much tonight. He had plans to make.

CHAPTER FORTY-TWO

December 22
Maverick Ranch

To Elliot's surprise, supper in the bunkhouse turned out to be a great success. Hayley had made a huge salad to go with the dozen pizzas that were delivered, and Dallas had driven to town and bought brownies and ice cream for dessert. When she served the brownies with ice cream and a cherry on top, she told all the men that she'd made it herself.

A few of the guys were playing guitars, and all were on their best behavior. They played through all the old country favorites. When Dallas asked Tatum to dance, all the men cheered them on.

Elliot stayed longer than he'd planned, but Jess seemed to be having so much fun he couldn't call it a night. He was seeing the ranch through her eyes, and she was seeing it through his.

"Did you have fun?" he said as they walked from the bunkhouse to the main headquarters.

"I did." She cuddled up to him as they walked. "It's a different world out here."

"I guess so." He thought about it and added, "It's my world."

"I know. Today I learned just how much you gave up even to dream in my world for a while. I didn't know the life you had here was so rich."

"It's just life." He'd never walked in her life, either. He had no idea what her days were like now. Living where she couldn't see the sky. Never walking on dirt.

She let out a sigh. "We never got around to finishing up today."

"It's too late tonight. The paperwork can wait. How about we work in the morning?"

She nodded. "All I have to do is make it back before six. Or as you'd put it, before dark."

He escorted her to the stairs and stopped.

Jess turned and looked up at him. "You coming up?"

"No. I don't think I could sleep next to you tonight without doing a whole lot more than sleeping."

"It's all right," she whispered as she hugged him. "I'd like loving you tonight. For old times' sake. We were always great together. I don't think we ever had an argument in bed." She tugged on his shirt.

"I can't." He pushed a few inches away. "You're planning to marry someone else. Before, all those years ago, I thought we were going to marry, we were almost married, already married in our hearts. Whatever you want to call it. But now it'd be something else." He studied her face, memorizing every curve. "I'm not a man who can settle for something else, Jess, no matter how much I wish I was right now."

He saw the disappointment in her eyes. "I can't be your fling before you walk down the aisle with Richard."

She started up the stairs, then turned. "You want this as much as I do."

"It's not fair, Jess. Not to any of us."

"It's not right, you mean." Tears rolled down her cheeks. "It's not right and Elliot Holloway always does what is right, no matter who he hurts."

The pain was back. They were going to part hating each other again. He felt he was going a hundred miles an hour toward a concrete wall and he knew he was going to crash and burn. Again!

"Do you love Richard more than you love me?"

"No. But it doesn't matter. I'm marrying him."

He saw that his hurt was hers, as well. "Ask yourself if getting what you want is worth sacrificing you and me for. I can't love anyone else while I'm still in love with you, and you won't be happy married to a man you don't love. You might as well send us both to hell."

She turned and ran up the stairs. He gripped the railing so hard he was surprised the wood didn't splinter in his hand.

The thought of going to bed without her seemed impossible. He grabbed his coat and stepped outside. He might as well be cold outside, because he felt frozen inside.

Tonight he saw none of the beauty of his ranch. There was no joy in his world; he'd gone deaf and blind to everything. Maybe the only way he could survive was to feel nothing, to see nothing, to love nothing.

The night was cool, but not freezing. Normally, he loved fresh air. He worked with his office windows open year-round, and he slept with his bedroom window raised. But tonight he could barely breathe. The air might as well be dusted with coal.

He moved to the rocker in the darkest corner of the porch. Logs shot out where a bay window had been built in the office. There he became invisible.

Part of him wanted to scream that tonight was not the time to do the right thing. For once he should have gone with his feelings. He should have climbed the stairs. He could be holding her now if he stopped thinking.

Music drifted in the air from the bunkhouse. He heard horses shifting in the corral, restless as the wind howling through the night. A barn owl hooted.

The ranch was still breathing, very much alive, but Elliot had turned to stone. He didn't feel the cold. He didn't care about the time. He couldn't figure out how to live without a heart.

The big old house seemed to settle with the night. One by one, the lights went out. Tatum opened a window on the second floor and howled at the wind, then banged it closed. Cooper and the doc went into the house by way of the side door. Probably planning to have a midnight snack.

Dallas didn't come in at all. Elliot knew she could take care of herself. She was the only coed who was in her seventh year of college and hadn't managed to get a degree in anything.

He remembered those carefree years with Jess by his side. He was happy then. His family was close and what they did here was rewarding. Maybe Jess simply wanted to go back to those days for a night.

Only life didn't work that way.

One question haunted his thoughts: If he'd gone with her into the business world all those years ago, would he be happier now?

The same answer kept coming back. *No.* She had to stay with her life plan no matter what it cost her, and he had to do what was right. He had to stay were he belonged.

Elliot wasn't sure if he'd gone numb or if he'd fallen asleep, but the blink of a desk lamp in his office woke him.

Jess was wearing one of her suit coats over her pajamas. She crawled into his desk chair and picked up the landline. For a few minutes she just held the phone, then she dialed.

"Hello, Dad."

Elliot could hear her clearly through the slit of the open window.

"I know it's late, Dad, but I wanted to tell you I won't be home tomorrow. I won't make the flight to Paris."

He watched her rub her forehead and listen for a while.

"I know it was our plan. I know everyone else is going. But, Dad, I can't."

He could hear her softly crying as she listened for several beats.

"Dad, it's over between Richard and me. I tried to tell you before I left. It has been for a long time. I felt like the only reason we were together was so we could take over the firm. Dad, I can't marry him when I still love another. I want more. I want my lover to be my partner, too."

She cried for a few minutes more, then said, "I know I'm throwing away the perfect life, but I've decided I don't want the perfect life. It didn't work out for you and Mom, and I don't think it will for me.

"I know. I will. I'm sure."

After a few minutes she put down the phone without saying goodbye, and Elliot wondered if her father had hung up on her. Her father had never visited Jess when they were in college. Always said he didn't have time. When she planned to go home most of the holidays, her dad would call and tell her to use her time wisely and study.

Elliot watched her crumble as she gave up on the dream she'd worked toward all her life. But it hadn't been *her* dream. Elliot only had to listen to half of the conversation to know that.

After a few minutes she dialed another number and waited. "Richard, I hate to say this in a voice mail, but it is time to tell our parents there will be no marriage. I can't pretend anymore, and you have to stop saying I'll see the light and give in. I'll give the ring back, so you can give it to whomever you're sleeping with tonight. There is no need to call. I won't be changing my mind. I won't be going with you to Paris. You were right about one thing: getting away did make me see more clearly, only I didn't have to go to France. I found the truth in Texas."

As she hung up, he watched her chin lift just a bit. Jess was a survivor. He wanted to go to her and hold her, but she'd done this alone. She hadn't mentioned to Richard that she'd found another.

He sat in the cold night and took on the sorrow that was in them both tonight. Her father didn't seem too happy with her. She'd lost any chance of becoming a partner and maybe she'd lost her job.

Where would she go?

He might not have been the cause of this mess, but he'd been the catalyst. Come morning, she might hate him as much as he hated cheating old Richard.

A misty rain started falling. Elliot watched as it turned to snow. Tomorrow, Griffin and his family would be home. It'd be two days until Christmas. Neighbors would come over. They'd go to the church service in Crossroads. They'd finish decorating the tree and hand out presents.

Elliot would live through another Christmas pretending to be happy.

What do you want for Christmas? the wind seemed to whisper.

Only one thing came to his mind. He wanted Jess in his life.

Like a man drunk on sorrow, Elliot stood and went inside. He walked through the big house, feeling so empty inside he wouldn't be surprised if he collapsed.

Cooper's door was open, and he was snoring. Elliot silently closed the door and moved down the hallway to his room.

He didn't bother to turn on a light. The glow of a snowy midnight offered him enough light to strip off his clothes and crawl into bed.

The warmth of another body made him jerk backward. He moved his hand into Jess's curly blond hair and, as always, the soft curls circled around his fingers.

"Jess. What are you doing here?"

"I don't want to be alone tonight. I want to be with you. Can I just sleep here?"

He pulled her close. "Of course. Go to sleep. We'll talk about it in the morning."

Suddenly the world didn't seem so black. He rested his forehead on hers.

After a while, he asked, "Any chance you'd say yes to marrying me?"

"Yes, there's a chance. How about we talk about it in the morning? I'm asleep right now."

CHAPTER FORTY-THREE

December 23
Maverick Ranch

Tye settled back in his room at the bunkhouse the next morning. The Franklin sisters said he could stay with them as long as he wanted to—with the relative discount, of course—but he wanted to move back to the ranch. He was more comfortable there, where Dani was near.

Strange how a woman could become part of you so quickly. For years, he hadn't thought he had enough heart even to love himself, but it turned out his heart was just empty. He didn't know what the future would bring, but he knew Dani would be in it.

A laugh rumbled up from deep inside. She was something. That day she was mad at him, throwing plates at him, was tattooed on his memory. He'd decided right then that she was the most beautiful woman he'd ever seen. For a man who rode wild horses for a living, Tye didn't need a sweet, meek woman.

As he headed toward the main house, he knew he wanted to walk to work every morning and walk back to Dani every night.

He'd checked on the horses before he'd unpacked. Someday, he'd have an operation like they had here in the white barn. He'd breed fine horses. He'd train them to be gentle. In ten years, he could have a big business.

When he stepped into the kitchen doorway, Dani was cooking. Her hair was pulled back in a ponytail, and her cheeks were red from the heat. He just stood and stared. "I swear, you get prettier every day, darlin'."

She laughed. "You're just hungry."

They were alone. He knew it wouldn't last, but he'd take what time he could steal. He walked up to her and kissed her lightly on the cheek. She pushed him away gently with a promise in her eyes.

"I want to say one more time that I'm sorry about the plates."

"Not necessary."

She studied him. "You're a man who forgives easy."

"I decided I don't mind a woman who gets fired up now and then."

"Then you're going to love me, Tye Franklin."

He smiled. "I already do."

Voices came from the main part of the house and their moment was over, but he quickly whispered, "Maybe I'll see some of that fire tonight for other reasons."

"I certainly hope so. Now, sit down. You don't have to worry about my boys. Cooper sent them over to the Kirkland place to wait for Griffin. Kirkland has a bigger airstrip and he lends it to Sunlan so she won't have to worry about sliding. The way it's snowing they'd better get in early or the roads between the ranches might be closed."

Cooper limped in, laughing, with the doc. Elliot made it in

next with Tatum following a few feet behind. The moment he saw Tye, the boy ran to him and gave Tye a hug.

Tye wasn't sure what to do so he patted the boy's back and said, "If you get time this morning, have Dani drive you over to the barn. I need help with that colt. He doesn't seem to want anyone to brush him but you."

"I will." Tatum plopped down next to Tye and poured honey on his biscuit.

Creed blew in with the wind from the open kitchen door.

As they all took their seats, Tatum asked, "Where is Dallas? She's going to teach me to dance today."

Creed took his coffee from Dani and said simply, "She's still asleep."

No one said a word. They all stared at Creed, but he didn't look up from his food.

Tye finally turned to the foreman and suggested they bring the tree inside after breakfast.

"Good idea," Creed answered. "We hammered in the boards for the stand yesterday."

Suddenly, everyone wanted to talk about the decorations. Creed finished his meal and silently drank his coffee, apparently having said all he'd had to say.

By midmorning, everyone on the ranch was working on hanging garlands or putting bulbs on the tree. Tye noticed the accountant was helping, instead of bent over her desk working. For once, she seemed happy. Maybe she'd finally finished her work.

Elliot returned again and again to her side.

By noon, the air was full of the smells of the holiday. Dani made spiced apple cider and put out a spread of sandwiches with all the trimmings.

Tye was watching all the chaos when Griffin and his family arrived. The toddler's hair was white blond, just like her mother's. She had a funny name, too—Jaci. Who would name a girl Jaci? Probably a mother named Sunlan.

It was like a three-ring circus had been set up in the great room. Everyone was shouting and hugging and laughing.

Everyone but Tatum. He sat four steps up on the staircase, watching.

Tye decided to join him.

"You all right, son?"

"I'm fine. I'm just trying to see it all, so I can remember."

"I know how you feel. I never had much family."

"Me, either."

Tye put his arm around the boy and changed the subject. They began comparing all the people to a herd and before long they were laughing. When Dallas wandered in, looking a bit like a stray cat, Tatum was into the game. He decided Dallas looked like a red fox who'd fought her way out of a trap.

As the women settled on the couches to talk, Tye noticed Elliot draw his brothers into the office. After a few minutes, Griffin stepped out and asked his beautiful wife to join the men.

Something was going on. A family meeting.

Sunlan had left the two-year-old with Creed, who did not look happy. As soon as the doors to the office were closed, Jaci began to cry. Creed tried to pass off the toddler to Dallas, but the redhead wouldn't touch her. She acted like she might catch something if she did. Hayley and Jess were standing on ladders, trying to hang the last of the ornaments, so they were no help.

Tatum glanced at Tye. "I've got to take care of this."

"She's just a newborn in a strange place. You know what to do," Tye answered.

Tatum stepped between Creed and Dallas, picked up the baby and sat her on the floor. While she cried, he began drawing circles in the thick rug. After a few minutes she began to watch. Before long her tiny hands were digging through the wool, making her own patterns.

When the office door opened, little Jaci smiled at her mother.

Elliot moved to the center of the room and waved Jess and Hayley down from their decorating. "I have an announcement that will not wait."

His brothers flanked him and all three looked down at Tatum.

Tye fought the urge to grab the kid. He knew what the boy was thinking. He remembered being about that age when his mother put him in foster care for the first time. She'd always come back and get him in a few months to take him to a new dump of an apartment to live until the money or the job ran out. Then he was back to being the state's problem for a while. News—any news—was always bad.

Elliot began, "We've been working with the sheriff and the courts to find the one relative Tatum might have. Yesterday they found her. A half sister of his mother. She's thirty years old and lives in Oklahoma City." Before anyone could say anything, he hurried on. "She wishes Tatum well, but said she has more kids than she can handle now. She did, however, give her written permission for Tatum to stay here until his adoption works it way through the courts."

"What does that mean?" Tatum sounded angry.

Cooper crouched down as far as he could with his cast and crutches. "Don't start packing for the hills, Tatum. It means that in a few months we'd like to change your name to Holloway. This place will always be your home."

Tatum shook his head, clearly not believing a word. "Which one of you is adopting me?"

Griffin lowered to one knee. "We all are. My name will be on the papers because I'm married. The lawyer thinks it would go through faster. But Cooper and Elliot will take care of you here, if you want to stay."

Elliot smiled down at the boy, who was starting to consider the idea.

"I can stay here at the ranch forever."

"You'll grow up here, unless you'd rather not be a Holloway. There will be times you might like to go to the ranch in the mountains of Colorado."

Tye watched Tatum study each man. "I'd better stay here. I've got a lot of work to do."

A cheer went up in the room, and all at once, everyone was hugging Tatum.

Dani came in to see what was going on and Tye hugged her right in front of everyone.

"I do love you, Danielle," he whispered against her ear. "As soon as I can save up enough to buy a little land, I plan to ask you to marry me. I own a few horses I plan to breed."

She studied him. "You own horses?"

"Twenty-seven, to be exact."

She straightened his hair and smiled. "I got land. What are you waiting for, cowboy? You do the asking and I'll do the saying yes."

He grinned. She did have land. She'd told him all about her place. Good water, good pasture. "What about your boys?"

"Griffin asked them if they'd like to move up to Sunlan's Colorado place. She said he could use a few men up there. The boys are excited to be traveling, seeing the world." She grinned. "Or at least another state."

No one noticed Tye and Dani slip from the room as they whispered about biscuits.

CHAPTER FORTY-FOUR

December 23

Elliot walked the sleeping house, smiling. He and Jess had never got around to the books today, but he knew neither of them cared. She hadn't mentioned leaving, either. He'd pulled her away from the crowd a few times, but they hadn't talked. There wasn't time; they were both too hungry to touch.

He had no idea where she was. With no crisis, she probably wasn't waiting for him in her bedroom on the third floor. He was positive about where they stood: he knew he still loved her, and she still loved him. Maybe that was enough for now.

When he opened his bedroom door, she was under his covers. When she rose onto her elbow he could see she wasn't wearing a nightgown.

"Did we change rooms and you forgot to tell me?"

"No. I'm sleeping with you tonight, Elliot." She wiggled her hand, showing off the engagement ring he'd given her in college, the one he hadn't wanted back. "Unless you're taking back your proposal, I'd like to sleep with my husband-to-be."

Elliot walked to her side of the bed, sat and picked up her left hand. "You kept this? I thought you'd probably tossed it away somewhere years ago."

"I locked it away for years, and then, when Richard asked me to marry him, I started wearing it on a chain beneath my blouse."

She sat up, seemingly unaware that she had no top on.

He, on the other hand, had lost the ability to speak.

"Richard wasn't the one who wanted me to come here. I was. Part of me still hated you, but somehow I still felt bound to you. Like you said, we were married in our hearts. I told myself I'd see to the books. See how you lived, and finally be able to toss the ring. I came here to prove I no longer had one drop of love for you in me."

"And what happened?" He forced himself to stare into her eyes.

"It didn't work, so if you agree, I'd say we continue the engagement until the wedding happens."

He kissed the ring on the third finger of her left hand. "I meant it when I said I'd love you forever."

"And a day," she said and smiled.

"And a day," he answered as he stood, removing his clothes. "Right now, I want to make love to you."

She pulled the covers up over her. "Are you sure it's right?"

"I'm sure. I can't even wait one more day."

His Jess was laughing. "In one more day, it'll be Christmas Eve."

"I know. It'll make it easy to remember our anniversary for the next fifty or sixty years."

"What makes you think I want to live with you that long?"

"Because, Jess, we're already married."

For once, she didn't argue with him.

CHAPTER FORTY-FIVE

December 24
Maverick Ranch

Hayley walked out of the front door of headquarters with her bag in her hand and noticed Cooper on the porch.

He'd been watching the clouds and wondering how long it'd be before he could ride again.

"I'm heading out," she said. "One of the Collins mules got in a fight with a pack of coyotes last night."

"The Collins place is forty miles away and the roads are slick. I'm not sure it'll be above freezing for a while."

"I know."

She looked so pretty he fought the need to tell her she was as cute as a bug...again.

"Drive safe." He grinned. "I'm still dreaming about that date we're going to have. As soon as I can, I plan to take you dancing."

She tilted her head like she always did when she didn't quite believe him. "You're not going to tell me to stay home? Or demand to come along to protect me? Or try to tell me how to drive?"

"I'm not. You know how to drive, and I know you've got an important job to do. By the way, I think you're a grand vet. The best around."

"All right, Cooper, I'll see you later."

As she walked toward to the barn where they'd stored her Jeep, Coop pulled out his cell and dialed the number on the card in his pocket.

"Hello, Johnson Sanders here."

"Johnson, this is Cooper Holloway. I've been wanting to call and tell you thank you."

"For what, Holloway? All you did was waste my time."

"I'm sorry about that, but I've been thinking, you were right. Hayley is dumb as a rock. In fact, I'm wondering why a smart guy like you would even want to be seen with her. You can do better. A medical doctor, or a brain surgeon maybe. You know, someone who makes six figures right out of college. You should leave Hayley to one of the dumb cowboys who lives far out in the country."

Johnson's tone changed. "I think you may be right. Why should I chase after a woman who isn't smart enough to realize what she has in a man like me? I'm on my way up, and she'd probably slow me down. Thanks, Holloway."

"Anytime. Oh, by the way, I'm that dumb cowboy who plans to marry her."

He clicked the phone off as Hayley pulled up in the Jeep.

"Coop, any chance you'd like to come along to keep me company?"

"I'd be honored. I'll get my hat."

As Hayley waited in the Jeep, Elliot stepped out with Cooper's hat and said the strangest thing. "Little brother, you're the smartest man I've ever met."

Cooper glanced at the open window by Elliot's office chair and realized his brother had been listening. "I plan to be."

CHAPTER FORTY-SIX

December 24

Christmas Eve came with laughter and love filling the ranch headquarters. Cooper couldn't stop smiling as he watched from the landing. Every woman in the house had told him to stay out of the way.

Tatum brought him a chair. "I figured you'd need this."

"You're right." Cooper leaned his crutches against the railing and lowered himself into the chair. "I seem to be a speed bump downstairs."

Tatum sat beside his chair and stared down at the crowd. "Reminds me of an ant bed."

"Me, too. I never liked decorating the tree and all that stuff, but it looks interesting from up here."

"Can I ask you something?" Tatum didn't look at Cooper.

"Sure, kid. Anything."

"Can I really stay here? Forever, I mean. Is this the place I get to land?"

Cooper nodded. "When you grow up, you might want to move away, maybe marry or find a job you love."

"Nope. From what I see, Holloways stay planted. I plan to follow the tradition."

Cooper looked down at his brothers. "It seems that way, and you are a Holloway now. You'll have to give up being a mountain man, and when we go up to the shack, it may not look the same. Dallas wants to decorate it. Near as I can tell, Dallas pretty much gets what she wants. She'll tell Sunlan, who'll tell Elliot, who'll tell me to ride up and rebuild."

The boy didn't look too interested in the details. "I got another question."

"Ask away." Cooper had already figured out that the questions never ended.

"I know I belong to Griffin and Elliot and you, but do you mind if I call you Dad?"

Cooper thought, for a moment, that his heart might explode. "I wouldn't mind at all, but I think we should shake on it."

The boy jumped up and offered his hand. "See you later, Dad."

For a while Cooper just sat in his chair on the landing and watched. He figured he was the luckiest man alive.

He smiled down at his sister-in-law. Sunlan finally made it home. Funny how he didn't even know her two years ago, and now, the family wasn't whole until she was home. Her father was still in the hospital, but Sunlan's mother was taking care of him. Griffin claimed his father-in-law would either be driven mad by Sunlan's mother or remarried to her by the time he left the hospital.

Elliot and Jess kept disappearing. They'd talked the preacher in town into coming out Christmas morning to marry them among the trees. Even if it was snowing the family planned to ride out to where the evergreens grew. Cooper had suggested that they wait until spring, but Elliot said he'd waited long enough. So Coop guessed he'd be riding out with the preacher in Dani's ATV.

Dallas's shout filled the great room as she insisted that Creed was hanging the last of the garland backward.

Cooper grinned as the foreman paid no attention to her.

"Jonathan Creed, you'd better listen to me."

"Jonathan?" all three brothers said simultaneously.

"And if I don't?" Creed said in a low voice, though everyone in the room still heard. He stepped off the ladder. "I don't like to be told what to do, Dallas."

"Well, then, you'll be sorry when the entire garland falls down on you," Dallas answered as she turned her back to him.

When he stomped toward her, she took off running and laughing. They were out the door before anyone thought to speak.

Tatum walked over and closed the door. "Where do you think they're going?"

When no one seemed to have an answer, Tye stepped up. "They're probably out feeding the horses."

Cooper barely heard Dani as she whispered to the cowboy, "That seems like a great idea."

The world was changing, and Cooper couldn't stop smiling. He watched Hayley dancing with the baby and remembered how he'd said that one day he'd dance with her before he asked her to marry him. He wanted to be able to stand on two feet in front of her before he asked. He wanted it to be perfect. That was important to a woman.

An hour later all was ready. The tree looked beautiful and the room was an explosion of red and green. Everyone said good-night and headed off, knowing that they'd all be down early to open presents.

Cooper was the only one who didn't call it a night. Hayley

had said good-night to the group, but not to him. He'd hoped for a good-night kiss, but it hadn't happened. She had to know how he felt about her. Hell, everyone on the ranch knew.

As he limped around, turning off the lights, he saw her standing on the stairs. She was in a cotton nightgown with her hair in braids.

"You forget something, honey?"

"No. I remembered something. Remember when I saved your life you said that you owed me one?"

"I do. Any favor you ask. If someone is bothering you or you're afraid, I'll be there."

"Good. Will you marry me?"

Cooper frowned. "Is that guy bothering you again? He's not frightening you, is he?"

"No. I'm afraid I might lose you."

He raised his hand to her cheek and smiled. "You won't lose me, Doc. You've got me for as long as you want me."

"How about life?"

Kissing her softly, Cooper whispered, "I have a feeling that won't be long enough."

★ ★ ★ ★ ★